C000065038

The Affair

Look out for other Black Lace short fiction collections

Wicked Words 1 – 10
Quickies 1 – 10
Sex in the Office
Sex on Holiday
Sex and the Sports Club
Sex on the Move
Sex in Uniform
Sex in the Kitchen
Sex and Music
Sex and Shopping
Sex in Public
Sex with Strangers
Love on the Dark Side (Paranormal Erotica)
Lust at First Bite – Sexy Vampire Stories
Seduction
Liaisons
Misbehaviour
Sexy Little Numbers Vol 1

Paranormal novella collections:
Lust Bites
Possession
Magic and Desire
Enchanted

The Affair

Edited by Lindsay Gordon

BL

This book is a work of fiction.
In real life, make sure you practise safe, sane and
consensual sex.

Published by Black Lace 2009

2 4 6 8 10 9 7 5 3 1

He Just Does © Charlotte Stein; The Weekend of Living Dangerously © Elizabeth Coldwell;
A Lavish Affair © Portia Da Costa; Delayed Gratification © Kyoko Church; Emrgency Exit
© Shanna Germain; Dirty Weekend © Primula Bond; I Spy © Rachel Kramer Bussel; The
High Ground © Janine Ashbless; Be Careful What You Ask For © Gwen Masters; The Judge
© Alegra Verde; The Interview © Justine Elyot; Playing the Part © Izzy French; Vetting the
Affair © K D Grace

*All characters in this publication are fictitious and any resemblance to real persons, living or
dead, is purely coincidental.*

This book is sold subject to the condition that it shall not, by way of trade or otherwise,
be lent, resold, hired out, or otherwise circulated without the publisher's prior consent in
any form of binding or cover other than that in which it is published and without a similar
condition, including this condition, being imposed on the subsequent purchaser.

First published in Great Britain in 2009 by
Black Lace,
Virgin Books,
Random House, 20 Vauxhall Bridge Road,
London SW1V 2SA

www.blacklace.co.uk/www.virginbooks.com/www.rbooks.co.uk

Addresses for companies within The Random House Group Limited can be found at:
www.randomhouse.co.uk/offices.htm

The Random House Group Limited Reg. No. 954009

Distributed in the USA by Macmillan, 175 Fifth Avenue, New York, NY 10010, USA

A CIP catalogue record for this book is available from the British Library

ISBN 9780352345172

The Random House Group Limited supports The Forest Stewardship Council (FSC),
the leading international forest certification organisation. All our titles that are printed
on Greenpeace approved FSC certified paper carry the FSC logo. Our paper procurement
policy can be found at www.rbooks.co.uk/environment

Typeset by Palimpsest Book Production Ltd, Grangemouth, Stirlingshire FK3 8XG

Printed and bound in Great Britain by CPI Bookmarque, Croydon CR0 4TD

Contents

He Just Does Charlotte Stein 1

The Weekend of Living Dangerously
Elizabeth Coldwell 20

A Lavish Affair Portia Da Costa 38

Delayed Gratification Kyoko Church 59

Emrgency Exit Shanna Germain 81

Dirty Weekend Primula Bond 91

I Spy Rachel Kramer Bussel 109

The High Ground Janine Ashbless 127

Be Careful What You Ask For Gwen Masters 149

The Judge Alegra Verde 170

The Interview Justine Elyot 196

Playing the Part Izzy French 218

Vetting the Affair K D Grace 237

He Just Does

Charlotte Stein

Vaughn says that Brendon is coming over tonight, and I don't think anything of it. He always invites God knows who at a moment's notice, and usually they're annoying and weird and I end up falling asleep before the evening news.

Which is when they'll depart for the patio, and drink and drink and drink until they do something stupid like paint themselves red and streak down Main Street. Or worse. Sometimes Vaughn will tell me about these things that are worse, as he sneaks a hand into my panties.

I can't say I mind.

Once he brought over a girl, a beautiful naughty little minx with saucer titties and a belly tauter than mine, and he made me watch while she gave him a long sticky blow job. Though really he didn't make me do anything. I just stayed, because I wanted to. I won't deny that I found it fascinating to see my boyfriend's cock sliding in and out of someone else's mouth.

I also didn't say no when he told me to lick her pussy. I had always wanted to try it with a girl, just one time, and even with him mauling me as I ate her out, it wasn't so bad. After he fell asleep, she licked my pussy. She was pretty cute, really – a nice girl.

And the whole thing got me a free pass on tons of stuff, for weeks after.

But now it's more than weeks, it's months, so it's no surprise that I'm wondering what the subtext for tonight is going to be. Though when Brendon turns up, he's less than what I expected. I expected someone seedy, somehow, someone into collars and cock-rings and other stuff I barely know about, but he isn't anything like that.

He's ginormous, true. Big broad shoulders and thick thighs in tight jeans. Hands like shovels. But he's also sort of . . . gawky. He's wearing a college sweater even though he's too old to be in college, and his hands are in the pockets of his too-tight jeans, and his upper lip keeps disappearing.

He's swelteringly handsome, however. His handsomeness is all over him, as though someone has covered him in their handsome handprints. His eyes are like big dark caves, and his hair is thick and shaggy and always falling into said caves, and his jaw looks as though it was cut along the length of a ruler.

I think I know what tonight's theme is going to be. Even if Vaughn hadn't told me to wear this tiny falling-off dress, I think I'd know. Even if Brendon wasn't faintly interesting – which he is, he talks about things that Vaughn knows I like, such as Ray Bradbury and gory horror films – I'd know. I know even more when the evening news rolls around, and Vaughn decides to put on something from his collection.

Brendon doesn't say a word – maybe he expected this. I don't say anything either, because I know better than to spoil the game. So we sit in muggy silence, watching Vaughn fuck two babes on screen.

The first is a tall spoilt blonde, who keeps telling him to fuck her now, fuck her now. When he doesn't immediately obey – and instead keeps fucking the tiny little Asian girl with the spiky hair – she pouts, and plays with herself.

I know. I've seen this tape a thousand times. He loves it, because of the way they fight over him. When he finally gives in and starts shafting the blonde, spiky hair squeezes in between and licks her clit – not to give the blonde pleasure, but to persuade Vaughn to put his cock in her mouth instead of the blonde's pussy.

The capper is both of them licking and sucking him as he kneels over them, pumping himself until he spurts in their greedy mouths.

'Oh, Vaughn,' they sigh. It's his crowning achievement.

When he sticks his hand up my skirt as the film rolls on and Brendon squirms on the other end of the couch, I don't protest. Mainly because the film is making me horny anyway, and I'm sure Brendon can hardly see. I press my clit harder against his fingers and he strums it until I'm slippery, then works his hand down inside my panties to my wet hole.

I don't really mind. I keep thinking about Brendon's too-handsome face and his big hands. I'll admit – I think it's more exciting because he's there, being all oddly bashful.

I let my head fall back against the sofa, my cheeks hot and my hips rocking, while on screen the threesome continues. They've not quite gotten to him filling their mouths; at the moment the blonde is fucking herself with a buzzing blue vibrator while spiky hair clambers around on all fours, pinching her own tits and backing up against his cock.

When the blonde arches her back and obviously comes around the slippery blue thing, I moan. Brendon moans. Clearly Vaughn intended a scenario much like the one on screen all along, only with a bit of a gender switch.

But he's got another thing coming, seriously. I don't mind him frigging me like he's doing, and I don't care if Brendon wants to wank off to it, but I'm not going to get fucked by the pair of them.

Still, I spread my legs wider. I get them nice and wide and then he fucks into my now sloppy pussy while his thumb worries my clit, and I can't resist putting a hand inside my thin dress to stroke and rub my nipples. In one way it's nice that I'm wearing barely anything, because it's easy to get at all the interesting parts.

'You wanna come?' he pants, in my ear. 'You wanna come?'

And I moan back *yeahhh, oooh, yeah*. Because I do. My clit feels like it's about to burst and I've soaked my panties and his hand. I now have both hands inside my dress and am pinching my nipples, spreading the glowing warmth that is building in my groin and my belly.

But then he removes his hand, and I'm left bereft. I move my own hand down there but he stops me, and tells me I can come – if I come while he's shafting me.

I say, 'Not here,' but I let him wriggle my panties off, anyway. It's always the way, really. I start out with good intentions and try not to fall into all of his games, but most of me likes them. I just get too turned on to not like them.

I know exactly what it will come to. Vaughn will fuck me until I'm steaming hot and wet and aching, and then I won't care what gets put in my mouth. I'll suck it greedily and without a second thought. And when I do, I'll come.

The thought of Brendon's cock is hardly off-putting, anyway. At least Vaughn has brought me something pretty and thoughtful, rather than brutish and nastily demanding.

'Look how wet she is,' he says to Brendon, but Brendon only looks flushed and startled, hand restlessly stirring in his lap. I can see how thick his erection looks through his jeans, and despite myself my pussy twinges and aches. Not even despite myself – my pussy just twinges and aches all on its own.

Vaughn isn't that big. But he'll do.

He gets out his tensely hard cock and spreads my legs, gently rubbing the head through my creamy slit. I moan and arch my

4

back, trying to keep that soft contact against my clit, but he just laughs and slides into me.

It feels good, though. I'm so sensitive that I think I might just come from being fucked, but unfortunately it's all over too soon. He grunts and lurches forward, his cock swelling inside me as he comes and comes, clearly over-excited by me letting him fuck my pussy in front of his friend.

Though I notice that he lasted a lot longer for the two babes.

He staggers away, allowing Brendon a good eyeful of my come-drenched pussy, my stiff clit. And Brendon isn't shy about looking. He rubs himself through his jeans as he stares at my spread slit, sighing and muttering.

'He's a virgin, you know,' Vaughn says, and I flash on the conversation we had not long ago, at the back of a ghost train. Later, while eating candyfloss and even later, tied up in knots in each other. Kissing and kissing and too excited to do anything but everything he wanted.

I should never have told him what I think of virgins. What I think of inexperience and over-eager excitement. I should have known he'd use it against me, and so spectacularly, too. Where did he find this Brendon? How did he even find out such a thing about him?

I'm sure he's lying, but then again Brendon does look embarrassed and excited and nervous all at the same time. I mean, that could just be because I'm lying against the arm of the sofa, legs spread and tits largely exposed, but that's not how Vaughn's friends usually react to me in a state like this.

Once, three of them lined up for me. They didn't hesitate.

But Brendon seems to hesitate. He flashes a look at Vaughn, but Vaughn just grins and tucks himself back into his jeans. He lights himself a cigarette and sits down at the dining table, waiting.

I think he might have to wait for ever. Either Brendon is a very good actor or exactly what Vaughn says he is, because he doesn't seem about to make a move without more of a say-so. Onscreen, the blonde is fucking spiky hair with the vibrator – her pussy perfectly split and obviously wet, just for the camera – while spiky hair sucks Vaughn's cock, but even that is not enough to persuade Brendon into action.

He just watches, and looks at my pussy, and watches.

Vaughn's smoke curls around us. It overlays the smell of sex softly, leaving it largely undisturbed. Brendon cannot escape.

'She hasn't come, you know, Brendon,' Vaughn says, eventually. I glance back at him and can hardly see his face through the dimness, and the smoke. 'Maybe you could have a go, for me.'

I ache at those words. I don't mean to. I just do. I'm weak for Vaughn and weak for this game and, well, at least it's something for me. This is just all for me, even if Vaughn doesn't really think so. He just wants to see some young buck embarrass himself between my thighs, I know, and then he can come in and show him how it's done.

I won't say anything about the first go around that Vaughn has already had, and maybe that's why he can be the big boss man in bed, after Brendon is done. Brendon won't either, because he's too much of a sweetheart.

Besides, I think Brendon looks as though his ship has come in. He can't seem to believe his luck, and that is nothing but pleasing to me. I am his ship. I am something coveted, a gift that he can't believe he's being given.

I like being given to Brendon.

The thought startles me, but I let it come on anyway. I shiver with it, and as he watches – the screen long since left behind – I slide the thin strap of my dress from one shoulder. My breasts are far larger than the ones that belong to the girls on

6

screen, but he doesn't seem to mind. Far from it. His eyes grow even bigger, like moons. Bigger still, when I lick one finger and circle my tight little nipple.

He swallows, visibly, so I expose my other breast to his big-eyed gaze. I pinch and pluck my nipples, sending pleasure straight down to my clit, but he doesn't make any sort of move until Vaughn gives him permission.

'Lick her pussy, first,' he says. 'Go on – she's gagging for it.'

I suppose I am, because I don't even mind that it took Vaughn doling out orders to get Brendon moving.

He leans forward slowly, slowly, his breath stirring against the bare skin of my pussy first, before he touches me for real. I tense with excitement but don't encourage him in any other way. If I do anything he might get too nervous, and dart away, and I couldn't bear that. I can barely stand waiting as he moves slowly towards me, and every thought I have seems designed to work me further into a frenzy.

He's going to lick up Vaughn's come, as well as my copious honey. He's going to bury his face in our combined juices, and the thought doesn't seem to bother him. I guess he's too excited to be bothered, just the same as me.

Things are easy, when you're all worked up like this.

I look at his long legs, trailing off the couch. His dark hair, between my pale thighs. He moans before he gets to anything other than nuzzling me, and the moan vibrates through my wet flesh, electrifying me enough to close my eyes and picture all of the things I'd like to do with big gawky Brendon.

It doesn't seem fair that Vaughn is still around. I want all night with his friend, to make my own videotape of us fucking and sucking and exploring each other. He moans again and it's such a lovely sound, such a gruff little *uh*, rough with need, that I almost come right there and then.

7

I imagine Brendon riding me hard from behind with nothing but that sound in the air, and squirm.

'Stop pussyfooting around and lick her cunt,' Vaughn snaps, and Brendon obeys. He pokes out his tongue and makes a wet stripe through my slit, right from my come-drenched hole to my stiff clit.

I cry out and he does it again – this time it's something I do that makes him act. Every time the flat of his tongue makes contact with my clit I let him know, until he's lapping there, just right there, oh God yes.

I buck and twist on the couch until he uses those big hands to hold me still – right on the sensitive high-up places of my inner thighs, which only makes it worse. He doesn't flick his tongue in that teasing way, as Vaughn does, but presses it firm and flat against my clit and then works it over and over me until I think I could go mad.

I think Vaughn knows I could go mad, because he says, gruffly: 'Leave her hanging. She loves it when you leave her hanging and fuck her just as she's right on the edge.'

But Brendon disobeys. I have no idea why. Maybe I climax close enough to Vaughn's command that it's all just down to chance, but I don't think so. I think maybe Brendon likes hearing my panting, and likes feeling my hips rock beneath his hands, and when I moan *ohhh, yesss, oh God I'm there, I'm there*, he moans right back at me into my soaking flesh.

Jesus, how my orgasm buzzes through me. I arch against it, but nothing can hold it down or make it less than what it is. I shake with it, and cream for him, and can't remember any time when it felt so good.

It feels so good that I don't even come down from it when Vaughn says: 'I think she needs to be shown who's boss, Brendon. She didn't listen to what I said.'

I'm drifting on a haze of bliss, so I don't feel the need to tell him that actually, he ordered *Brendon* to do something, not me. He never said *I* couldn't come. He said that Brendon shouldn't let me. He should leave me hanging.

Brendon was just too nice to obey, I like to think.

Not that there's anything wrong with keeping someone waiting. Sometimes I like it. Sometimes it's great. For instance, I can imagine Brendon tying me up and teasing me with his big thick cock for hours. Just hours and hours and hours until I'm insane and raving. Covering me in oil and licking me and sucking me and always leaving me hovering just on the brink, aching for him and –

I get on all fours on the carpet when Vaughn tells me to. I think he's having a joke at Brendon's expense, but I don't think Vaughn knows quite what the joke is. Because when he tells Brendon to give me a spanking and I squeal like usual and say no, inside I'm thinking *yes*.

For the first time, I think *yes, yes, God yes. Spank me, Brendon. Cover my ass with those big hands.*

I tug my dress up and over my head with frantic and fumbling hands, sure that I look just like usual, when Vaughn wants to smack my ass. Nervous and reluctant. Rather than what I actually am – more turned on than I've ever been in my life.

When I kneel on all fours on the carpet, naked, I'm aching as though I haven't just had one huge orgasm. I have no idea why. I barely know Brendon and it's not as though he's all that different to Vaughn.

Except that he is different. Clearly, obviously different. I'm betting as wicked, in a lot of ways, but also . . . also I'm sure that he wants me. He wants me so much that I bet he'd do anything to get me, even this. He'd probably do anything I asked, as much as he's willing to do anything Vaughn asks.

'Smack my naughty ass,' I tell him, and only then do I hear him stutter out an *OK*.

He kneels behind me on the carpet, and before I feel his hand on my ass, I hear him unzip his jeans. Vaughn chuckles but doesn't tell him not to, and as he tentatively slaps me, I feel him tugging at his cock.

'Harder,' Vaughn says, and Brendon barely obeys, so I help him out. I wriggle my ass back at him, and beg him for more.

'Yes, yes, punish me,' I gasp, and he brings his hand down hard enough to burn.

I jerk forward, grazing my nipples on the carpet and sparking myself up higher, and then he spanks again before I can catch myself. Liquid trickles down my inside thigh from my gaping, aching pussy, and I think of the sight I must be making. I think of him jerking off until his thick come covers my bare ass. I think about him thrusting into me roughly, and using me to bring himself off.

I think about all of these things, and then he spanks again.

Onscreen, Vaughn is splashing his come all over their faces and into their mouths.

'Fuck me,' I say to Brendon. 'Fuck me hard.'

Vaughn is magnanimous. He doesn't tell me off or stop Brendon from doing what I demand. Instead he says, 'Go on. Go on and fuck her pussy. Look at how much she wants it, the slut.'

But still it's a surprise when he sinks into me. So much so that I'm sure it must really be Vaughn, even as Brendon's startling thickness spreads me open. I can feel him trembling against the backs of my thighs, too, and oh, how large his hands are as they work into the cup of my hips.

He tugs me back against him insistently, eagerly, groaning loud and long.

'Come on, get going,' Vaughn says. 'She likes it when you fuck her hard.'

I like it when Brendon fucks me hard. His hips and pelvis butt against my bare and almost-sore ass, solidly. He isn't as jerky as I would have expected, but I can feel his nervousness, and his excitement. He's so swollen and tense inside me that I'm sure I can feel every pulse and leap of his cock, and the hands that cup my hips are slick with sweat.

His groans are quavering, breathy things. Almost like a girl. Almost like the way I should sound, instead of all these mannish grunts that keep coming out of me.

'Oh, you're so hot,' he whimpers, and I shouldn't really believe him but he sounds so fucking excited that it's hard not to. 'I can't last.'

'Don't worry about it,' Vaughn says. 'Fill her pussy, go on.'

I groan somewhere in between, half in bliss, half in despair, as I see Vaughn's fancy shoes crossing the carpet. He's going to make me suck him off while another man fucks me, I know it, and though part of me likes the idea another part just wants to finish getting fucked by Brendon. Just Brendon, who actually makes me feel like I'm hot stuff. Like I'm a sexy piece of ass. Like he just can't resist fucking me and fucking me just as he is doing, oh, Jesus.

But Vaughn doesn't kneel down before me. Instead there is the plastic-y sound of him changing tapes, and then the over-exposed image of me sucking his cock flickers to life onscreen.

I know exactly which one it is. My curly hair has practically been straightened with all the sweat and humidity – it's his favourite part on the tape, when I'm all exhausted from the marathon fuck session we've been through and he's gagging me with his cock. The me up there still hasn't come, and after he's plundered my mouth for a bit he makes me turn around so that the video camera can see my blushing, swollen, honey-drenched pussy.

'Look how excited she is,' Vaughn says, and I know he's looking at the screen, not at the real me, as he says it.

Brendon just groans out a little 'uh' for my delectation, and works into me harder. I don't think he could ever make me do so many things, and still not have me come. I think I could just come from him looking at me, across a crowded bar. I think I could come watching him jerk off, gleaming with perspiration and twisting before me.

I think I can come now, with just his cock in my cunt and his groans and his hands now rubbing and soothing my sore ass. And then I don't have to think, because he gasps and reaches around my thigh to get at my clit, and rubs as he fucks me.

It only takes a second. My back arches and shoves his cock in deep. The screen shows Vaughn giggling, and telling me to make myself come. My own eyes stare back at me, pained and pleasured, as I clench tight around Brendon's cock and he spills inside me.

'Oh, Jesus Christ,' he cries out. 'I can't believe how good this feels!'

And I say the same thing back to him, in my head: I can't believe it, either.

Sure enough, Vaughn fucks me again once Brendon is done. Brendon doesn't seem as happy to watch it as last time, however. He sits on the couch, dark eyes burning, watching Vaughn *show him how it's done*.

It seems pathetic, really, after what came before. I mean, I've had better than Vaughn a few times – his friend Greg was very good. But somehow this feels different, a different sort of bad compared with good. I suppose Vaughn is as handsome as Brendon, and in many ways I like the games he plays.

But I'm still laid on the floor, Vaughn between my legs, returning Brendon's gaze.

Of course I shake it off. He's just a kid even though he clearly isn't at all. It was just a good fuck, even though it was probably just the thought of taking his virginity that made it exciting.

Though I wonder if he really was a virgin at all. True, he was eager and excited and like he'd never seen a woman naked before, but he was also knowing. He knew what to do to please me. He knew how to lick and stroke and fuck me. His smacks weren't too hard, his words were just right.

You need to learn that stuff, right? Most men aren't like that, right?

I don't know. I shake it off. I do not lie awake next to a snoring Vaughn, thinking about Brendon on the pull-out bed downstairs.

What would he do if I went downstairs to him, now? What would Vaughn do? Though I suppose Vaughn need never know. I'm sure he fucks plenty of women he doesn't tell me about, even if I know that isn't true. He loves to tell me about his exploits. He loves to film them, and show me. What fun is it, if I never find out about it?

Not as much fun as never telling Vaughn at all.

I get out of bed inch by inch, and pad across the bedroom floor. Just the effort of keeping quiet thrills me, and despite all the excesses of earlier I feel myself getting warm, and wet. Vaughn shifts and grunts and I freeze, but then his snoring becomes steady again.

I risk it.

I close the door gently behind myself so that hopefully I'll hear, should Vaughn get up for a drink of water. But somehow I doubt I'll have to worry too much – after a great big bout of sex, Vaughn can sleep for England.

I hope he sleeps for ever. If he does, then I can –

But when I get downstairs the pull-out bed is empty, the covers rumpled. I didn't realise how much time had passed.

Blue dawn light is already creeping through the curtains, and Brendon is probably long gone. Likely he left as soon as we went upstairs – the whole thing must have been quite embarrassing for him. Fucking someone's girlfriend, getting told that he didn't know what he was doing.

He couldn't have known how I really felt, or sensed anything about the experience above fleeting sensation. I know all of this. I understand it. I'm not the sort of person to regret or fancy things that aren't there.

I like real. I like gritty. I like pleasure.

I like Vaughn.

But I sit on the edge of the pull-out bed anyway, and wonder what sort of life Brendon leads. Like whether he really goes to college, or if he wouldn't mind seeing a Halloween double bill at the Rialto with his girlfriend, and if he was a virgin then why? Why did he want to be involved in all of this?

I wonder if Vaughn paid him. It's possible. He's done that before.

And then the downstairs shower rumbles the water pipes to life, and almost makes me fall off the pull-out bed.

I don't know why it startles me. Why would Vaughn have come downstairs and got into the shower? And even if he had, what would it matter that I was sat on the empty pull-out bed? Why am I so afraid? Why am I so afraid if Vaughn and I have such a perfect, open, sexually flexible relationship?

I don't know. I don't know. I know that I get up and walk down the hall to the downstairs bathroom, though. The light isn't on, but I can hear the water pitter-patting against the tiles Vaughn paid too much money for. He paid too much for the whole bathroom, and his study across the hall, too.

He pays too much for a lot of things. I think he's going to have paid too much for tonight, as well.

I don't knock on the door. It would be pretty weird to knock when I've already seen and felt so much of him. And yet I feel shy, anyway, without Vaughn's voice at my back telling me to go on. Go on, go into the bathroom. Open the shower door. Lick him from head to toe.

I can hardly do it on my own. I just go into the misty blue light-streaked bathroom and stand before the shower door, staring through the frosted glass and the thick steam. I can just about see the shape of him through all those damp clouds, and I eat it all up with my eyes.

Maybe he never has to know that I was here – Brendon, I mean. That way he never has to reject me and I never have to know that it was all in my head – some sort of tiny connection. I didn't even know I wanted something like a connection, so why should it be so?

Connections are stupid things. Stupid new-age arty-farty things, for people who float around in kaftans and eat lentils. Connections aren't raw and real, like what Vaughn and I have.

But I put my hand against the glass, and feel more than I have through years of all that raw realness, all that sexual ecstasy, with Vaughn. I feel more desire than I have in a century, and it blooms up inside me so strongly that I think I'm going to be sick. It's a fist inside me, rising up.

He doesn't say anything, when I open the shower door and step inside. He doesn't even say anything about the little slip I'm still wearing. The water pours immediately over me and soaks the material through, but that doesn't seem strange to him. He stares down at me with something like heat and something like pity in his eyes, but I don't feel ashamed.

I don't feel small, in the face of his pity. I swell up and up, and shut the door behind myself, and let the water pound down on me.

'Kiss me,' I say, and he does. I don't think I even have to ask him, or tell him to – I think after another moment he would have just done it. That is the sort of person Brendon is. The sort who just does, and maybe you don't have to beg and plead and humiliate yourself.

And then when it comes time to play games like that, they're not so bad.

He pushes his fingers into my now wet hair, scraping against my scalp just enough, rubbing just enough. When his mouth comes down on mine I'm already weak-legged and moaning, but he holds me up. He puts one arm around my shoulders and holds me to him.

The heat builds inside this tiny space. I think the heat inside me kind of cancels it out, though, because I hardly notice it.

I put my hands on his big hips, and then stroke over his stomach – Vaughn's is harder, but all I think of when I consider Vaughn's taut belly is how proud he is of it. Brendon self-consciously sucks his gut in, but I slap it and kiss him harder. He doesn't need to hide anything from me, least of all his gorgeous body.

It's the body of someone who keeps in shape because he likes swimming. The body of someone who doesn't pose every morning, in front of the mirror. I like his body against my body. We fit nicely, partly hard and partly soft.

He whispers against my cheek: 'Does Vaughn know you're here?'

And when I say no he doesn't look afraid or bothered in any way. He grins, broadly – though not smugly.

'I knew,' he says. 'I knew.'

And even though he doesn't say what it is he knew, I know it just the same: that I wanted something just between me and him.

'I promise I won't tell,' he says.

'How many times do you think you could never tell?' I ask, and he smiles even wider at that.

'If you leave him, it won't matter if I never tell or not.'

My heart pounds in my head, in my stomach, in my legs. In every part of me but my chest. I think it has vacated my chest.

'Let's just start here,' I say, and drag his mouth back down to my hungry one.

I eat him alive. I eat his face and his neck and his shoulders, the tuft of hair below his navel and each one of his fingers. His trembling thighs and the soft tender place behind his knees. His tiny sensitive nipples and the curve of his firm ass. I bite that flesh hard and he calls out my name, hoarsely, before turning around and demanding that I now get the same treatment.

His teeth scraping over my stomach, the arch of my back, while all the hot water runs away and time ticks on and Vaughn could catch us any minute. His tongue in the cleft of my ass, on the nape of my neck, in all the hills and hollows that I didn't know I had.

I'm trembling by the time he lifts me against the shower wall. As I wrap my legs around his waist and stroke his seal-slick hair down flat, I ask him if he really was a virgin. His reply is sweeter than chocolate melting on my tongue.

'I'm glad I didn't seem like one.'

I moan when he works his cock through my folds, and then pushes into me. I cry out when he jerks in harder.

'As soon as I was done, I wanted to fuck you again,' he gruffs out, and I think, *oh God yes, me too*.

But I don't tell him that. Let him work, for some things. Let me be the one who is wanted, for once, wanted so badly that he doesn't care how loud he is – that Vaughn might hear and catch us and kill him. He surges in and out of me roughly, quickly, clutching at my ass with his face in my shoulder, calling out my name.

He tells me how hot and wet I am, how he can't get enough of fucking my tight little pussy. He doesn't call it snatch or cooze, and he doesn't tell me to take it like the little bitch I am. Instead he pants, 'Come for me, come on my cock,' and when I don't immediately obey he changes the angle that he's fucking into me at, slides his mouth down to my tits and sucks, gets a stroking hand between my legs.

His fingers pinch my clit and he tugs a nipple hard into his mouth, and oh, God, it feels good. It feels amazing. I can feel my pussy clenching and fluttering around him, and he mutters against my breast that I'm getting so wet.

He buries his face in the curve of my throat and pants, and asks me if I like that, do I like it, do I like it, is it good, and I marvel over the idea that he doesn't know. How can he not know that I like it?

But oh my Jesus, it's nice to be asked. So nice that I think I come just from hearing it, twisting and bucking on his cock, trying to escape from him and all of this too-much-ness. And then scrabbling to get back to it.

He grabs me by the hair and pulls my mouth down to his, so that when he comes he can voice all of his pleasure directly into me.

I shout it right back. I shout all of me right back at him, and thank God, thank God for letting me see what it is to have someone who can actually hear it.

It isn't that Vaughn is awful. In many ways he isn't. He has loved and cared for me all these years, and expanded my horizons, and made me the person I am today.

But he isn't Brendon. He can't ever be. He's just one way, and doesn't know anything else. But Brendon does. He says,

'What do you want to do next?' and I know he means anything at all. He is open, he is asking and telling, he is everything, he is both ways, he just does.

Goodbye, Vaughn.

Charlotte Stein is the author of the Black Lace collection *The Things That Make Me Give In*. Her short fiction appears in numerous Black Lace anthologies.

The Weekend of Living Dangerously

Elizabeth Coldwell

Drew gave me a last, lingering kiss in the hallway. His hand moved up under my coat to cup my knickerless pussy, which he had filled with his come such a short time ago. I wriggled under his touch, knowing how easily it could reignite the passion we had shared for the last two days, but aware that I simply had to leave. My phone vibrated briefly in my pocket; I didn't have to reach for it to know it was the cab firm texting me to let me know my taxi was waiting outside.

Reluctantly, I pulled away from Drew's embrace. 'Take care of yourself, OK?' he murmured.

'Don't worry, I'll be seeing you soon enough,' I replied. In a little over nine hours, to be precise, but by then we would have returned to being office colleagues, rather than the lovers we'd finally been this weekend. But I couldn't complain about leaving him; when I walked out of his flat I was going back to my gorgeous husband, after all.

I didn't bother slipping my shoes on until I was down the stairs, and I closed the front door behind me as quietly as I could. Close to midnight on a Sunday night, most of the residents of this Victorian conversion, and all the others on the street, would already be in bed and dreaming of the working week to come. I didn't want to wake them and draw any attention to myself. I knew exactly what I looked like, and the expression on the taxi driver's face told me how I would look to others. While it wasn't immediately obvious that all I had on beneath my coat was a pair of stockings, it was easy to see how ripped and laddered those stockings were. My hair was tangled and sticky with sweat and lube, though I had done my best to comb it out, and though I had sprayed myself generously with perfume before leaving Drew's flat, beneath the vanilla and ylang ylang I still stank of sex. It was all exactly as my husband had requested it. I was to return to Richie looking, smelling and tasting like a woman who had spent the whole weekend being magnificently fucked.

Dark eyes met mine in the rear view mirror as the taxi pulled away from the kerb. 'You look like you've had a good time.'

I could hardly keep the smile from my face as I replied, 'Oh, it's been better than good.'

'So why don't you tell me about it?'

It wasn't the sort of story I would normally divulge in the back of a cab, but I was still on such a high that I was more than in the mood to share. 'OK, then . . .'

And as the taxi sped through the darkened streets of Crouch End, radio tuned to smooth jazz and a light rain beginning to fall, I thought back to the events which had led to this incredible weekend, and how it had all begun with a photograph.

'You look like you've had a good time.' Drew put the magazine down on the desk in front of me. I glanced at it and recognised it as one of the monthly trade publications to which we subscribed; Drew always pounced on it as soon as it was delivered, looking for potential new sources of advertising revenue. I couldn't understand at first why he was showing me the write-up of the magazine's awards dinner, until I saw the photo of the party at table 17. Sitting next to a balding man in a tuxedo, twirling a strand of her blonde hair between her fingers and trying not to look bored, was a woman who looked unbelievably like me. Indeed, if it wasn't for the fact that I didn't own a strapless blue evening dress like the one she was wearing and hadn't actually been at the dinner in question, I would have assumed it was me.

'Incredible likeness, isn't it?' he said, as the realisation of what he was talking about dawned on my face. 'I wonder who she is?'

'I have no idea,' I told him. 'And to be honest, I don't particularly want to know.'

'Really, why not?' He perched on the corner of my desk, settling in for a conversation. Nick, his line manager, glared over at us, as he always did when Drew appeared to be favouring chatting to me over working. If Drew had seen him, he gave no impression of taking any notice.

'Well, you shouldn't ever meet your *doppelgänger*,' I told him. 'It'd be like matter meeting anti-matter. You'd probably get sucked out of existence.'

'Now, that's the way I've always wanted to go . . .' Drew gave me a dirty look. I tried not to blush as he turned back to the magazine. 'I tell you what, though. Whoever she is, she's obviously having a better time than you.'

'You think so?'

'Well, who's the one who's at the swanky dinner in a sexy little dress, eh? I mean, you're always moaning that Richie never gives you the opportunity to dress up for him – or undress for him.'

Now I knew I was blushing. A couple of months ago, at the company's monthly after-work drinks, I had found myself wedged in a corner with Drew, knocking back gin and tonics like they were going out of fashion and complaining that I just wasn't having sex often enough. It wasn't that Richie and I had any problems in our marriage – quite the opposite, in fact – but my husband worked odd hours and late nights, and recently we'd been seeing so little of each other that sex had somehow slipped further down the agenda than either of us would have liked.

It wasn't the only frank conversation I'd had with Drew. From the day he had first joined the company I had felt I could tell him just about anything. He was one of those men who seemed to genuinely like being with women, rather than simply paying attention to them in an attempt to get into their knickers. And he was a good listener, which was useful when I needed to vent my anger at the latest departmental fuck-up. The trouble was that I enjoyed being around Drew just that little bit too much. Physically, he was very similar to Richie – dark-haired and lean with a luscious, tight arse – and the chemistry between us was almost overpowering at times. He often joked that I was his 'office wife', and if I'd been single I was pretty sure we would have ended up in bed together long before now. As it was, there were still moments when I was seriously tempted.

'There are things I tell you that I don't want blurting all over the office,' I said, sounding more annoyed than I felt.

'Oh, come on, Dale, you know me better than that. The one thing I can do is keep a secret. And just think how much fun you could have with this. I mean, you could do a swap one weekend. She could go home to Richie and see how long it took him to notice the difference.'

'OK, and what would I do?'

'Whatever she normally does – which I admit wouldn't be too much fun if that fat, dull-looking bloke at the side of her is actually her husband. More importantly,' Drew continued, warming to his theme, 'you could do whatever you wanted. It would be your chance to misbehave. You could pick up a man in a bar and spend the weekend having wild, depraved sex with him –'

I couldn't help thinking that as Drew suggested this, he had a particular man in mind – and I was looking at him. 'But what would Richie say when he found out I'd tricked him?' I asked.

'Well, I don't know about him, but if I was your husband and you pulled a little stunt like that, I'd give you a bloody good spanking.'

An image flashed into my mind: I saw myself lying face down on Drew's lap, bottom bare and knickers down round my knees. Drew's big, solid hand was raised, ready to come down hard on my unprotected cheeks till they burned a fiery crimson, while I kicked and yelled and promised tearfully never to misbehave again. And when he had spanked me, he would pull his cock out of his fly, hard and imposing, and order me to suck it. The thought sent a sudden shiver of lust through me. And then the phone rang, giving me the perfect excuse to put an end to the conversation before I blurted out just how appealing I found Drew's suggestion.

He left the magazine on my desk as he walked away. 'Think about it,' he mouthed, and winked.

I thought about it for most of the rest of the day, and when I went home that night, I took the magazine with me. For once, Richie was home at a reasonable time, and after we'd eaten, I made Irish coffees, his favourite, and took them through into the lounge. Richie was sprawled on the settee, watching football on TV, and he gave me a sleepy smile when I pressed the mug into his hand.

'What's this in aid of?' he asked, taking a sip and registering the sharp bite of whiskey in the coffee. 'Don't tell me I forgot our anniversary? Sorry, Dale, I –'

'No, it's nothing like that. Budge up, I've got something I wanted to show you.' I curled up beside him on the settee, settling into his embrace as he wrapped an arm around my shoulders. 'What do you think?' I asked, thrusting the magazine under his nose.

It took a moment for the penny to drop, just as it had done with me that morning, and then he burst out laughing 'That's fantastic. Where did you get this?'

'Oh, it's something Drew at work gave me. He reckons that's my evil twin.'

'Really?' Richie gave me a squeeze. 'Then he obviously doesn't know you all that well. You can be pretty evil when you want to be.'

'He told me we should do a swap,' I continued. 'She should spend the weekend with you, and I should spend the weekend with –' I almost let the word 'him' slip out of my mouth and corrected myself hurriedly '– with her husband, and see if you noticed. Of course, I said I could never trick you like that.'

And then Richie said something which totally floored me. 'Maybe you should.'

'I'm sorry?' I said.

'Maybe you should – spend the weekend with someone else, I mean. You know I wouldn't mind.' I gaped at him, speechless. On the TV, the commentator was describing how a group of players were surrounding the referee, disputing a decision to send one of their teammates off. The footballer who was being shown trudging off the pitch after receiving the red card, a look of utter bafflement on his face, would have understood exactly how I felt at this moment, unable to believe the turn events were taking.

'You can't be serious,' I said eventually.

'I've never been more serious,' Richie replied. He took a gulp of his coffee before continuing, 'Dale, I can't tell you how much it turns me on to think of you having sex with another man. Don't ask me why. I just know that I'd love to be able to watch you being fucked by someone else, but if that couldn't happen, I'd like you to do it, then come back and tell me about it.'

As he spoke, his hand had snaked up under the hem of my top and was gently stroking my breast through my bra, his fingers circling the nipple. It was one of his moves which was always guaranteed to turn me on, and my body gave in to the caress even as my mind struggled to make sense of what he was telling me. How long had he felt like this, and why had he never mentioned it until now?

'It wouldn't mean we didn't love each other any more,' Richie went on, 'because there's no one else I want to be with apart from you, and I'd know that whatever you did, you would be coming back to me afterwards. But I just get so horny at the thought of you sucking another man's cock, or taking it up your arse.'

I was beginning to realise just how long it had been since Richie last talked dirty to me, and how much I had missed it. I put my hand on his crotch and felt the hefty bulge there. He clearly hadn't been lying when he said he found the thought of me with someone else a massive turn-on. Unzipping his fly, I reached in and stroked him gently through his boxer shorts.

'So you'd really give me permission to fuck someone else?' I asked, feeling him stiffen even further against my fingertips.

'Well, it's not like you haven't got someone else in mind,' Richie replied.

I stopped what I was doing and sat up. 'How could you say that?'

'Come on, Dale, I'm not daft. This Drew, the one who gave you the magazine. Have you ever caught on to the way you talk about him? Do you think I haven't realised you fancy the arse off him?'

I couldn't pretend I didn't know what he meant. A couple of my girlfriends had had affairs, and the first clue that they were playing away from home was always the way that person's name suddenly appeared far too frequently in their conversation. Now I started thinking about it, whenever I was telling Richie about my day at work, Drew always seemed to figure quite prominently.

'Well, if you want the truth,' I said, 'I did think that when Drew was suggesting I sleep with someone else, he kind of wanted to be that person.' My hand closed around Richie's cock again. If we were discussing fantasies, I supposed I had to be honest about my own. 'And he also said that if I was his wife and I spent the weekend with someone else, when I came back to him he'd spank my bottom. And I thought that sounded really sexy.'

'You know,' Richie said, in the moment before his mouth clamped down on mine and he gave me a kiss that I felt all the way down to my pussy, 'I think we just might have a deal . . .'

And so I was charged with the task of letting Drew know that if he wanted me, I was his for the weekend. He could do whatever he wanted with me, and I would go home and describe it all to my husband afterwards. It's not the easiest conversation I've ever had; it took a couple of glasses of wine before I finally felt relaxed enough to make the offer, but as soon as I began to explain what Richie wanted, Drew started smiling as though he would never stop.

'I've never met your husband, but he is clearly a fine and honourable man,' he said.

'There are a couple of ground rules, though,' I told him. 'Richie says I have to turn up at yours in a coat and my underwear and nothing else. That's so you're not tempted to take me out anywhere, and we just have to stay in bed all weekend.

And he's buying me some toys to bring along that he'd like you to use on me.'

'He's really thought about this, hasn't he?' Drew commented.

More than you'll ever know, I thought. 'And most importantly, he'd like this to happen as soon as possible.'

As soon as possible turned out to be the following weekend. Drew claimed not have any plans, though I had the feeling he would willingly have cancelled almost anything to make this happen. On the Friday evening, Richie started work a couple of hours later than usual so he could help me get ready for Drew. I came home to find a bath waiting for me, filled to the brim with foamy, scented water.

'I could get used to this kind of treatment,' I said, as Richie handed me a glass of wine to enjoy in the tub.

'Yeah, maybe I should spoil you a little more often,' he said, half to himself. 'When you're ready, your clothes are laid out on the bed.'

'Clothes' was overstating it a little, I thought, as I wandered out into the bedroom, wrapped in a warm, fluffy towel. I'd been expecting matching bra, panties, the full works. Instead, all that lay on the duvet was a black satin suspender belt cut in a Fifties style, with broad suspender straps with gleaming metal fastenings, and nylon stockings with a seam up the back and a fully fashioned heel. Classy, and yet somehow sleazy at the same time.

When my minimal lingerie was on, lashings of mascara and scarlet lipstick had been applied and I had stepped into the highest heels I possessed, I stood admiring myself in the mirror. The suspenders really drew attention to the triangle of hair on my mound, trimmed down to almost nothing for the occasion. If Drew had got hard at the thought of me dressed for sex, as the way he'd been shifting in his seat when we had discussed the plan had suggested, then how would he react when he actually saw me?

I was still pondering his reaction when Richie came into the bedroom. He stood behind me, pressing his groin against the bare cheeks of my arse. I could feel his erection through the layers of his clothing. 'I'm almost tempted to tell your mate Drew the plan's off and fuck you myself,' he said, his voice a feral growl in my ear, 'but a promise is a promise. Come on, let's go.'

Even so, as the car engine idled outside Drew's flat and I looked up to where I was sure I could see him, silhouetted in a second-floor window, I began to wonder whether it wouldn't be a better idea to do as Richie had suggested and tell him we wouldn't be going through with it. Richie was the man I knew and loved, Richie was safe. Yet wasn't that the very reason we were sitting here now, because we had both realised that we needed to step out of our safety zone, and see what happened if we walked on the wild side, just the once.

I kissed Richie before I got out of the car. 'I'll see you on Sunday night,' I said. 'Wish me luck.'

'I'll be thinking of you,' he replied. From the tone of his voice, I suspected it would be with his cock in his hand.

With my heart in my mouth, I knocked on Drew's door, feeling incredibly self-conscious despite the fact I looked outwardly completely respectable in my knee-length winter coat. When he came to greet me, I realised that until tonight I'd never seen him out of a suit. Now he was casually dressed in faded jeans and a black polo shirt, the beginnings of a five o'clock shadow on his chin, and it suited him.

'Hey, Dale, lovely to see you,' he said, ushering me inside with a peck on the cheek. 'Let me take your coat.'

I hesitated for a long moment before unfastening it, knowing it would leave me next to naked within seconds of stepping inside his home. This, though, was what Richie had wanted, so I took a deep breath, undid the buttons and allowed Drew to see just how little I had on underneath.

He stood there, devouring me with his eyes. Finally, he murmured, 'Your husband is far too good to me. And I think you deserve a glass of champagne.'

I went to sit on his sofa while he busied himself in the kitchen, emerging in a couple of minutes with a tray on which were two glasses of champagne and a plate of cocktail blinis topped with sour cream and caviar. He handed me a glass, then clinked his to mine in a toast. 'Here's to living danger-ously,' he said.

'I did have something else I was to give you,' I said when I had put my glass down, and went to fish it out of my bag.

He smiled at the gift-wrapped package. 'Is this your custom-ised toy box?'

I nodded. 'And I have absolutely no idea what's in it.'

Drew tore off the paper to discover a pair of handcuffs which fastened with Velcro, a string of anal beads, fat, pink and shiny, a little bottle of peach-scented lube and a couple of packets of condoms. I stared at them, realising I was learning more about Richie that I had never suspected. He had never shown any interest in fucking my arse and now here he was, including anal beads in my care package.

'And I absolutely have to use these on you?' Drew gave a mock sigh. 'The sacrifices I'm being forced to make . . .'

As we sat sipping champagne and nibbling on the blinis, it almost seemed possible to forget that I was sitting there in nothing but stockings, my breasts, bottom and pussy blatantly on display, while Drew was fully dressed. Almost, but not quite: the tell-tale wetness and prickling heat between my legs were hard to ignore, particularly when he encouraged me to lick sour cream and salty fish eggs from his fingers. As I tasted him for the first time, my gaze kept flickering to the package of toys Richie had given me. It wouldn't be the first time I had been restrained during sex – Richie loved to fasten me to the bed frame with a couple of his ties so he could go down on me while I lay there, thrilling to the feeling of helplessness – but the anal beads were something new, and I couldn't help wondering how they would feel inside me. A wicked little part of me hoped I might be able to persuade Drew that I should use them on him, but I didn't think that was what Richie had planned when he'd bought them. Which was a shame, because I would have loved to describe that little scene to him later.

As if sensing what I was thinking, Drew put his arms round me, pulling me to him. 'I can't help thinking what you're going to look like when I cuff you to the bed.' He kissed my neck, nipping the flesh with his teeth, and for the first time I really registered the difference in size between us. In his casual clothes, the muscularity of his build was more obvious; his body would be heavy on mine, like Richie's, dominating me and making me his. The thought was undeniably exciting, and I shuddered under his touch.

Drew's big hands cupped my breasts, thumbs rubbing the nipples. At that moment, I just wanted him to unzip his fly and shove his cock up into me. No ceremony, no niceties: just a rough fuck that would have Richie fisting his own hard-on as I told him all about it.

Drew, however, had other ideas. He pushed me back so I was sprawling on the couch, then crouched down between my thighs. 'This isn't just about your husband getting off on this, you know,' he said, as his hands gently stroked their way up my legs.

I moaned by way of answer as his mouth settled on my pussy, searching through the soft folds of flesh till he found the centre of my pleasure. He knew what he was doing, switching between long, lapping strokes of his tongue and hard, fast ones directly on my clit. The stubble on his cheeks tickled the soft flesh of my thighs. For a moment, I imagined him naked, his hands cuffed behind him as I ordered him to lick me until I just wasn't capable of coming any more. When he pulled away, just as I was beginning to buck my pelvis up into his face, my excitement peaking, I almost wished I'd acted on my fantasy.

'Not yet.' He smiled at my pout of disappointment, my juices glazing his mouth and chin. 'You haven't earned it yet.'

'And what do I have to do to earn it?' I asked.

'You can start by showing me just how good you are with your mouth,' he told me. Immediately I reached for the belt of his jeans, but he slapped my hand away. 'Your mouth, I said.' As I was wondering whether he was expecting me to undress him using my teeth, he snatched up the Velcro cuffs from the coffee table and quickly fastened my hands behind my back. I looked up at him as he stripped down to a pair of black briefs that clung enticingly to his cock and balls. I was impatient to see him remove those, too, but Drew strung the moment out, refilling his champagne glass and taking a long gulp from it before offering it to my suddenly parched lips so I could sip. Finally, he took off his underwear, revealing himself in all his glory: a cock which was nicely in proportion to his six-foot frame, rising up hard and ready for my attention.

I shuffled forward on the couch as he presented himself to my mouth. Swallowing him was a little awkward in my bound position, but it felt like coming home, and I breathed in the salty, indefinably male scent of him. At the same time as I was sucking him, using all the little tricks I knew to have him groaning with pleasure and telling me how fantastic it felt to be lodged in my hot, sexy mouth, part of me was thinking how I would recount this later: how to describe Drew's urgent grunting as he took hold of my hair, pulling my head down further on to his cock, and how to describe the sudden, earthy excitement I felt at being used in this way?

Just as rapidly as he had brought me to the verge of climax, I was doing the same for him, and just as he had done before, he called an abrupt halt to the action before I could make him come.

I thought Drew was going to uncuff me, but to my surprise he hauled me over his shoulder and carried me into his bedroom. Incense had clearly been burning for a while, giving off a heady, musky aroma, and the sheets had already been turned back, leaving no doubt that this bed was going to be used for sex, rather than sleep.

Drew had brought the condoms Richie had so thoughtfully provided through with him, and he carefully rolled one into place before lying back and inviting me to straddle him. I looked back ruefully at my bound hands, hoping he would make things easier for me, but he was now firmly in charge – and I couldn't deny that I was enjoying it. Finally taking pity on me, he held his cock steady and I shuffled into position. Slowly, I lowered myself, the thickness of him opening me up deliciously. Drew had clearly settled back to enjoy a long ride, but the almost smug look on his face began to evaporate as I ground up and down on his shaft, using my muscles to grip and squeeze him in ways he didn't appear to have expected. 'Now who's in control?' I wanted to ask, until he responded by reaching down to stroke my clit where it peeped from between my widely parted lips. Now, we were locked in a battle of wills, each of us trying to force the other to come without surrendering ourselves. Drew had the advantage, of course; I was only able to ride him, rather than play with his heavy balls or run my finger along the deliciously sensitive seam of skin that led to his arse. Inevitably, I was the first to peak, dizzy from the intensity of the sensations which were rushing through me, though Drew was only moments behind, tormented beyond endurance by the feel of my pussy clenching around him. I slumped forward on to his chest, feeling his heart pounding as he stroked my hair and murmured his thanks into my ear.

That first fuck set the pattern for the rest of the weekend. Whenever the mood took us, one of us would begin kissing and touching the other, reawakening the passion which was barely given the opportunity to lay dormant. We fucked in every room in Drew's flat, even on the cold, slippery slate tiles of the kitchen floor. As Drew had promised earlier, he cuffed me to the bed, face down and with a couple of pillows under my stomach, raising me up so he could fuck me from behind. We ate very little, neither of us having much of an appetite for anything other than sex. Richie and I had not discussed whether this weekend would be a one-off, but if it was, then I didn't want to waste a minute of it. Drew seemed to catch my mood; his hands were constantly on my body as he encouraged me to talk about all the things we could do if we had more than just a couple of days together. He would love, he said, to take me to an expensive restaurant, or even the awards dinner which had started this whole unlikely chain of events. I would be bare beneath my skirt, so he could play with me all evening; he liked the idea of trying to make me come while the stuffy chairman of the awards ceremony was up making his speech. In return, I told him about my fantasy of him becoming my slave boy, naked, bound and forced to give me pleasure whenever I demanded it. I couldn't help but notice the way his cock twitched in my hand as I described the scene. But what really turned me on more than anything, I told him, was the thought of inviting him into bed with me and Richie: two sets of hands, two mouths and two hard, beautiful cocks, all dedicated to making me come – that was my idea of heaven.

Richie had wanted to watch Drew and me fucking; I would be more than happy if he decided he was going to join in.

Perhaps that was what inspired Drew to do what he did on the Sunday night. We had woken late, having made love till the early hours of the morning, and then I had gone to take a shower, though I had barely stepped under the hot spray before Drew had joined me, cock already beginning to rise to the occasion once more, and lovingly soaped every inch of my body. I thought he was going to take me in the cramped confines of the shower cubicle, but he had other ideas. Richie had requested that when I finally went home, I was to do so freshly fucked and ready for him to clean and, as he put it, worship with his tongue. So Drew spent the day keeping me largely frustrated, teasing me but never letting me have his cock inside me.

It wasn't till we were back in his bedroom, aware that we had less than a couple of hours before I was due to leave, that it suddenly occurred to me that the one thing we had never done was play with my new anal beads. I should have realised that was what Drew had in mind as we lay twined together on the bed and his finger strayed down, not to toy with the entrance to my pussy or my clit as it had done so many times this weekend, but to stroke my rosebud with the lightest of touches. 'Does that feel nice?' he asked, between lingering kisses.

'Mmm,' was all I could reply, drowsy with pleasure. If I had been paying more attention, I might have noticed that he had used the peach lube to lavishly grease up the anal beads, but I was too busy wondering whether Drew was going to replace that finger, which was now probing more insistently, with his gifted tongue.

'So have you ever had anything up your arse?' he asked, still circling and teasing the tight, sensitive hole.

I shook my head. 'No, I've never wanted to.'

'Do you want to now?' he continued.

'It might be nice,' I said, surprising myself with my response.

'Well, I'd hate to disappoint a lady.' There was a pause, then again something was probing at my arse, but now it was something fatter than a finger, something cold and slightly sticky. I realised it had to be the first bead on the string in the moment before it pushed through the tight ring of muscle, lodging itself inside me. 'How does that feel?' Drew asked.

I had to admit that it felt slightly dirty, but surprisingly good. His response was to shove a second bead inside me, then a third. When he began to move them slowly back and forth, I grabbed a handful of the bedcovers and almost screamed with delight.

'God, you look amazing,' Drew murmured. 'But you'd look even better with my cock in you, too.'

As he spoke, he pulled me down on to him, his cock unsheathed for the first and only time this weekend. Now I was full in both holes, with Drew's hardness in my cunt and the fat plastic beads in my arse. I had never experienced anything like it, and I told him so. Drew's response was simply to say, 'Now just think how it would feel if that was your husband's cock in your back door.'

Just the thought of being sandwiched between the two horniest men I knew, crammed to bursting point with hot, thick cock, was enough to push me over the edge. The orgasm I had been building towards all day was just beginning to burst inside me when Drew tugged the beads out of my arse. The wholly unexpected sensation left me shrieking and shuddering in the most powerful climax I'd ever known. I was barely aware of Drew shooting his spunk inside me, as the spasms of ecstasy seemed to go on and on. Then, finally, it was over, leaving both of us spent and unable to speak. What could we say after that, apart from thank you for the most filthy, stunning, unforget-table weekend of my life – and is there any chance at all of our being able to do it again?

'And then I called you, and here we are.' As I spoke, I noticed we were passing the gates of the local park, firmly locked at this time of night, and realised we were almost home.

'And that's how the story ends, is it?' my driver said. 'No more naughty adventures planned, then?'

I shook my head. 'All I have planned is a nice, hot bath and a good night's sleep. But before that, darling, you can lick me clean of Drew's come, just like you said you wanted to. And then maybe tomorrow we can talk about that spanking I deserve for misbehaving.'

Smiling at the thought, my gorgeous husband parked his taxi in front of our house, and took me inside to thank me properly for making his dearest fantasy come true.

Elizabeth Coldwell's short fiction appears in numerous Black Lace collections.

A Lavish Affair

Portia Da Costa

'So this is really quite a lavish affair then?'

Edward glances sideways at me from the driver's seat as we scud along, looking as handsome as the very devil done up in a sexy dark suit. It's quite a shock seeing him in formal wear. I'm used to him in leather, or partially – or completely – naked.

'Yes, ultra posh. Beauchamp Manor belongs to Mandy's rich relations and they've given her the reception there as a wedding gift.'

'Sounds like fun,' he says, eyes back on the road.

Fun? What does that mean? My innards tremble. I know Edward's idea of fun. And even though I like it, it's sometimes scary.

I'm still fizzing with excitement that he's agreed to be my escort. We've been involved for quite some time now, but we've never come out like this in public before. I'm a bit nervous. After all, it's not often a fairly straight woman in her forties nabs a gorgeously hot sexy master nearly half her age. And there'll be lots of people from work who'll remember him as the fit young freelance IT guy who set up our new computer system. The one they always speculated about as they wondered just who he was banging.

It was me, everyone! Average old Jane Mitchell from Human Resources. He was fucking me, and spanking me, and God knows what else . . . and he's still doing it!

I can see he's scheming. He loves to make even the simplest of dates an event.

We go out for a meal and he'll make me give him a blow job in the car park. On a trip to the movies, he'll play with me in the darkness. Out for a walk in the woods, and he'll bend me over a fallen tree trunk and thrash me long and hard with his leather belt.

And when we're at his flat or mine, he's even more imaginative.

We drive on for a few miles. It's countryside now. Wooded copses on either side of the road. I think of that tree trunk, and my pussy gets all wet and my panties sticky. I try not to smile, but my heart races and excitement bubbles even more.

'What are you smiling about?'

Ah, it seems I didn't hide my smile after all. He's noticed, and he's smiling himself in that way I know so well.

'Oh, nothing much . . .'

He gives me the swiftest of glances out of the corner of his blue eyes.

Uh oh, I know that look too.

'Somehow, I think if this affair is as posh as you say it is, we need to have you on your best behaviour, don't we?' He pauses, scanning the road side, as if looking for something. 'I think I need to give you a little something to settle you down.'

I can't breathe. I feel faint. My heart turns over and my pussy ripples with longing.

Almost immediately, he's signalling, and we pull off the road and turn into a narrow lane. It winds away from the main drag and around a few corners then amongst some trees. When Edward finally stops the car, we're out in the wilds and invisible from the road and civilisation. He steps out and hurries round to my side, opening the door and handing me courteously out on to the rough path. He might be cruel as sin sometimes, but he does have gorgeous old-fashioned manners.

'Raise your skirt, will you?' he says conversationally, as we stand beside the car. To him it's a perfectly normal request, and it's one I've become used to myself. It still has the power to thrill me to my core though.

I'm dressed up to the nines, in high heels and a dark suit with a long, narrow skirt, rather Forties style, and glam. The jacket's tightly fitted, plunges low, and I'm not wearing a blouse. I haven't informed him what I'm wearing underneath, but it's a treat I know he'll appreciate, even if he thrashes my bottom for being so brazen.

'Come on, get a move on, you don't want us to be late, do you?' His voice is mild and amused. He's having fun. So am I.

Teetering on my heels, I put one gloved hand on the car, and with the other I snake up my skirt, not hesitating until it's all in a clump at my waist. My stockings are smoke-grey hold-ups and my panties are rose-pink lace, and a pretty lavish affair too. Deep, scalloped lace at the front, and cleverly scooped up at the back, thong-style, to leave my buttocks virtually bare. Just the way Edward likes them. The way his eyes darken as he appraises them is a dead giveaway – even though he looks as calm and cool as ever on the surface. Automatically, I turn, as I know he wants me to, and show him the plump cheeks of my bum.

'Very nice, but very pale. We need to do something about that, don't we?'

I stand, shaking, as he walks towards me. When he's so close I can feel his breath on the back of my neck, he pushes on my shoulders, making me dip over the bonnet of the car, skirt still up.

'Good. That's just right.'

My heart feels as if it's in my throat and I can barely breathe.

I hear the jingle of his belt, and simultaneously think, *oh no*, and *goodie*. I'm still not sure how I can hate pain and love it at the same time. Perhaps, though, I don't? Maybe I just love him?

'OK. As it's a special occasion, you may finger your clit at the same time as I beat you.'

'Thank you, master,' I whisper, resting on my elbows, awkwardly, so I can peel off a glove. Then I reach under myself to find the hot spot, and almost come when I make contact, I'm so ready.

Edward steps away, and with no further warning, I hear the hiss of flying leather and there's an explosion of pain and heat across my bottom.

Oh God! I'm never ready for this. It's always a shock. The feeling of a stripe of agony across my flesh. Without control, I whine loudly, shuddering and shaking. Beneath my fingertip, my clitoris pulsates.

He strikes again – harder – and I bite my lip, trying to keep silent. In the all too brief hiatus before the next blow, I rub my pussy, furiously slicking at my clit.

As he hits again, I collapse against the shiny black paint, coming and crying. The waves of pleasure are so hard and wrenching that I barely notice another wallop, the last one for now.

'We'll be late,' I gasp on regaining the power of speech. I'm still gulping in air, my entire body tingling, my bottom burning. I seem to have lost the ability to move, but energy returns to me when Edward strokes my back, encouraging me like a horsemaster coaxing a steady old mare into action. He's gentle, though, almost tender, and it makes my heart twist in a strange, non-sexual way.

He's a BDSM freak, but he can be kind, and very sweet.

'Come on then, love,' he says brightly. 'Let's move it, shall we?'

He helps me with my skirt, brushing me down lightly, then straightens my jacket. Licking the corner of his handkerchief, he delicately tidies my eye make-up where it's run a bit from my tears. Finally, he hands me my glove. 'There! You look gorgeous, old girl.' He gives me a light, reassuring kiss on my cheek.

'And you look as if you desperately need a shag,' I answer cheekily, glancing down at his crotch. He's got a massive hard-on that's tenting his elegant trousers.

His blue eyes narrow. Threateningly, but with a twinkle. 'If it didn't mean we'd be late, I'd thrash you again for your insolence.'

My head comes up. I like to challenge him sometimes, and he likes it too. He winks at me as he opens the passenger door for me. I hiss through my teeth when I resume my seat in the car, my stripes stinging, but after that I'm quiet and full of thought as we race towards the wedding venue.

I like him. I like him probably more than I should. He's fabulous. Utterly gorgeous. A real catch, handsome as sin, a beautiful man. Tall and dark and roguish with his neat goatee beard, his brilliant eyes and his wicked, teasing smile.

He's everything I want, but I should have found him twenty years ago.

Now stop that, you silly woman. Just don't go there . . .

The wedding itself is charming, and takes place in an old country church, but the pews are very hard and unforgiving to my punished bottom. A fact that clearly delights Edward. His eyes glitter, and his smirk is salacious as we share a battered hymnal.

The way he looks at me makes me want to do things that one shouldn't even *think* about in church. Like kneeling the wrong way round in the pew, while everybody else praises the Lord, to give *my* lord and master an extended blow job.

I drift through the reception on a wave of heightened awareness. This whole affair should be about Mandy and her new husband, but somehow they seem distant, on the periphery of my attention. All I can think about is Edward and his hands, his mouth, his cock. Speculative glances follow us wherever we go. I can see the surprise, imagine the muttered comments. Isn't that the IT guy with Jane Mitchell? The hot one who set up the new system a while back? How come those two are here together?

You don't know that half of it, people. And if you did, you wouldn't believe it.

Edward takes every opportunity to touch me, obviously aware of the interest in us. He guides my arm as we enter the house. He touches my back as we head towards the bridal receiving line. He pats my bottom, making me gasp, as we step forward to meet Mandy and her spouse, and, preoccupied as she must be, she seems to notice what he does.

'So glad you could come, Jane, and nice to see you again, Edward.' She grins widely, accepting our congrats.

Throughout the champagne swigging and canapé nibbling, Edward keeps eyeing me, that wicked, arch look on his face. His glance keeps drifting to my frontage, and the deep V of my suit jacket, as if he's speculating about what lies beneath it.

Wouldn't you like to know, mister.

After I've adjusted my lapels a couple of times, to let him know I've noticed his interest, he suddenly takes my champagne glass from me, knocks back the half-inch in it, and grabs me by the elbow and steers me towards the open French windows that lead to the garden. One or two people watch us, including Susan Grey, who works in my office, and I think, *Yes, it's exactly what you're thinking!*

Always clever at finding a secluded spot to have his way with me, Edward directs me around the side of the house until we happen upon what seems to be an old stable block. There are no horses there now, but we find a stall that's filled with old boxes and clearly used for storage.

'Show me!' he commands.

I don't have to ask what he means, and with shaking fingers I unfasten my jacket.

'Oh, very nice,' he breathes, in genuine admiration.

I've crammed myself into a deliciously naughty and very beautiful bustier. It's all pink satin and lace and it matches my skimpy thong. The cups are next to nothing, just a bit of frothy gauze, almost transparent, and my nipples are dark and hard, poking and pointing. In Edward's direction.

He reaches for me, and them, immediately. Cupping and stroking, he rolls the sensitive crests between his thumbs and fingers, squeezing a little as he manipulates me, but not hurting.

'Just gorgeous . . .' With respect for a garment that cost a fortune, and which I would only ever buy to please him, he scoops my breasts out of the fragile cups so that they rest on top of them, flauntingly offered. Then to my astonishment, he swoops down and kisses each teat, using his tongue, licking and anointing.

When he touches me again, the faint film of saliva adds a new layer of sensitivity. I moan and work my hips as he flicks and tickles me.

In these sorts of situations, I usually have to wait for permission to touch him, but right now, I can't help myself. I grab his head, digging my fingers into his thick, shampoo-fragrant hair. When he sucks a nipple again, I groan out loud, loving the sweet tugging sensation that's echoed in my clit. Caressing his scalp, I throw my head back, almost swooning.

I love this man. It's mad but it's true.

Still sucking and toying around my teat with his tongue, he

grips my bottom and stirs the flames that are simmering there. It burns hard, yet in my sex the honey flows. I shift my hips about. I can't keep still. I need him in me.

As if he's heard my plea, Edward straightens, his dark head cocked on one side, that knowing smile framed by his goatee.

'If you have it now, you'll have to pay, you know,' he says all low and serious, even though I know inside he's laughing.

'I know.' My voice is small, affectedly submissive. I'm laughing too, inside.

'OK then.' All business, he glances around, looking, I realise, for somewhere for us to fuck that won't ruin our posh wedding clothes. He nods towards an old wooden door, oaken and solid, that leads into an adjoining room. The surface is smooth and looks passably clean. I totter towards it, feeling shaky but horny as hell. Edward follows, pushing me onwards, a force of nature.

He backs me up against the wood and it's hard against my punished bottom. The stripes from his belt are fading now, but I still let out an 'oof!' of breath when he throws himself up against me and starts to kiss me as if I'm a hunk of prime filet mignon and he's a starving wolf. Worry for my make-up shoots through my mind then evaporates. It can be fixed, anything can be fixed. I've got to have him.

'Skirt!' he orders. Rocking back on his heels, he's already unfastening that devilish belt of his, then attacking his trousers and underwear to expose his cock. As I rumple up my clothing, ready and eager, I stare downwards.

And now I'm the ravening she-wolf, slavering over *his* meat.

He's prime, hard and high and reddened, his glans shining and the veins in his shaft sublimely defined. A work of art. And mine. For the moment. For a split second, I scrabble around for the itsy-bitsy little bag that's still dangling from my shoulder, but he just says, 'Leave it!' and reaches into his pocket.

So, we've both brought condoms to the occasion. I have to smile, and he nods and smiles back at me, his blue eyes suddenly beautifully young and merry.

'Great minds think alike.' I grin at my own cliché as he efficiently enrobes himself.

He gives me a despairing yet indulgent look, and then summarily grabs my thigh, lifting me and opening me while pushing aside my thong and positioning his cock at my entrance with his free hand.

No preliminaries. No niceties. No foreplay. Who needs it?

He shoves in hard, knocking me against the door and making me wince at its impact against my bottom. Throwing his weight against me, he starts to thrust, in and up, in a steady rhythm. I grab his shoulders and grunt in sync as he ploughs me.

Oh God, I'll never be able to get enough of this! The fucking and the spanking and the games – and the quieter moments too. Even as he bangs away at me relentlessly, there's a part of my consciousness hovering above us, marvelling at the sexy sight we make.

A beautiful young man, and an older woman made beautiful by the lust for life he's stirred in her. It might be another old cliché, the one about sex making you bloom, but by hell, it's surely happened to me with Edward. I feel doubly alive, full of juice, full of energy.

He thrusts and thrusts, going deep, slamming my back, my bottom and my head against the oak. I feel dizzy and it isn't only from arousal. Or from the way each plunge of his mighty penis knocks my clitoris. I hold on as if my life depends on this. Maybe it does? Orgasm barrels towards me, huge and breathtaking, and I bite my lip, keeping in a scream as it hits me full on. Everything jerks and wrenches and contracts in a delicious spasm. My heart soars even as pleasure tumbles down through me.

Climaxing, I haven't an ounce of strength left. I'm pinned to the door by Edward, and the way he holds me and powers into me with his cock. He makes a growly noise that's half-way between a laugh and groan of pleasure, and then he's coming too, his hips pounding, pounding, pounding me against the unyielding oak. The soreness in my bottom seems a million miles away.

'God almighty,' I pant, when my brain eventually re-engages. We're sort of propped in a general tangled heap against the door, and for all his usual sang-froid, Edward seems as shell-shocked as I am.

'I couldn't have put it better myself,' he says with a broken laugh as he levers himself off me, and straightens up, pushing against our support with both hands. Still not quite with it, I watch as he whips off the condom, knots it and flings it away. Wonder what someone coming to search the boxes will think when they find a used rubber johnny in the corner of their old storeroom?

Within seconds, Edward is zipped up and immaculate again, and with a couple of swipes of his hand, his smooth brown hair is tidy too. I suspect it might take rather longer to bring my appearance to order, but when I start to fiddle with my bustier, he dashes my hands away. Before I can draw breath he gives my nipples a squeeze or two.

'What a shame to have to cover these. They're so pinchable.' The squeezes turn to little nips, and even though I've just come like an express train, my body starts to be aroused again. It's always like that with him. I'm virtually always ready. 'Wish we had some clamps with us. I'd love to parade you about in front of all these posh folk with your tits on show and clamps dangling from your nipples.'

The way he's touching me, and what he says, make me feel faint. Because I can imagine it so clearly, almost feel it. All eyes on me and my bare breasts, adorned for his pleasure. It'd be shaming, but at the same time I'd feel proud. Like a prize, a barbarian slave girl . . . well, slave woman . . . all captured and tamed by my hot young warrior.

Still playing around with me, he kisses me again, hard and possessive. Where his pelvis is pressed against me, dear God, he's hard again. What is it with us two today? Is it the wedding, a traditional celebration of fertility and sensuality? Is it getting to us and making us extra horny?

Pulling away again, he laughs and reaches for the buttons of my jacket, fastening them up while my breasts are still uncovered beneath, resting on the flimsy cups of the bustier. The sensation of the jacket's satin lining sliding against my sensitised nipples is breathtaking, and I gasp as I move to try and set my skirt to rights.

As if he's loath to cover up my pussy too, Edward reaches down and gives me a rough fondle there, before unfolding the bundle of my skirt and sliding it down over my thighs and my stockings. With a wicked wink, he licks his fingers, savouring my taste.

'Well, I doubt if there's anything as delicious as that at the buffet, but shall we mosey on back inside and see what's on offer?' He smacks his lips wickedly, and gives my crotch a last quick squeeze through the cloth of my skirt.

'I'm going to have to tidy myself up first.' I try and comb my hair with my fingers, even though I know it'll take more than that, and a better mirror than the tiny one I have in my handbag. 'I must look as if I've been dragged backwards through a bush.'

Cocking his dark head on one side, he gives me a strange complex smile, and brushes his fingers lightly against my face.

'You look fabulous. Bloody amazing. And if I didn't think I was depriving you of all the festivities, love, I'd have your skirt up again and fuck you again right now.' The smile widens, becomes salacious. 'Maybe up the arse this time, for variety. Would you like that?'

Desire grinds in my pussy. Dark, twisted desire. The sort that blooms from pain, and strangeness, and intense sensations that dwell in the confused hinterland of discomfort and perverted pleasure.

Oh God, I really want that. I really do.

'Would you like that?' he persists, his blue eyes dark and stormy, vaguely satanic.

'Yes . . .'

'Yes, what?'

'Yes, master . . .' My voice is tiny. I feel light as air, as if I could fall over. But as if he's more attuned to me than I am to myself, Edward holds me by the arm and keeps me upright.

Leaning in to whisper in my ear, he says, 'Very well then, slave. I'm going to have your arse before we leave here, I promise you that.'

Luscious fear chokes me, and between my legs I feel a new rush of liquid. 'But . . . um . . . won't we need lube?'

'Never you worry, dirty girl. Don't you know by now that I'm always prepared?' He squeezes my bottom, and stirs the fire of my earlier punishment again. 'Now let's go.' He pushes me forward, towards the outside, still cupping my buttocks.

I complain, even though I like it, how I like it.

It's later and we've circulated, we've eaten, and I've drunk some more. Edward is a god over this. After a couple of glasses of champers, he's switched to mineral water with a twist of lime. I don't know whether it's simply his responsible driver ethic, or that he prefers to keep a clear head for our little games. I suspect it's a bit of both, but I'm not complaining. I've had more champagne and I'm feeling frisky and crazy and horny, and generally pretty fabulous.

People look at us. They look at us a lot. I still think they wonder what that old bird is doing with the gorgeous young hunk, but I don't care any more. I pretty much stopped caring altogether very soon after Edward and I started seeing each other. And fucking each other. And doing all the other things we do together. Apart from the fact that his face is smooth and unlined, and his body is like a male supermodel's, he doesn't seem like a younger man to me. He's in charge. He's authority personified. He knows the world.

There's a very impressive and disproportionately loud firework display going on now, and people are filtering outside to watch it. Edward winks at me, takes my glass from my hand and leads me out into the hall.

Oh. Game on. Desire charges through my veins and races to my pussy. He nods towards the stairs and urges me up them, touching my bottom as we go up. Just the simple contact makes me want to clutch myself, I'm so turned on. I can barely believe it.

He scans the landing, and we turn right along a corridor. Ahead of us, we see one of the groomsmen, a tall, fit individual I might have yearned for if I'd never met Edward. What the hell is he up to? All of a sudden, he opens a door that seems to lead to a cupboard of some kind, then slips inside, with a secret smile upon his face.

Edward gives me a secret smile of his own. 'Come on,' he says, 'let's find a cupboard of our own, eh?'

This is a rambling house, and exploring more corridors and a staircase brings us to a door that's slightly ajar. Confidently pushing it open, Edward steps inside then beckons me to follow.

It's an old study, someone's private retreat. Small and cluttered, and a bit dusty, it's still cosy in its own way. There are books around the walls, and a couple of old leather armchairs that nearly fill the space. On a sideboard, there's a candelabra, set with fresh, never-lit candles. As I step forward into the room, Edward crosses behind me to turn the key in the lock. I spin around and his eyes are narrowed yet glinting as he runs his gaze over my body.

If I wasn't already primed, I would be now. The way he looks at me seems to own me, and I love that. His scrutiny lingers over my breasts, and my crotch, and when he tips his head, it's an unspoken indication that I should turn around and show him more.

'That arse of yours, love. I'll never get tired of it, you know. Never ever.' There's such honesty in his voice, real enthusiasm. He loves to play the master, but he doesn't fool about with feigning disinterest and aloofness. He never hides the fact he's really into it. 'Come on, show me the goods, you sexy creature.'

Craning to look at him over my shoulder, I ease up my slim skirt, the glide of the silk lining a subtle caress and also a lick of simmering heat over my bottom. The places where he hit me earlier have settled now, but there's still heightened sensitivity and subtle fire there.

'Lean over. Put your hands on the chair arms, and brace yourself.'

I obey him, my heart fluttering. God, I love to show myself to him in this kind of blatant and faux demeaning way. It doesn't actually demean me – it's really the opposite – but the sense of theatre in it excites me as well as him.

He comes over to stand behind me, and nudges my heels apart with the toe of his polished dress shoe. As my thighs separate, I feel the sticky folds of my sex part as well. My thong is sodden, has been for hours, and the odour of my arousal seems to fill the room.

In an action of ownership, Edward thrusts two fingers into my sex. 'Always ready . . . I love that. I love that you're so horny, sweetheart.'

Only for you . . . only for you . . .

I bear down on the intrusion. I love it that I'm so horny too. I love that this beautiful young man has come into my life and switched everything on to full power that was only ticking over before. Right now, I don't care that it's probably only a temporary situation. Knowing Edward – and yes, loving him too – has given me the gift of being able to live for the day, for the moment.

'Oh, you like that, don't you?' he whispers, leaning over me, the smooth cloth of his jacket sliding over my bottom. With his breath whispering against the back of my neck, he parts his two fingers to stretch me. My pussy ripples around them and my clit swells and pulses.

'Answer me,' he growls softly, flexing his fingers even more and making me gasp and moan in my throat.

'I like it.' I force out the words as he tests me, pushing me and making me rise on my toes.

'And would you like it if I put something else inside you?'

Push, push, push . . .

'Yes. Anything,' I answer boldly.

'And how about in your arse? The same?'

'Yes . . . the same . . . in my arse.' With his free hand he slips a finger under the ribbon that bisects my buttocks and flicks lightly at my anus, syncopating the touches with the thrust of his fingers inside me.

I can hardly breathe. I can hardly think. I can only anticipate, and feel intoxicated by luscious sexual anxiety.

'Good girl . . . good girl . . .' He continues to fondle me and plague me. I want to tell him to get on with it, to do his worst. But he'll do things in his time. He's in charge. He always will be.

And yet I can't stop myself from moving, hitching about, tensing and stretching. This pose is killing the backs of my legs, but in my ever-gathering anticipation I barely notice the discomfort. It's like being a mechanism that tightens, tightens, tightens, ready to discharge its energy in a huge, frightening burst.

'Be careful, slave,' he warns softly, still working me. The words are stern, but there's that softer, more tender note again.

That's what makes me come. It's too much. Too sweet. Too great a pleasure. Unable to contain or control myself, I pitch forward in the chair, face first into the cushions, resting on one elbow while with the other I reach down disobediently and press on my pulsing clit to sweeten the moment. My hand jostles Edward's where it's down between my legs.

He doesn't reprimand me, or go all 'master' on me. He just works with me, through the furore, making things better for me with his clever, loving fingers.

'Well, that didn't work out quite how I planned,' he says at length.

I'm sort of in a heap in the chair, crumpling my posh suit and ruining my make-up yet again by burying my face in the cushions. I feel a bit teary and I'm hiding it from him, although I suspect he can probably tell. He's perched on the chair arm beside me, and he's stroking my dishevelled hair slowly.

'Sorry.'

'Don't be, baby . . .' His hand pauses, and he tucks a few thick wayward strands of hair behind my ears. Lord knows what's happened to the hairdo that cost me a fortune. I must look like a well-dressed bag lady by now. 'I like to see you having fun. I like to feel it.'

I roll over, trying to sit straight and adjust my skirt to make myself half-way decent, but he stops me. Quite gently, but he still prevents me from covering myself up.

'No, don't hide it yet.' His blue eyes gleam. 'When I said things didn't quite turn out how I planned, that doesn't mean I've given up altogether.'

Oh, there's that delicious thread in his voice again. Command. Confidence. Control. Even though I've come so much already today, I start to want again. Want him. Want . . . want whatever. With him. I risk a slight smile, then unfold myself from the chair, and assume the position again. In readiness.

'Good God,' he breathes, 'You are a very special woman.' For a moment, he's quiet and awestruck, and then it's like a cloak of power falls back over him and he's all business again. All sex.

'And you have a very special arse too,' he observes, beginning to fondle me there again. 'A very fine arse. An arse that should have things done to it.' He pats and plays around the little vent between my buttocks for a moment, and then pauses and reaches into the inside pocket of his suit jacket. A second later I feel something cool and slippery being poured between my bottom cheeks, saturating the string of my thong.

'Oh, so that's what you mean by coming prepared,' I snip at him, forgetting my role, but he just laughs and continues to lube me.

Oh, it's exciting. This feeling. The wondering. The waiting. We've played like this often enough before, but somehow my brain seems to forget how it's going to feel, how it's going to go. It's always new. Always a cause for apprehension and longing in equal parts. And it always makes me moan, and gasp and pant.

'Steady,' he whispers, firm yet sensitive to my chaos. He slides his sticky hand up beneath my bunched skirt and rubs the small of my back like a trainer calming a skittish horse, then, still rubbing, he reaches away.

A second later, I realise what he was reaching for. There's firm pressure on my anus, something quite narrow but unforgiving, not a part of Edward.

The absolute devil! He's pushing one of the unused candles into my bottom!

Everything surges inside me. Messages along my nerves, pumping hormones and juice, feelings, sensations. I gasp harder, fight for control as he penetrates my rear with the candle.

I hate it. I love it. I can't bear it. I want more.

And all the time he murmurs, 'Steady, steady . . .' to calm my struggles.

He inserts it just an inch or two, not a long way, and just leaves it there. My crazed innards don't know what they want to do. My pussy is awash, slick and flowing, my own lubrication, rather than the artificial kind, streaming down the insides of my thighs and wetting the tops of my hold-up stockings.

With the candle still inside me, he starts to play. Both with me and with himself. I hear the smooth whir of his zip and I know he's got his cock out, even though my eyes are tight shut to help me cope with the overloading of my senses.

He fingers my clit. He pushes a digit inside my vagina. He gives my bare bottom one or two lazy slaps, stirring the heat there. Quite at his leisure, he alternates these various attentions, although he returns most frequently to my clitoris, fondling and petting it.

I'm sobbing now, at my wit's end, but happy with it. The sob sharpens to a wail as he pinches my clit lightly and compels me to come, setting the candle bobbing in and out as my pussy clenches.

With difficulty, I hold my position. I barely know what I'm doing apart from being rocked on waves of dark sweet pleasure.

As if from a great distance, I hear the small distinctive sounds of a condom being unwrapped, and a second or two later, I feel the brush of his latex-covered cock against the under-hang of my bottom.

'Decisions, decisions.' His voice is sweet with humour, deliciously devilish. 'Cunt? Arse? Cunt? Arse?' It's like he's a boy choosing a hand for that hidden marble. And then he ends the debate, makes his choice, and I feel the candle slide out of me. Then I hear it hit the carpet as he flings it away.

More pressure on the tender, resisting hole. And this time the intrusion is bigger. *Much* bigger than a candle. He pushes in and my senses riot again; dangerous, forbidden, transgressive messages fly about inside me. But as he forges on, he's still gentling and soothing me with soft words, soft caresses. He holds me steady and rubs my clit as he starts to thrust.

I'm not soft though. I shout and blaspheme, out of my mind with pleasure. I buck about, collapsing again, grabbing at his hand, holding it between my legs, forcing him to fondle me and pleasure my clitoris, and to go on and on doing it as I come wildly, my entire lower body pulsing and clamping and rippling in furious, kinetic movement.

He holds on. He fights for control. But eventually loses it too. His voice is hoarse and passionate as he pumps and climaxes in my bottom. His words are twisted, but I understand them, and my joy is doubled.

A while later, we stagger out of the little study and manage to find a bathroom that doesn't have a queue of waiting guests. Even though they're all filtering back in from the firework display now, heading for the main ballroom and the disco.

We tidy up. We calm down. We exchange hugs and smiles like an entirely normal couple. Maybe we are a normal couple, for all our quirks and our disparate ages? In the aftermath of stormy passion, all is tranquil, all is easy. It's as if we've been together decades, comfortable yet still adoring.

The music's good and we dance, bopping about with the best of them. People seem to have got used to us as an item. Smiles abound. When the slow tunes come along, we drift into each other's arms, to smooch.

'So, weddings,' whispers Edward in my ear after a song or two. 'Big, lavish affairs . . . or small, intimate registry office jobs with a few folk round the pub afterwards?'

I almost freeze on the dance floor, but he buoys me up, keeping me moving to the rhythm, strong and unwavering.

Am I imagining things? Is he asking what I think he's asking?

'Are you asking what I think you're asking?' I didn't mean the words to come out loud but they have.

'Yep,' he says, his hand on the small of my back, gentling me as he did before when he was doing wicked, naughty things to my bottom. 'I'm asking.'

I should weigh things up, think things through, consider this carefully, but instead I just say, 'Yes!'

'Brilliant!' he answers, then kisses me, long and sweet and hard.

When we break apart he smiles and asks again, 'So, small affair or big and lavish?'

I laugh and kiss his cheek. I don't care which, but I answer, 'Lavish!' in his ear.

'Good girl,' he whispers, and moving closer, we slow-dance on . . .

Portia Da Costa is the author of the Black Lace novels *Continuum*, *Entertaining Mr Stone*, *Gemini Heat*, *Gothic Heat*, *Gothic Blue*, *Hotbed*, *Shadowplay*, *Suite Seventeen*, *The Devil Inside*, *The*

Stranger, The Tutor, In Too Deep and *Kiss It Better*. Her paranormal novellas are included in the Black Lace collections *Lust Bites* and *Magic and Desire*. Her short stories appear in numerous Black Lace anthologies.

Delayed Gratification

Kyoko Church

Here they were, again.

Lola had promised herself. Never again. And after nearly four years she thought she was fairly safe. Four years of passing hellos. Four years of polite conversation and platonic smiles. Graduation for her. A divorce for him. He seemed happier now and she, well, she had reclaimed the person she once was. Lola, the honest person. Lola, the good friend.

So how was it that the two of them were in this hotel room? About to do something she'd thought of over and over but had sworn. Never again. Only in her head. Fantasy was OK. But this was not fantasy.

Looking back at the past few weeks it seemed like maybe she had planned it. Had she? Not consciously, anyway, she didn't think. Exams finally completed and university behind her, she was home for the summer. She made plans to hang out with Hailey, like she'd done so many times before. And, like so many times before, Hailey said, 'Yeah, come on over, we'll rent movies, eat popcorn.' And now, since her parents' divorce was finally settled, her mom had moved out and calm had been restored, she could stay over again. 'It'll be just like old times,' Hailey had said.

Like old times.

She forced herself not to think about that too long, in the days and hours before going over there. Not to let her mind wander back to the many nights four long summers ago. The slumber parties. Girlfriends just hanging out, gossiping, texting their friends, dishing on guys. And what would happen – after.

The first weekend after graduating high school she and Hailey were celebrating by sneaking slugs from the various bottles in her parents' liquor cabinet. Not that they had to be too secretive. That year the tension in Hailey's house was at its peak and both parents were too embroiled in their own fighting to really notice what the girls were up to.

'Do you think your parents still do it?' giggled Lola, as she took a swig from the bottle of peach schnapps Hailey had passed her.

'Oh my God, Lola! Fucking, ew!' Hailey grimaced. 'Is your mind always in the gutter?'

'I don't know, I just wonder about shit like that.' She smiled slyly. 'I know mine do. I've heard them,' she whispered, handing the bottle back.

Hailey threw a pillow at her. 'You're a freak, girl.'

'I'm sure yours do too,' Lola teased her friend. 'Your dad's a total hottie. His sandy hair and blue eyes – he looks like that plumber on *Desperate Housewives*.'

'Lola! That's my friggin' dad you're talking about!'

'Sor-ry,' Lola sang out, though she was clearly not. 'But God, everybody else's dad is, like, ancient. Yours is, what, like barely forty?'

'Yeah, well, I guess that's the benefit of getting your girl-friend pregnant in high school,' Hailey said with a shrug.

'They told you that?'

'I pretty much figured it out on my own when I was twelve. It wasn't hard, I knew the relevant dates,' Hailey scoffed. 'I confronted my mom and she admitted it.'

There was an awkward silence. Then Hailey sighed. 'It's no big deal. Now, anyway. At least I know why I got the sex talk so early. Plus, my mom put me on birth control, like, two years ago.'

'Really?' Lola asked.

'I swear, she thinks she's my friend, not my mom,' Hailey said.

'That is so cool. I think my mom would die if she found my pills. I'd love it if she would relax a little.'

'You think so,' said Hailey, 'but really it sucks. You should hear some of the things she tells me. T-M-I, Mom!! So I actually happen to know they don't do it any more.'

'Oh my God, she talks to you about that?'

'She told me she's not into it. Personally I think she's still messed up about getting knocked up in the first place. It's like she wants to punish him.' Hailey took a big gulp of the schnapps, winced and let out a belch. 'I know she's my mom and everything but she's a total whacko. I mean, how screwed up is it to be talking to your daughter about your sex life?'

'Pretty screwed up,' Lola admitted.

'Whatever. I don't even care any more. Because –' she paused dramatically as she sat up on her bed '– they're letting me take that summer acting course,' Hailey sang out, a big satisfied smile across her lips.

'What?' Lola said. 'It's like an hour away. I thought your dad didn't want you driving there at night on your own!'

'My mom's taking me.' She grinned. 'That's the upside of having your mom trying to be your best friend. I can talk her into anything. Besides, it'll give her an excuse to shop downtown every Monday and Thursday night.'

The schnapps rendered the girls sleepy early. But Lola woke up at about 2 a.m., parched. She tottered down to the kitchen, her long wavy brown hair spilling messily down over her full breasts, still slightly tipsy and only vaguely aware of her state of undress in just a T-shirt and panties. She opened the fridge, searching for juice, when she was suddenly aware of a presence behind her.

She turned and there was Hailey's father, seated at the kitchen table in his bathrobe, hair dishevelled, looking for all the world like a man with the soul sucked out of him. Lola was used to seeing him in a business suit, arriving home from work, confident, busy, quickly kissing his daughter on the cheek before disappearing into his den. This was a different man. A broken man. Vulnerable.

She apologised and quickly got her drink, embarrassed and trying to pull her shirt down. And he looked embarrassed too. But then, there was something else. Underneath that beaten-down exterior emerged a little look. Like an ember. She only saw it briefly after she fled down the hallway to the staircase and glanced back. There he sat at the table, framed by the doorway. And he was staring, just where her T-shirt ended and the slightest bit of her bottom was exposed. Heat rose to her face, and down, as she dashed up to Hailey's room, her heart pounding.

She left her book there. She needed her book.

That's what she told herself the following Monday. Putting out of her mind the fact that she had spent all of Sunday thinking about him, about what Hailey had told her and about that look she saw on his face, she finally remembered Monday night that she'd left a book in Hailey's room. That is what she repeated over and over in her head as she watched her feet on the sidewalk, hitting the pavement, tramp – tramp – tramp, propelled, it seemed, by a mission all their own. A chant in her head as she went. Tramp – tramp – tramp, need – my – book, tramp – tramp – tramp, need – my – book, tramp – tramp. Tramp?

He opened the door. 'Oh, Lola.' He seemed surprised, nervous. 'Hailey isn't here right now. Her mother's taken her to her acting class.'

'Oh, I'm sorry, I didn't realise.' (Tramp.)

Pause.

'. . . Need my book.' It fell out of her mouth.

'I'm sorry?'

'I, I left my book here on the weekend.' She managed a weak smile. 'I have to study.'

'But it's summer vacation,' he said, but he was smiling too. And as she stepped inside she saw the look again, the same ember of fire that she had seen two nights before. This time she was sure what it meant.

She stood awkwardly, wordlessly rooted to the spot in the front hall with him. He was so close she could smell his clean scent, soap and shaving cream. Her mind reeled as she remembered Hailey's words – *they don't do it* – *she wants to punish him* – while she gazed up at his dark-blue eyes. Suddenly, before she could think too much about it, she leaned forward to kiss him. He tasted sweet, like apples. His lips parted but he barely moved.

She moved into the den, the room beside the front door she had seen him disappear into a million times before. He followed her. It was dark. The shades were drawn. The walls were painted a forest green and the mahogany shelves were filled with hockey trophies, books on sales strategies, model race cars. On the built-in desk, beside his laptop, there was a small framed photo of him and Hailey. Lola swallowed and quickly looked away.

He had a small loveseat in there and that's where they landed. She kissed him and her kisses were like questions, seeking out his attention, his attraction. It was unlike anything Lola had experienced before. Granted her experience was fairly limited to high-school fumblings in cars and parents' basements. Those encounters had always made her feel like she was playing defence, blocking this hand here, heading off this pass there. Guys called her a cock-tease. They didn't understand. She wanted to be touched and caressed. How badly she did! At nights she lay awake in her bed, her head brimming with horny fantasies of faceless men working her to shuddering orgasm after orgasm. In her favourite ones, the faceless man's head moved down, between her legs. The thought of a slick, warm tongue sliding repeatedly over that sensitive little button sent her over the edge every time. She had never experienced it. Never dared ask for it. But she craved it.

In reality the boys she had been with always went for broke way too early. They'd just barely be alone together and suddenly she'd be under attack. She spent way too much time playing defence to get horny. And the one time she had allowed it to go further, when she lost her virginity, it was over before she had time to register what happened.

But not this time. And while she was glad – no, glad didn't cover it: ecstatic – while she was ecstatic to finally enjoy slow, passionate kisses, to revel in the way it made her feel, pretty soon she was wondering why he wasn't trying to touch her. And that wondering gave way to desperately needing his hands on her.

He broke the kiss and she looked at him.

'Lola, you are such a beautiful girl,' he started. And then she saw it. The lust mixed with tortured conflict in his eyes. The simultaneous wanting and self-loathing. And she realised that, though he might want her – and she gathered by the huge bulge in his pants that he did – badly enough that he couldn't stop what they were doing, he also wouldn't allow himself to push forward. That would have to come from her.

So when she started kissing him again she put his hands

on her body. And she guided them where she wanted them to go. She slid his hands over her breasts, her breath catching as he grazed her taut nipples under her thin T-shirt and bra. She pulled them under her shirt, undoing her bra so she could feel his bare hands on her flesh. She guided his fingers to her nipples and he pinched and pulled at them as she exhaled audibly, the sensations going directly to her increasingly wet pussy. Swiftly she pulled her shirt off and guided his head to her breast. Slowly, almost timidly, he began licking at the puckered tip. His lips surrounded it and he sucked on it softly as he continued pinching the other one between his fingers. She could barely sit still, could only squirm and sigh and moan.

She pushed him to each new level. Several times she faltered. What was she doing? This was Hailey's father! What about Hailey's mom? But her libido pushed those thoughts aside, urgently compelling her to act in this brazen way that seemed like a different person.

By the time he was naked from the waist up and she was clad only in her panties, her body felt like it had been plugged in and charged up, fairly humming with pent-up desire. At her urging he had kissed and caressed, licked and tugged every part of her exposed skin. There was only one place he hadn't kissed. And although she desperately wanted him to, though her clitoris was pounding a relentless beat between her thighs, she just couldn't bring herself to guide him there.

Instead she went to undo his belt. As she started to pull the tongue out from the buckle, he stopped her. And, taking the lead for the first and only time that day, he knelt down on the floor in front of where she sat on the sofa.

She could barely breathe as he slid her panties down her thighs, exposing her cleanly shaven sex. When she saw the dark spot where her wetness had seeped on to the material, her cheeks burned bright with embarrassment. She saw him notice it too. It seemed to spur him on.

Wordlessly he pulled her hips towards him so that her pussy was even with the edge of the couch. Gently he parted her legs. Her embarrassment over how wet she was almost made her want him to stop. Almost. But then his thumbs were on her labia, carefully pulling them apart. His head was inches away. She felt his warm breath on her. He dipped his tongue deep into her well, pulled the slick honey up and spread it over her clit with his tongue.

Her mind could only register one-syllable thoughts. Fuck. Fuck. Oh. God. She pulled her feet up on either side of her, opening her cunt up to his mouth more fully. Her clit was beyond sensitive after the hour of drawn-out foreplay. It was a jangled bunch of nerve endings all crammed into one hard little bud. And now his wet tongue was stroking it, lapping that bud over and over.

'Oh God,' she moaned. She was shaking uncontrollably under the slow stroking ministrations of his tongue. Then he sucked her clit into his mouth, she bucked and gasped, and he started flicking it rapidly.

'Ah! Uh, uh, oh, uh, guh, guh,' she panted and grasped at the couch. She was vaguely aware that the sounds emitting from her mouth were like those of a heart-attack victim or mental patient. But she couldn't control it. His tongue! Oh God, it just kept flicking her clit, faster, faster, licking, licking it, over and over, harder now, harder, oh God, oh God, she was coming.

She had only ever experienced an orgasm before by her own hand. And now, to have the explosion licked out of her by his strong, persistent tongue was almost more than she could handle. She screamed wildly as her body convulsed but he held her steady, one hand firmly on each hip, and continued to lick and suck until only soft whimpers escaped her lips.

Afterwards when he came up to sit beside her she tried again to unbuckle his pants. But again he stopped her.

'I'm sorry, Lola. I want you so badly,' he said as she glanced down at that bulge in his pants. He chuckled and sheepishly bowed his head. 'Obviously,' he muttered. 'But this is such a mistake. I feel terrible that I let it go this far.'

'It wasn't you. I pushed you. I wanted you to,' she said.

'But I'm the adult here,' he argued.

'Mr Thornton,' she said, and he groaned and put his head between his hands. 'I'm nineteen now. I was a willing part of this.' She bowed her head. 'And I should have stopped too.'

'At least call me David,' he whispered, still with his head in his hands.

He made her leave him then. And they didn't see each other for the rest of the week. But every night she dreamed of him. Dreamed of how he made her erupt with his tongue, of how his cock would feel deep inside her throbbing pussy. When she stayed over again that Saturday she held her breath as she descended the stairs, again in the wee hours of the morning. But she knew he would be there. Sitting at the kitchen table. Waiting.

They made their confessions in a hushed, hurried torrent of words.

'I dream every night of you licking me.'

'I jerked off on to the couch where your pussy was.'

'I finger myself while I imagine your cock.'

'I could still smell you.'

That night he let her put him inside her for the first time. There in the darkened kitchen, ears primed to perceive the first hint of movement from upstairs, she straddled him urgently, no talking now, no thinking, only body parts: cock, pussy. Though they could barely move for fear of making noise, though she could only rock her clitoris slowly against the base of his hard shaft, she came with all the intensity of the first time; more so, it seemed, as her sex clenched hungrily around his steel-like rod. When she whispered in his ear, 'Fuck me, fuck me and come in my tight little pussy,' he let out a strangled cry and released inside of her.

And so began the whirlwind of that summer. For a few weeks they were satisfied with the Monday and Thursday nights and the few stolen moments whenever she stayed there on weekends. But soon they needed more. Then there were hotel rooms, he bought her presents, she emailed him long, explicit fantasies.

It was one such night, blissfully alone in a hotel room and free of all the usual hindrances of time and keeping quiet, that he first teased her. He was lying beside her on the bed fingering her pussy. During their first encounter he had been so reluctant to push forward, and after she worried that without that barrier he might turn out to be just like the other boys she had been with, pawing at her too quickly. She needn't have worried. His usual pace was dawdling at its fastest. She grew addicted to his frustratingly unhurried tempo.

After about fifteen minutes of his fingers moving inside her she was gasping and thrusting her hips up, a flush moving from her cheeks down to her breasts.

'Oh, baby, oh, David, yes, yes,' she panted as he continued his slow stroking. 'Oh, God, I'm getting close.'

'Are you going to come?' he whispered in her ear.

'God, yes,' she sighed, eyes closed.

'Ask me.'

'Wha–?' she gasped as he sped up his fingers just a fraction.

'Say, "May I come?"'

Confused, but too horny to protest, she blurted out, 'May I come?'

'Not yet,' he replied, and stroked a little faster still. She tried to obey him, to hold herself back, but her pussy seemed to have a mind of its own, especially now that he was supplying the faster strokes it was hungry for. She felt her juices flowing out of her and dripping down. Her orgasm loomed and her muscles clenched once.

'Oh, oh, I can't help it! I'm gonna come! Please, please, may I come?'

His lips brushed her ear as he whispered, 'Just hold back a little longer. Relax into it . . .'

'OK, OK, I'm trying,' she panted and forced herself to unclench. She breathed deeply as he fingered her for another thirty seconds. Then he withdrew his hand and she let out a frustrated moan.

Her eyes flew open and she saw him pull himself on top of her. Slowly, slowly he eased his pulsing erection into her sopping hole. 'Ah!' she exclaimed. Her slippery tunnel sucked him in in one smooth stroke. She closed her eyes again, lost in sheer sexual bliss. He was so wonderfully hard, he filled her so entirely. He pushed the base of his dick against her throbbing clit and her pussy immediately clamped down eagerly around his cock.

'Oh, fuck, I can't hold back. Please may I come, please, please, please?' she pleaded, her voice panicked.

'Open your eyes,' he commanded. She obeyed. She stared up at him, still panting, stared deeply into the dark blue of his eyes and felt the intensity thrum between them as he continued to saw steadily in and out of her. 'Now you can come,' he announced, and he fucked her hard then, fucked her faster, rubbing her clit each time and she finally, finally let go, let herself explode, her pussy contracting wildly around him as she gasped for air. And the whole time she kept her eyes locked on his, watched the fire burning in their depths as he worked her gushing quim over the edge with his monstrous cock. At that moment there was nothing else. Just him. And her.

Soon she felt one impossibly powerful throb deep within her and, with a loud groan, he pulled out and jacked that enormous shaft until her stomach and breasts were covered in his milky load.

It went on like this for two more months. Two months of fiery, blistering passion. Two months of him slowly teasing every orgasm out of her. Two months of making her ask, beg, plead and scream to be allowed to come. In between their meetings she was constantly wet. Once she had to take the bus out of town, to the university that had accepted her, to spend the weekend at the residence that would soon be her home. She could barely stand to be away from him but she couldn't arouse any suspicion by not going. On the way home, seated by herself at the back of the bus, she stared dreamily out the window and thought about the last time they were together, when he licked her pussy for an hour without letting her come, no matter how she begged. The vibrations of the bus buzzed up through the inseam of her jeans that was pressed firmly against her swollen nub. Suddenly she came, came right there on the bus, making her gasp and clutch the seat in front of her. It wasn't a full orgasm, just short, shallow spasms that somehow left her hornier than before, aching for him in a way that was almost tangible.

She knew, of course she knew, that what they were doing was so glaringly wrong and would have to end. Occasionally thoughts of Hailey and of Hailey's mom would enter, unbidden, into her harried brain. But she worked hard at keeping them at bay, wouldn't allow them to land and fester for too long. Part of her knew that if she thought about it, let herself acknowledge what she was doing to her friend's family, she would have to stop. And she so badly didn't want to stop.

Then came the day when she couldn't prevent reality from forcing its way in, from insisting that she take stock.

Hailey called her in tears. 'I heard him, Lola,' she managed between sobs. 'I've been suspicious for a while now that he's seeing someone. He's been away so much more, he's always so distracted. I guess I just didn't want to believe it.'

Heat rose to Lola's face. 'What did you hear?'

Hailey sobbed again. 'I heard him on the phone with her.'

Panic. 'You were listening on the line?' Lola choked out, then cleared her throat. 'Did you hear her voice?'

'No, I was walking past the den and I heard him in there. I couldn't tell exactly what he was saying. But I didn't have to. I could just tell by the way he was speaking to her.' She started crying again.

'Lola, I know my mom can be a royal bitch. I hate her half the time too. But I really thought he would try to work it out. If he leaves us for this woman, what are we going to do?'

That's what brought reality crashing down on her. She ended it the next day.

For a while she was worried that Hailey would put two and two together. Would start to realise that every time her father hadn't been around, strangely Lola had been busy too. Or that it was after her teary phone call that her dad seemed to come around, to be less distracted. But no. Really Lola knew that in her wildest imaginings Hailey would never think that Lola could be the one, that Lola could do this to her. And that made her feel even more guilty. That's what made her swear to herself that no matter what happened, she would never let her body overtake her common sense again.

Never again.

Truth be told, it had been a long four years for her.

She had figured that, away at school, out on her own for the first time, she would have lots of exciting experiences. Turned out university guys weren't that much different from high-school guys when it came to sex. She'd had a couple of longer-term boyfriends, one that lasted over a year. But nothing came close to matching the illicit passion she'd had with David. Occasionally she tried encouraging her partner to slow things down. Timidly once, she even asked one guy to make her beg. He treated her like she was a total freak. She never saw him again after that.

'I'm glad you're here tonight, Lola,' Hailey said. 'It's been too long.'

'It has been a while,' Lola agreed as she sipped at the wine her friend poured her. 'But I understand. Things were tough around here.' She paused. 'I'm sorry I wasn't really around for you. You know, through your folks splitting up and every-thing.'

'It's OK,' Hailey said. 'Really, it's better now. No more screaming matches. My mom's better on her own. And she's finally getting counselling.'

'That's great, Hails.' Lola took another gulp of the dark-red liquid before she ventured, 'Your dad's doing better too, then?'

'Yeah, I guess. I mean, he's definitely around more often, which is nice.' She paused. 'But I don't know, he seems a little . . . vacant. Like sometimes I look at him and he's a million miles away. I wish I knew what he was thinking.'

After Hailey fell asleep that night, Lola lay awake staring up at the ceiling. She felt suffocated, like a weight was on her, wondering, desperately wondering if he could be down there, waiting for her. The thought consumed her. Finally she could take it no longer. She stole down the steps. Crept down the hall. At first it looked empty. Then. There he was.

He stared at her, wordlessly. In his stare were all the things she was dying for. Heat. Fire. Passion. And most of all lust. Lust stripped down and bare, this time with no encumbrances. She drank it in and returned it with a look filled with all of her own unfulfilled desires. Finally she took a breath and whispered, 'I dream . . . of sucking you.' She felt giddy, drunk on wine and the deliciousness of saying the words out loud after so long, of him hearing them. Horny, thinking, *now he knows. I've said it.* She closed her eyes and relished that feeling for as long as she could.

When she opened them he said, 'Not here.'

She nodded her silent agreement.

So it didn't happen then. Not then. But then there was an email, a phone call. Then a couple more. Pretty soon it was: Meet me here. Just this once. One last time. We'll have all night. One whole night.

So. Here. Again.

He was already there, in the hotel room, when she arrived. And when he opened the door it all hit her: the familiarity, the inevitability, the momentum leading them to this. It was intoxicating and knocked the wind out of her for a moment. Despite all the circumstances that dictated to the contrary – that deemed this wrong, deceitful, bad – in that moment it felt undeniably exciting, sexy and right.

They kissed, passionately, standing in the middle of the room, the door still open. He broke their embrace for a moment to close the door and when he turned back to her she was holding something in her hands.

Handcuffs.

He chuckled. 'Seems you've gotten a little kinky.'

She shrugged and grinned. 'Right. *I'm* the kinky one.' Then she motioned with her head. 'Sit in the chair.'

'Yes, ma'am,' he said and obliged, still chuckling, amused by her seriousness.

She had three pairs of handcuffs. She used one to restrain his hands behind his back, around the back of the chair. The other two pairs she used to secure each of his ankles to the front two legs of the chair. Then she sat gently in his lap and kissed him again, harder this time, while she unbuttoned his shirt. When she got up to undo his pants and slide them as far down as his restrained legs would allow, her face was so close to his crotch he pressed his pelvis up off the chair towards her.

'Hmm. Now that's going to be a problem.' He looked at her quizzically as she stood back and surveyed her work, contemplating. Then she took his belt out from his pants and hers from her jeans. She took down his briefs to join his pants and then strapped his belt around his knee and the top of the chair leg, so that his knee was fixed to the corner. She repeated this task on the other side with her belt so that he was now almost completely immobile with his legs parted in a V.

'Much better,' she said, and for the first time he started to look a little nervous.

That done she put on some music and began to strip for him, very slowly. She watched his eyes as she slowly unbuttoned her top. His gaze fixed on her breasts, clad in a black French lace demi-cup bra with just a touch of pink. 'Do you remember this bra?' she asked him softly. He only stared back, unsure. 'You bought it for me. This, and the thong.' She turned around and eased down her jeans so he could see the black lace disappearing between her ass cheeks. She stepped out of the jeans. Arching her back, she looked at him over her shoulder, enjoying his expression as he took in the picture of her with her ass pushed out in front of him, of her clad only in the bra and thong he had bought for her and a pair of stripper heels she'd bought when she was taking that pole-dancing class. Swaying to the music she turned around, took a few steps closer and slowly circled her pelvis in front of him. Her breasts spilled out of the demi-cups, which just barely covered her nipples. 'Do you remember it now? I know it was very expensive and I've kept it all this time.'

'I can't believe you still have it,' he finally managed, his eyes still glued to her swaying body. 'I always loved it when you'd strip for me in this. Baby, you look so fucking hot. Why don't you come over here and let me touch you.'

'Mmmm, soon, baby,' she replied, relishing his total attention on her. 'But first I want to dance for you while I tell you about some of the naughty fantasies I've had.'

So, as the bass of the music pumped slow and steady, she swayed her body to the rhythm and ran her hands up through her hair, down over her breasts, playing idly with her nipples before sliding them over her belly. And as she danced she told him of all the times over the past four years she lay in bed alone, wanting him, wondering if he still thought of her. So horny, unrequited and fantasising about going down on him, about having his cock in her mouth, her fantasy playing out in her mind while in bed she quietly fingered herself to a slow, pulsing orgasm, choking back her moans. Telling him was so freeing, once she got started she couldn't stop, and the words flowed out of her. It was as if she had built a dam across her desires, a dam filled up with all the fleeting hellos, the chaste kisses on the cheek appropriate to greeting her friend's father. Now it was just him. And her. Alone. And her true feelings, all the fantasies she kept bottled up inside her spilled over and flowed out, filling the room.

'Sometimes when I'm all alone, I'll watch porn for an hour without touching myself. Until I'm really horny. Then I imagine you're there with me and you make me masturbate for you. You tell me to finger myself until I'm really close to the edge and then stop. You make me edge myself like that ten times while you watch. Watch and count. By ten I'm so close I can hardly touch my clit without going over. I'm writhing and moaning and begging you to let me come. Finally you say you'll finish me yourself, with your tongue on my clit, but that you're going to do it slow. Then with my finger slowly rubbing I imagine it's your tongue. You keep it going back and forth firmly but achingly slow so that even as I'm going over the edge you never speed up. I scream and contort as the spasms rock through my body and I come and come and come.'

Her chest heaved and the sound of her blood pumping through her veins filled her ears as she came out of the trance she was in while she relayed her favourite fantasy. She looked at him, his cock rock-hard now, his breathing shallow, his arms and legs pulling at their restraints. 'Come here,' he said, and it came out a growl, low and dangerous.

She sauntered slowly over and, careful not to touch his cock, sat on his lap. 'Have you ever tried going slow at that point?' She ran her fingers through his hair and then held his face so she could look straight into his eyes as she whispered, 'Do you know how hard it is, when you've held back that long, not to speed up and stroke really fast as you're going over the edge?' He swallowed hard. She smiled seductively. 'Do you know how much more intense it is? When you finally come?' Then she kissed him, deeply, with her tongue in his mouth and her hands moving down over his chest, pinching what she knew were his sensitive nipples.

She pulled away and he glanced down at his bound limbs. She saw the understanding slowly register, the realisation that this wasn't just another fantasy but information. A hint of what was to come. She saw him begin to understand this even as he asked, 'What are you going to do?' A quick kiss and she went to her bag.

'I thought we'd make it even more fun,' she exclaimed, as if she were a girl at a slumber party who'd come up with a great game. Reaching in, she pulled out a pair of dice. 'I'm going to roll these,' she explained as she walked back over and knelt in front of him, her head only inches away from his hard flesh. 'Whatever number comes up is how many times I'm going to get you close and stop before I let you come. In my mouth.' The look in his eyes then was so tortured – she felt her pussy throb and moisten. He opened his mouth to protest but she rose up and kissed him again. 'Baby, I've been dreaming about having your big cock in my mouth for so long. I'm going to make sure it lasts as long as you are possibly able.'

He smiled then. 'How about only using one die?' But she gave him a reprimanding look.

'I have a third one in my bag I'll add if you keep protesting,' she said. She held the dice up to his mouth. 'Wanna blow . . . for luck?' she said teasingly.

'Why don't you?' he said. So she smiled, blew on the dice and rolled.

He closed his eyes and swallowed. It seemed that somehow he knew, even before he opened them, what he would see.

Double sixes.

'Twelve,' she sighed, her eyes twinkling. Kneeling again between his legs she grinned up at him. Devilishly. But as she gently took his cock in her hand and he groaned at this first touch on his hard member, the grin vanished. Putting him in her mouth for the first time was almost her favourite part. Almost. And so as all her fantasies were coming to fruition she did this slowly. Savouring each moment.

She gazed at the head, the skin taut and shiny, almost a cherry colour. She looked up at him one more time, licked her lips and then bent to slowly ease the sensitive flesh between her moist lips. He groaned and her sex melted. She ran her tongue round and around the head two, three, four times before she pushed the length of his dick into her mouth, until the head touched the back of her throat, listening to him moan and feeling herself getting wetter by the moment. Suddenly she wasn't sure if *she* would be able to handle all twelve edges without jumping up, straddling him on the chair and riding him hard with wild abandon.

She looked up, 'OK, you have to tell me when you're too close. When I have to stop.' He nodded. 'If you come before twelve there are going to be consequences for being so naughty.' She winked. Then she went back to work.

She shunted his cock in and out of her mouth at a steady pace now as one hand cupped and massaged his balls. She interchanged sliding her mouth over him with sliding her hand and mouth up and down, stopping every so often, to swirl her tongue over his velvety smooth cockhead. His groans got louder and louder as she worked him until he finally breathed out, 'Stop!' And she did. She let him recover for a few moments. 'Baby, I can't do this twelve times,' he said. 'You're killing me. Just uncuff me and let me fuck you. You know you want to.' She smiled and he watched as she pushed two fingers inside her pussy, pulled them out and put them to his lips. They were covered in her shiny wet juice. She watched him breathe in her familiar scent before he parted his lips to taste her.

'Yes, I know I do,' she said. 'But waiting is even more fun. As you've taught me.' And she went back to his cock.

After five edges he was puffing and sweat sprang to his temples. After seven he started cursing her. After nine while she sucked him she began rubbing the spot between his balls and his anus that she remembered he loved and he nearly lost it. She gave him an extra minute to compose himself then. At eleven he stopped her after two up and down strokes of her wet lips against his sensitive flesh. She gripped him then and watched as pre-come came in big drops to the tip of his cock and she licked and savoured each one. He gasped each time her tongue came in contact with the aching tip until his head swelled, turned purple and she felt one hard pulse in the hand that held him. She quickly let go.

'Hold on,' she commanded. 'One more.'

'I can come now?' he asked, pleading in his eyes.

'One more and then you can come,' she said firmly.

'Oh, God,' he groaned as she started to push his cock into her mouth again. Down. Up. 'Stop!' His whole body was shaking now, sweating and quivering with the need and the effort of holding it back.

'Now you can come.' She waited a moment. And this time, when she began stroking him again with her mouth, the strokes were slower. Much slower.

'Oh, oh, God. Oh, fuck, baby, please. God, please, I've held on so long, please just go a little faster.' But she maintained the slow tempo and rubbed his perineum for a little extra pressure.

After what was only a minute but she was certain seemed like an eternity to him his body started to spasm uncontrollably. 'Oh, oh, fuck. Here it comes . . . baby, oh, oh . . . fuck . . . suck my cock, you little slut, God . . . I'm coming, oh, oh . . .' But she only continued her slow pace, relishing his nasty words and his quaking body and the feeling of power she had with the centre of his world at this moment here in her mouth, under her control. She didn't stop or speed up as she felt the first orgasmic wave crash over him and begin to flow into her mouth. He was utterly silent then, as if frozen, suspended. Then as the next spasm hit he cried out, a sound purely animalistic and involuntary, his body jerking violently. She knew the intensity of each spasm was jacked up from the pressure of having it built up and held off for so long and she gloried in the feeling of bringing him this much pleasure. And the whole time she just kept slowly stroking and swallowing, trying to keep up with the river pouring out of him.

When he was done, spent, drained of every last drop, she unlocked the handcuffs, untied the belts and they went, both a little shaky, and fell on to the bed. She had been totally caught up in his pleasure for the past hour and now she was urgently aware of how horny it had made her.

After they kissed and cuddled wordlessly for a few minutes he reached down and, for the first time, slid his finger down over her clit and into her pussy. She gasped loudly as her starved centre was finally touched and moaned as his finger filled her. She was a sopping, slippery mess. 'You are so fucking wet,' he said and kissed her again.

'Yeah, well . . .' She looked down at his cock which was now soft, barely stirring.

'I think I can help you another way.' He smiled lasciviously at her and sucked his wet finger into his mouth. The thought of his head between her legs and remembering how good he was with his tongue made her pussy pulse harder.

Then he started to get up out of bed.

'Where are you going?' she asked in a panic.

'To get the cuffs,' he replied. 'And, baby,' he added. 'Payback's a bitch.'

'Delayed Gratification' is Kyoko Church's first appearance in a Black Lace collection.

Emrgency Exit

Shanna Germain

Half-way through the conference, the company I work for rents a school bus to take everyone to a warehouse for a party. I don't get on it. Someone I know knows someone else who has a car, and he offers me a ride. I say yes.

I regret it.

Me, squished in the backseat between two guys I don't know, guys who show me pictures of their kids on their cell phones for the entire traffic-filled hour that it takes to go from the hotel to the company's new facility. I am work-dressed: mid-length black skirt and knee-tall boots, a shirt that opens in the front to show the curves of my small breasts. My boots don't fit anywhere, so I sit with one foot on each side of the back hump and my knees tight together, and I think, 'I'm the same age as these men. My husband is the same age as these men.' I look at digital pictures of baby food smeared on faces and birthday presents and I think, 'Save me, please.'

On the outside, I'm going to this party because it's one of those things you have to do at conferences. It's business-a-business. Making an appearance, rah-rahing our business relationship and their beautiful warehouse.

On the inside, I'm going to the party because Sean is likely to be there. I don't say this to anyone, of course. They would find this strange, partly because I have a husband, a man that my co-workers know and adore. They describe him as 'adorable'. As 'sweet'. As 'kind'. He is all of those things, yes.

They would also find it strange because I barely know Sean. We met once in Germany. Again in Montana. At the kind of work functions where you have dinner, or talk over cold snacks and warm beers at a cocktail party. Where you could lock eyes across the table in an outdoor restaurant in Hamburg and realise that his eyes aren't leaf-green, as you'd thought, but blue-green. Water. Deep water. The kind you might drown in.

Those work functions where you could accidentally drop an olive at a country-western bar in Bozeman and laugh at the same time. And you notice that he doesn't offer to pick it up like so many others. Instead, he watches as you bend down, his eyes sliding over the movement of your ass. He stuffs his hands in his pockets as though to keep them contained.

He has good hands. He bikes. He told me this at the Hamburg dinner. The same dinner where he told me he'd noticed me at previous events, but thought I was a snob. I've heard that before.

'Shy,' I said.

'Seliah,' I said.

'Sean,' he said.

'Sub,' I did not say. All those S-words. All of them true.

When the regret car finally arrives at the party, I climb out of the backseat and enter the warehouse, doing the thing that you do. I greet the business owners by the door. I ooh and aah over the boxes of boxes as though they mean something. I pretend I'm not looking for him. Someone hands me a beer. It isn't someone. It's a guy that I know, that I've known for years. But he's barely in my vision. He's not there even as he's there. I'm looking, scanning, screening. I'll know if I see it. Those deep-water eyes. The sandy curls that make waves across his forehead until he sweeps them back with those hands of his. If I tune my attentions right, I believe I'll feel those hands even if I don't see them, the waves they push across the air, across the room.

I sip the beer, talk. Listen with my eyes. Look with every cell that spills in his direction. I am pulled toward him as though by some force other than gravity, and I follow its course. There: corner pocket.

I excuse myself, head to the table where the food is. It's his laugh that guides me, although I've only heard it once before, in Hamburg. I'd told a story about riding my bike into a tree and he'd laughed like that. Like he was laughing at himself, even though it was my flub, my black eye.

By the time I make my way through the crowd – hello, hello, hey, how are you? – to the corner, he's not laughing any more. His mouth is full. Still chewing, he offers me half of whatever he's eating. His hands, good hands, bike hands. I would take those if they were being offered. But it's only the nasty sandwich-looking thing. I shake my head.

He swallows and holds up the food. There's a ring on his finger that wasn't there before. Thick and silver, no stones. He has good hands. He bikes. He told me these things. He didn't tell me he might be married. I didn't tell him I might be married.

'I just got here,' he says. 'Starving.' His hair's a little longer than in Montana. He doesn't sweep it away.

'Me too.' Both things. Now that I'm here, in front of him, I wonder if I've made it up in my mind all these months. The connection over the table, over a bowl of olives, a funny story. Not the way I want to swim in his eyes – that's real – but the way I thought he wanted me to. I've read the depths wrong. Again. Bubbles of air.

He puts the sandwich down and wipes his fingers on the

tablecloth. People swim through the air around us, but I don't see them. Only his eyes. Only the way he tilts his head sideways at me, the way he watches. Sees through me.

'First bus is leaving, back to the hotels,' he says. 'Want to get on it?'

'Yes.'

I follow him, cells retuned, jumping. I don't let myself think about what the others see. Gossip runs rampant in any business. But maybe they're all so busy telling their tales, tuning their bodies to their own stories, they won't notice this one unfurling.

'Heya,' he says to the bus driver. I watch Sean's ass climbing the stairs. I don't raise my eyes to the driver. It is a school bus, an old one. There is no one else on. Why would there be? Most people just got here.

Sean leads the way to the backseat. He holds his hand out. 'Want the inside?' I scoot by without touching his fingers – it's too much, too early – and slide next to the window.

We sit. Silent with our mouths. My skin won't shut up, hollers *hello, touch me, slide over, turn me over.*

'Look,' he says. 'No way out.' He points. Over a window, *Emrgency Exit.* Spelled just like that. Not that a letter's fallen off. But that there never was one.

'Oh my God.' I have to laugh. It breaks up some of the clench in my belly. 'No wonder American kids are stupid.'

'Zen koan: is an exit really an exit if it's spelled wrong?' he asks.

'Maybe it's just a false escape,' I say.

'Like a door you go through and then it's all bricked up?' He does an impression of punching through a wall, his fists battering the back of the seat in a light, fast rhythm that makes me laugh but also pushes a sliver of something between my thighs.

'I was thinking more something that gives you . . . hope. Like, it's always there but you don't take it, so you don't know it's fake.'

'Or that it's real.'

The fast banter opens something. We talk music, biking, movies, books. He is funny and kind. He doesn't tell me that. I see it anyway. His ring flashes in the semi-dark. I can almost put away my need. I keep it under the seat for now, hidden beneath fun, smart banter and getting-to-know-you-a-little-more conversation.

After a long time, people climb on. They pretend they don't see us. Or we pretend we don't see them. I point out the *Emrgency Exit* sign to the couple sitting beneath it. The four of us laugh. Two couples. Almost.

The driver brings the bus to life, and it rumbles beneath us. He shifts, we shift. Sean's leg touches mine. The hard fabric of jeans. He leans across me, but doesn't touch. Puts his finger to the window and wipes away the condensation. One lone line across the glass. I want to lick the wet from his fingertip. I can't ask though. Somehow, it has to come from him, to start with him. I don't know how I know this.

I put my knees up against the seat in front of me and scootch down a little. My skirt slides up, exposes thigh. Sean's still talking about something, the moon I think, and I wonder if he even notices my bare thigh, whiter than the moon. Once again, I think, *this isn't*. I settle in, telling myself I'll be content with letting Sean step off the bus with a little 'It was great to see you again' wave. For going home and masturbating with my skirt still on, my boots. We'll be friends, I think. It's OK. I could use more funny, interesting male friends. I could.

I look out at the moon, waning. Its crevices and hidden hollows. I think about how it pulls across the sky, dragging the stars, the sea, the two of us, all gathered in its arc.

While I'm staring at the moon, Sean puts his hand on my leg, sliding it down. His palm and fingers create an upside-down basket for my knee. All my cells rush to that point of contact, spinning and dizzy. The space between my thighs rushes and wavers. When I turn back, Sean is closer than he was, without having moved. I can't look at his hand on my knee, so I look at his eyes. Blue-blue. They don't change colour this time.

'Emr-gency exit,' I say, stupidly. Rolling my r.

'Broken,' he says. 'Can't get out.'

'Can't get out,' I whisper.

He moves his hand from my knee to my thigh, beneath the fabric of my skirt. The bus bumps along the highway. Makes his hand and my leg shake. His fingers grab, my thigh hard. Leave marks. I can feel them blossoming already, know that I will shower later and press my fingers to those spots.

'What do you want?' he asks. Does he say it aloud, or do his eyes ask?

His hand slides up the inside of my thigh, his palm hard on my skin, scraping it.

'I want . . .' I'm not sure if I say that part aloud, but he doesn't let me finish. Knuckles the hand at my thigh into a fist, presses the hard bony edges of him against the thin fabric that covers my clit. The other hand to my mouth, flat palm, hard against my lips.

If I leaned I could see over the seat in front of me. Could see who might be looking, turning their head even now to this sight of me in the backseat, a near-stranger's hand over my mouth, my eyes wide. It's dark on the bus, but not that dark. They could see if they looked back, if I looked up. I don't lean up, I turn to look at Sean instead. His eyes are close to me now. Fuck. I could drown there. And I can tell he hasn't even started.

'I've been dreaming about you,' he says, into my ear. I can barely hear it above the rumble of the bus, above the rush of water in my ears as he knuckles my clit. Without taking his hand off my mouth, he uses his thumb to trace the half-curve beneath my eye. His thumb is soft, and I have the urge to take it in my mouth, suckle it. 'You and that black eye.'

And you'd think that would turn me, make me get up or get off the bus. The feminist in me, if I could find her, would surely do that. But I know, somehow, that he doesn't mean he wants to give me a black eye. He means something else, something dark that I understand only in my body. I inhale around – through – his fingers, tasting the dry salt skin of him in my air.

He is still knuckling me, so hard, too hard for one moment, and then my body opens against his pressure and I'm wet. That fast. He feels it too because he moves his knuckles tighter against me, bruises, one time, and then takes his hand away. Not far, not out from under my skirt. I can still feel the heat of his skin.

My clit, relieved of the pressure, sends out a pulse-beat into the air, calling for his return. It begs, loud and solid and unashamed – exactly how I would if I could, if I knew how.

'If you go one step farther, it will be like that,' he says against my ear as he points at the *emrgency exit* sign. 'No way out. Do you want that?'

I inhale him again. I hear the sound – that suck of my breath through his skin, his very cells – and it's a sound that fits my ear perfectly. I think of the regret car – me, stuck there in the middle, surrounded by photos of kids and carpets, going nowhere fast – and how it might be my future. I think of 'sweet' and 'nice'.

I nod. Not with my head – he has my lips and chin captured

under his fingers – but it seems my very skin splits to let him in.

'Good,' and this time his whisper turns into his teeth at the fold of my ear and then his mouth hard at the base of my neck. Suckling the skin, breaking the cells so they ache into a darker colour. His hand kisses my lips, mashes my teeth hard against the inside of my mouth, and I suck in air through my nose. I raise my hips off the seat toward his fingers, but he doesn't let me make contact.

'Please,' I say, but of course it's nothing. No sound but the press of air against his hand.

'This?' he says, as though he heard me. He pinches bits of my thighs between his fingers. Little stings of pain that flash and recede, quick as tides. At the same time, his mouth and teeth at my neck and collarbone, biting. Sucking my skin in between his teeth as I suck his skin in between mine.

'Or this?' He knuckles me again, blooming my clit into something so close to pain that I can't tell if it is. I spread my legs, whimper through the strength of his hand.

Someone in front turns around. I hear it and feel it more than I see it. I try to duck my head, to slide down in the seat, but he doesn't let me. Soft laughter, and a voice that says something I can't hear. My cheeks burn and I struggle to be let out, my skirt sliding higher up my thigh. I nip at the skin of his fingers, but he doesn't let go.

His lips leave my collarbone and return to my ear. He nips the curled edge of my skin so hard I feel the pain in my eyes.

'Can I make you come, just like this, do you think?' His knuckles twist against me, pain for sure now. Pain that lights up through my stomach, but is diluted by how wet I am, by how much I want just what he's doing. And behind the pain, that other thing . . . unexpected. The wax and wane of it as it slips me closer toward the dark, or the light. I'm not sure I can tell the difference any more.

'I've been waiting for this' is what he says.

'Come for me' is what he says.

I don't want to tell him the truth, that I'm already coming, that I've been coming for him since I first saw him. Not like this, not the way my body is cracking up for him now, splintering, but in my own mind. And, now, here, at his words and his teeth and his knuckles, I am coming, for real this time. The kind of pleasure and pain that twists, spirals down and out, crashes outward and then draws back. How I've imagined this moment: my breath hard against his hand, my clit hard against his knuckles and that voice in my ear, telling me there's no, never, not any way out.

His hand slips away from my mouth, catching my bottom lip for a moment. He pinches it between his fingers, a soft bruise of pain that somehow goes straight to my tender, pulsing clit.

The bus stops, nearly sending my body tumbling off the seat, and I hold to the base of it just by his fingers against my mouth.

'My stop,' he says.

I sit, dazed, as he stands, my clit slow-slowing in its swollen dance. Am I supposed to stand? To follow? We don't say.

I sit and watch him step to the front of the bus, his hand trailing over the seats. Through the window, his hotel. A fountain throws water at the moon but doesn't quite reach. I wonder what's in the dark space between spray and sky. And then Sean appears in front of it, framed by the spray. He turns as the bus begins to pull away. He mouths something. I can't make it out. I wipe away the fog from the glass in an arc.

In the pulling away, he raises a fist, the skin glistening as it rises, round and shiny as a full moon, a blackened eye, a ring of gold.

Shanna Germain is an award-winning author of erotica. This is her first appearance in Black Lace.

Dirty Weekend

Primula Bond

We'd sworn never to do it, and here we were doing it. With knobs on. In the rain. In the middle of nowhere.

Devon is beautiful for a holiday, sure, whatever the weather, and the rose-swamped cottage was adorable. The beach was down a rocky path at the bottom of the garden.

In the brochure Mandy showed me, the sun was shining. White umbrellas fluttered outside the boutique hotel/gastro-pub along the cliff. Boats bobbed on the calm sea.

'At least Charlie will be on the water all day or the golf course and out of my hair. He's nutty about sailing, so we won't see him for dust. Or surf.' She wiped coffee drips off the spout of her cafetière and filled up my cup. 'He's not built for city life.'

'I don't know about that.' I leant back in the creamy armchair in their new, all-glass extension and relished the way my jeans felt a little bit looser round my waist since my crash diet. 'He must work like a dog to afford all – for you to live in such a sensational house. I've seen him at the station sometimes. He cuts a dash in a business suit –'

'He's like the Incredible Hulk, always trying to bust out of it!' She snorted, unrolling a pale-pink orchid petal between her fingers. 'He's happier barefoot.'

'Hmm, that sounds sexy!' I laughed, and glanced round the

room for more clues about this never-seen husband of hers. 'He like the Hulk in bed, too?'

I peered around for some sign of him. Some Calvin Klein boxers hanging on the line in their impeccable garden? A guitar, or an expensive camera, maybe. Books. Even a photograph. There was one in a silver frame, the picture you see in marital homes everywhere of the two of them ramrod-straight and done up like figurines on a wedding cake. But it was stuck behind the tropical fish tank.

'Oh God, no. Typical Englishman.' Mandy sniffed, as if I'd let off a bad smell.

'But look at you, Mandy! Slim, blonde, classy – and your Charlie's sex on a stick! Come on, spill. We all reckon you're at it like rabbits!'

'Looks can be very deceptive, Natasha. And I'm not sure I like the idea of "we all" gossiping about me.'

'Oh, it's all said with love!' I laughed.

But she shook her head. 'Sex with my husband is pretty useless, if you want to know. Oh, he's got tons of boyish energy, know what I mean? But it's all wham bam. Miracle we ever had kids at all!' She laughed, making light of it all. 'Why? Is the Hulk supposed to be a stud?'

All I could see in the wedding photo was a tall man in a dark suit, with a shock of wild blond hair.

'I don't know. If a green six-pack's your type!' I mused, flicking to the price-list. 'He's so strong. He just looks as if he goes like a train!'

Mandy licked sprinkles off her cup cake. 'Well, the Hulk might be sex on a stick, but my husband hardly ever – well, let's just say it takes a lot to get him going these days. He has some really outrageous ideas, comes home *begging* me to try these toys, games, parties, you know – honestly, like something out of a Swedish blue movie, some of them –'

'Oh God, that's so kinky, Mandy, I can't imagine you –' I went all hot. I fanned out the centrefold of the brochure. *Perfect for dirty weekends*, ran the text under a brightly coloured photo of an Aryan young couple sitting outside the gastro-pub on the cliff, clinking big glasses of rosé. I imagined them kissing each other chastely for the camera, getting turned on, hands all over each other, knocking over the glasses of wine, getting heated and frantic, rocking on the hard wooden bench, then pulling each other's tops off in the hot sun, yanking at shorts and miniskirts, stripping off and getting tangled in front of all the other grinning guests, pushing each other down on to the grassy clifftop, the boy's cock rigid, the girl's waxed cunt pink and wet, and then without a hair flying out of place fucking each other's brains out, there in the beer garden, while everyone watched and clapped.

I couldn't breathe as the images undulated. Mandy must have said something. I glanced up. 'Do you mean, like, wife swapping?'

'Oh God, Nat, swear you'll never tell?' There was a catch in her voice. Her eyes were a bit glassy, and she also looked out of breath.

I put the brochure down. I leant forward, hands clamped between my knees. My voice came out in a hoarse whisper. 'What's it like?'

'It's all so civilised on the surface. Sherry to start with, all standing round in this prim little house dressed up to the nines, prawn cocktails, buckets more sherry, and then the most incredible, filthy goings on behind net curtains –'

'Really? That's just wild!'

'I know! What would the neighbours say, eh?' She slapped at my arm. 'Your face! I had no idea you were a horny little bitch, but you're creaming yourself just thinking about it, aren't you?'

'Don't be daft,' I squeaked. I picked up my cup again. 'Each to their own. Just makes me look at you with totally new eyes, that's all –'

She laughed, making me jump. A glamorous hyena. 'I'm joking, darling! You don't honestly think I'd be bothered with all that pervy nonsense?'

'Of *course* not, Mandy! You, giving blow jobs to the bank manager on the shag pile?' I rolled my eyes, blushing furiously and wishing the other girls were here.

'Parquet floor, actually!' Her face was poker-straight.

It was my turn to laugh like a hyena. 'I mean, you're so, I don't know – so conventional?'

She waited for me to calm down. 'Charlie can pleasure himself over a magazine for all I care. He's just an overgrown, over-sexed schoolboy knocking things over, getting in everyone's way.'

'He sounds like a real handful!' The cup was shaking in my hands. 'Not sure he'll get on with my husband, then. Jim's the ultimate slob. Never stirs from his chair if he can help it. That's why he's put on so much weight.' The coffee was too hot, and scalded my mouth as if it was chiding me for disloyalty. But I said it anyway. 'Quite turns my stomach, if I'm honest.'

'Oh, he's a cute teddy bear. He always makes a lady feel like, well, a lady. But enough about me!' Mandy held the milk jug in mid-air, antennae pricking. 'You two having problems? Maybe you'd rather go away somewhere on your own rather than hang round with us?'

'Getting cosy with you two will be just what the doctor ordered!' I tossed my hair back and stared at a pair of scuffed brown brogues. They been kicked off by the back door, one in front of the other, as if making a bid to escape. 'Now all I've got to do is tell Jim we're off to the seaside next weekend!'

Her pink lips parted at my raised voice and flushed face.

She couldn't have known that my despair was not at the idea of a dirty weekend with my overweight, sweaty husband, but at this whole arrangement, the impending reality of sharing a cottage with the ultimate Alpha Mum and her scary husband.

But her eyes gleamed with the whiff of marital discord and all the attendant scandal. Not to mention all that potential for juicy gossip at the tennis club. She poured me another cup of steaming hot coffee.

'In that case, my sweet, I'll make bloody sure this trip will sort you out once and for all.'

So there we were. With knobs on. In the rain. In the middle of nowhere. Waiting for our dirty weekend to start.

'You swore we'd never go away with another couple, Natasha. So why now?'

Jim and I were well into our second bottle of Merlot as the rain lashed down outside. Mandy and Charlie were late.

'Mandy bullied me into it.'

'Oh, she's a pussy cat really. I swear she purrs when she's happy –'

'When have you heard her purring?'

'Why are you so anti shared holidays?'

I glugged down another glass. 'Oh, arguments over cooking Money. Housework.' The wine was heating me up nicely. 'Sharing a bathroom. No privacy.'

'Well, it's not as if we've got anything to hide, girl. They can wander round naked for all I care. I'll be off to bed with a good book as soon as it's polite.'

Oh God. The swish of tyres in the pitted lane outside. The door was thrown open, letting the cold air slice through the low-beamed sitting room. Mandy had morphed from yummy mummy to sexless dog-breeder in dung-coloured Barbour and muddy cords.

'Dreadful traffic on the A303?'

Jim, bless him, leapt up to take Mandy's jacket. I tugged at my soft jersey dress which kept falling open over my exposed cleavage.

'Not helped by Charlie being summoned to the office at the last minute. Idiot.' She rudely shrugged her coat off into Jim's hands and frowned at me. 'Aren't you cold in that little scrap of an outfit, Nat? No one dresses up in the country, you know.'

My stomach twisted with anxiety and the prickling realisation that we were well and truly trapped.

'That's old-fashioned bollocks, Amanda. She looks absolutely lovely.'

Mandy glared down at the suitcases and as Jim bent to help her I looked across their fussing, hunched backs and saw Charlie.

I swear the candle flames dipped in awe as he crashed through the door, all rain-drenched hair and tired blue eyes and long, long legs, a picnic rug thrown over one shoulder as if he was some kind of Mexican bandit, and holding what looked like a set of golf clubs. He brought in with him the wild manly scent of, I don't know, the ocean and wood smoke.

'Hi. You're Natasha.' He stepped round his wife and my husband, dropping the canvas bag to shake my hand. He dipped his chin and focused calmly on me. 'I can tell this is going to be fun.'

I am an Amazon. I tower over Jim, who doesn't care, my children are already giants and my girlfriends are mostly Dresden dolls in ankle boots and sparkly cardis. But Charlie made me feel slight, delicate. My fingers were lost inside his, curling round his palm. Then our hands went still.

'Better find the bedroom,' he murmured, still staring at me.

My stomach twisted again, but this time it was into a knot

of excited confusion. His voice was very deep. Almost a groan. I looked for the hyperactive sleazeball his frigid wife had described, but this wasn't him.

'God knows where we're sleeping!' Mandy squawked from the freezing pantry where she and Jim were now unpacking jars of her home-made chutney. 'I suppose you bagged the best beds, Nat?'

'All the bedrooms are nice, Amanda. Four-posters, you said.' Charlie slowly loosened his grip on my hand. There was an angry flush across his cheekbone. 'That's why you chose this place.'

'And why I chose Nat and Jim to come with us. They're not getting any. They need a good romp in a four-poster –'

'I'll show you,' I said, leading the way. 'You can hardly get lost.'

'She prefers to be called Natasha,' I heard Jim say. Mandy's reply was drowned in the rattle of wine bottles and they both snorted with laughter. My anxiety lifted.

'Those two have always got on well. Movers and shakers when the kids were at school, I gather,' Charlie remarked, close up behind me. 'I'm amazed you and I have never met.'

'Same.'

I stumbled on my silly heels at the top of the stairs, my skirt flipping up over my bottom. He took hold of my hips to steady me but when he touched skin instead of fabric he pulled me hard against him. His warm fingers brushed over my stomach under the dress.

'Fuck, I'd forgotten how lovely a woman feels when she's properly tarted up,' he breathed into my hair. 'Sexy dress. French knickers. Your Jim's a lucky man.'

I heaved myself upright on the banister. I could smell the worn leather of his jacket as his fingers drifted down the back of my legs and away. I caught a whiff of my own scent as the silk slid across my pussy, leaving a sticky hint.

'This is your room.' I leant weakly against the wall to let him pass. He was unshaven and golden hairs curled above his collar. I could see the pulse drumming in his neck.

'Thanks, Natasha.' But he didn't move. Heat radiated off his body. 'So tired. I wish we could stay up here, don't you?'

'I didn't expect you to be so –' I bit my lip quickly. Handsome. Gorgeous. 'Quiet.'

'What's she been saying?' he asked. His chest touched my shoulder. 'That I'm some kind of dickhead who likes lap-dancing clubs and plays golf?'

I couldn't help smiling, and he smiled too. His tongue ran across his teeth and his mouth looked wet. He was looking at my mouth. I licked my lips for him and made them tingle.

'We'll forget the dick bit, for now, but those are golf clubs, right?'

'As always she's got it all wrong.' He sighed. His breath smelt of coffee. 'It's an easel. I like to paint. I like to get as far away as possible and paint.' He dipped his head to look closer at me. 'So you didn't have me down as the sensitive type?'

'No. She made out you were a bit out of control, actually. Into swinging, and all sorts –' I clapped my hand over my mouth and blushed scarlet, glad of the darkness on the landing. 'But why would you need stuff like that? You two – you could have anyone –'

'She said swinging?'

'Er, something like that, yes!'

'You mean wife-swapping? Fuck, what's she like?' His voice grated with momentary anger, but then he looked at me again and moved closer, pushing me against the wall. 'On the other hand, maybe it's not such a bad idea –'

He rubbed his mouth against mine, paused as if for permission, pressed again harder and rougher, making my stomach plunge. My mouth opened right up. I tasted the tip of his warm wet tongue, sucked it, and we started to kiss. Downstairs a cork popped. My thighs went weak and opened too. He lifted my dress and slid his fingers up my thighs under my knickers. Christ, he'd know I was already so wet. I strained against him, hooking one knee round his leg, opening his jacket to touch the hard outline of his cock.

'Put her down, Charles!' yelled Mandy from the sitting room. 'It's time to get sloshed!'

He pulled away. And then the lights went out.

Supper and wine by candlelight painted everyone in a sexy glow. Charlie watched me through the flickering flames, making me wriggle on the sofa as we all slurped spaghetti and wine and played games. The clock ticked noisily round to midnight.

'OK. This truth-and-dare lark is far too tame.' Charlie finished stoking the fire and clapped his hands. 'We'll spin the bottle once more before bedtime.'

Jim had forgotten his good book and was clumsily play-fighting with Mandy on the sofa. Oh, fuck it. I was so horny I was going to have to grit my teeth and climb on to his cock tonight to get myself off. Either that or do it for myself. I pushed my hands down between my legs, touched my wet knickers under my dress.

The bottle stopped spinning and was pointing at my husband.

'Truth.' Jim chuckled and dug Mandy in the ribs.

'So, Jim lad.' Charlie stared straight at me. 'Would you ever consider wife-swapping?'

An After Eight froze half-way to Jim's lips. I smothered the urge to scream and run away. Mandy was grappling with the corkscrew. Any minute now she'd realise I'd spilled the beans about her little joke. I clamped my legs together, waiting for the explosion.

'I mean, in exchange for you having Amanda,' Charlie added, pouring out wine into all the glasses without taking his eyes off me. 'Would you ever let me fuck your wife?'

At last Jim calmly put the mint in his mouth. 'Only if I could watch.'

'Yeah, right, honey.' I laughed shakily. 'In your dreams.'

But nobody else was laughing. Mandy laid a hand on his knee and nodded at Charlie.

'So, the old man's given us *carte blanche*, Natasha. So shall we act out his fantasy for him and put me out of my misery? I've had a socking great hard-on for you all night.' Charlie came and sat beside me and took my face in his hands. 'Cut the crap, shall we, and go upstairs?'

'Stop teasing me, all of you.' I groaned and inhaled his smell, but I was shaking like a schoolgirl. 'Mandy? Tell them to stop joking!'

Mandy started rubbing her hand up Jim's leg and splayed her fingers over his crotch. He already had a huge erection. The dead cool look in his eyes as Mandy's hand reached his straining flies was an incredible turn-on.

'You go right ahead, sweetie. It's no joke,' cooed Mandy. 'Don't look so shocked! We've had our eye on you two for months.'

'Jim?' I pleaded, as Charlie started to pull me to my feet. 'It's just a game, right?'

'Look, love, no point pretending I'm jealous. I've got my own handmaiden right here. Just glad it's all out in the open.' Jim eased back on the sofa and spread his legs. 'You wait. You'll hear her purring when she gets the cream.'

'You and her?' My mouth was hanging open by now. I felt a weird new jab of jealousy as Mandy unzipped my husband's trousers.

'Oh, honey. This is old news. What else do you think we used to do to liven up those dreary PTA meetings?'

Mandy winked at me. Then she took his stiff cock out and slowly, still looking at me, she bent her head, flicked out her tongue and started to lick it.

'The only rule is you do it right here, just the once, where I can see everything,' ordered my Jim, tangling his fingers in Mandy's blonde hair and pushing her face hard down into his lap. 'Yes, Charles. I want to watch my beautiful wife being fucked.'

'See, Natasha? Your husband's having a ball. My wife's having his balls. You'll be pleasing everybody. Not so perverted, is it?' Charlie's hands were soothing and warm on my skin as he pushed me down on my back. 'You want me, don't you?'

'Yes.' My voice was a croak. 'God, yes.'

'So relax. Stop thinking. Amanda said you were the unconventional one. So show us how sexy and low-down you can be.'

I fell backwards on to the sofa. Jim's groans and the slurping of Mandy's tongue and mouth on his cock merged with the crackling of the fire and the singing of the wine in my ears. Yes. I wanted to stop thinking. I lay back on the big sofa and felt Charlie pull my dress open. Instantly my nipples pricked up hard, nudging against my bra, and I arched my back with pleasure.

'Can you see, Jim?' Charlie crooned, stroking my breasts over the bra, making them lift towards his hands for more. 'You want to see me sucking your wife's tits?'

'Yeah,' Jim groaned in response. I turned my head lazily and saw that actually his eyes were closed as Mandy worked on him. Charlie turned my head back to him and started to kiss me.

'They're not even looking at us. I could carry you away, and they wouldn't notice,' he whispered. As his tongue pushed inside my mouth he reached under me and unclipped the bra. As he pulled it off it scraped across my nipples, making them burn with longing, and my body was crackling and singing, like the fire. 'You're all mine, Natasha. I'm going to do this again and again. Not just the once.'

Words, words, I thought. Just pretty words. But they were working their magic. I felt like an X-rated Sleeping Beauty –

'Suck her tits, man!' growled Jim, pulling Mandy's head roughly in and out of his groin by the hair as she sucked his cock. 'Play the game!'

'I wanted to rip off your dress the moment I walked in,' Charlie murmured into the corner of my mouth as he pushed my tits together. 'Now I know why she's always stopped us meeting.'

'Stop talking, Charlie. Go ahead and fuck her.'

Jim's voice was really brutal and another shock of excitement at this dirty new side to him stabbed at me. And something else. Something deliciously wicked coiled inside me.

'My voyeur husband can bloody well wait,' I hissed, raising myself up to kiss Charlie harder. I couldn't get enough of his lips. They were firm, like a man's should be, and yet they had a softness in them, and I was making them wet with kissing. I could taste port, and coffee, and the outdoors, and I wanted to drink him.

But the rest of me was aching now, as his tongue, warm and slippery in my mouth, probed and pushed. My pussy was hot and tight and already I wanted his cock inside me. It was too soon. I didn't know what to do with myself. I'd forgotten how just licking someone's mouth can send desire rippling madly right through you.

I felt for his hips, tried to hook my fingers into the waistband of his jeans, tried to pull him closer, but he stopped kissing me and let his tongue run down my throat towards my breasts and I groaned out loud. Jim and Mandy would hear me but not only did I not care, I actually *wanted* them to see. I thrust my breasts out, knowing how good they looked in the firelight, heavy and round, nipples jutting out like berries, all offered to him, bouncing with my heartbeat, throbbing with the desperate urge to be fondled and sucked.

'Your wife's horny, isn't she, Jim? Look how stiff and red her nipples are! You must have had hours of pleasure playing with these. God, so gorgeous!' Charlie laughed, lifting my tits towards his mouth and brushing his lips across them. I pushed harder, aching for him to suck them. But he let me drop down on to my back and pinned me there with one hand. 'Shall I show her what she's getting?'

'Go ahead, if talking dirty gets your rocks off,' muttered Jim, eyes still closed, away in a world of his own. Well, his and Mandy's world of cock-sucking –

So Charlie opened his jeans. He was wearing tight black trunks and my pussy twitched, hot and wet, as I got a good look at the outline of his cock, the tip poking over the top of his pants. I tried to wrap my legs around him but he lifted himself further away from me, slowly peeling off his sweater and his shirt and with every inch I saw of shoulder, chest, stomach, I shook with lust and the unwelcome reminder that this all belonged to Mandy. She owned that gorgeous body. She had touched and been fucked endlessly by him.

But she'd said he was no good.

Over on the sofa I saw her pushing Jim on to his back and kneeling over him. His head was tipped sideways, looking right at me now. Mandy pulled off her huge woollen sweater and her naked breasts dangled down over Jim's face. She started to lower herself over Jim's cock, swinging her silky hair about as she swallowed it inside her cunt.

'Fuck me, Charlie,' I hissed, scrabbling to get hold of his

trunks. I yanked them down, my heart knocking somewhere in my throat. And there it was, his cock banging out of his pants, hot and hard and jumping with its own beat.

'What do you think, Jim? Ready? She's gagging for it now. Shall I fuck her, or make her wait?'

'Bastard! Why can't you leave him out of it!' My hand flashed out and I scratched his face.

Charlie caught my wrist. 'You're not playing the game, Natasha. He watches, and gives the order, OK? Otherwise it doesn't happen at all and we all go home.'

'Stupid fucking games!'

He pinned my arms back over my head to stop me scratching at him again and bit my nipples, hard, making me screech and forget my fury as the pain licked into pleasure and silenced me. As he pinched one nipple and bit the other, all I could think about was his tongue teasing me, my nipples rigid, burning for him to keep sucking and hurting them, and the hot delicious shame of my husband watching insinuated in between us and made me arch and writhe violently under Charlie's mouth, trying to push my tits into his face, my pussy up to his cock, but the more I kicked and struggled the more he kept himself from touching the places that were burning for him.

'Fuck my wife, God damn you, or I'll do it myself!'

My laid-back, lazy slob Jim was really shouting now as Mandy rode him faster, her bottom tensing and bucking over his cock. Her fingernails dug into his buttocks as she reared backwards and plunged down on to him. We had all gone too far now. There was nothing anyone could do to stop the wife-swap.

But his anger kept firing me up. I lifted myself up to Charlie and licked my lips greedily like a witch as he bit hard, and let my head fall back with bliss. His cock was quivering and jumping, nudging and pushing against my thigh. I wrapped my legs round him and stuck fast to him like a limpet. I tipped myself so that my red, swollen pussy lips slapped and smeared against his balls before sliding up his cock and, as they opened to kiss it and my cunt opened ready to take him in, my clit popped out, burning and tingling. I started to rub myself against him, desperate to scratch the itch.

He let go of my breasts and raised himself on his strong arms. There was too much air and space between our bodies. Through that space I could see the fire burning and Mandy still rocking on my husband's cock. She was discovering how long he could hold out. There was one way to make him come explosively and yes, she'd found it. Like she already knew? She was fondling and rolling his balls with one hand and as I watched I saw her extend one finger and circle it round Jim's arsehole, poking at it with her fingernail, opening it, pushing inside, sliding out again.

'They've done this before,' Charlie murmured, watching also. 'You can tell.'

Mandy jabbed her finger violently right into Jim's arsehole and he jerked violently and lifted her half off his cock with a sudden strength and then slammed her back down. They bucked and screamed together, two of her fingers poking in and out of his arse as she screwed herself on to him, her breasts swinging like a stripper's, until they came explosively together. His head fell back and Mandy collapsed on to his chest, both momentarily forgetting they were supposed to be watching me.

Charlie paused, waiting for them to calm down. Then he looked down at me.

'Ready?'

I pulled him closer, trying to get back in the mood. I could feel his warm heavy body, his elbows shaking with the effort not to squash me, but when he kissed me again my body melted and I sank into the soft sofa beneath him, raising my hips to meet his, feeling at last the warm tip of that beautiful cock.

'She says you fuck like an Englishman,' I murmured. 'So how does an Englishman fuck?'

He didn't know what I meant, but he smiled and eased his cock slowly inside, just the first couple of inches inside, stopping and starting, driving me wilder with wanting. My ready cunt made an easy slide for him but still he was putting it into me agonisingly slowly and I whimpered and shook with the effort of holding myself back. I could hear Jim and Mandy shifting about on the other sofa, sighing, clearing throats, the zipping up of jeans, the refilling of glasses.

'Remember, Charles, it's just the once,' Mandy said suddenly into the crackling silence, as if she was reminding him to put petrol in the car. 'When we all go home, this weekend never happened.'

'Shut up, bitch!' he muttered, and pulled his hips right back.

'Fuck, they're really going to do it!' Jim's voice was an excited squeak. 'I don't believe I'm going to watch them doing it in front of me! This is so bloody filthy!'

'We do it all the time, Jim. Didn't you guess?'

My eyes met Charlie's. A split second's hesitation and I would have wriggled out of the whole thing. But Charlie shook his head sharply and started fucking me, hard. My cunt gripped his cock as it rammed up me, pushing me across the sofa, banging my head against the arm, my tits wobbling and bouncing in the candlelight as my husband watched. My body welded into Charlie's, sticking him into me so that I couldn't tell where my stomach and pussy and legs ended and his stomach and cock and legs began.

He slowed again, resting on his forearms, kissing me again

as if we were alone in the room, nudging my mouth wide open so that his tongue could imitate what his cock was doing, pushing his tongue into my mouth, nibbling my lips as he fucked me and stopped my cries.

But as soon as his mouth slid sideways I started moaning again, louder and higher.

'Go on, Charlie, go on!' roared Jim.

Charlie thrust hard inside me and drove us both up the gathering wave of ecstasy and we thrust together faster and faster. I was vaguely aware of my husband hollering something in the background. Mandy was going, 'Yes, yes, yes.' My knees locked round Charlie's hips. My mind washed through with colour from the candles and fire and sensation from Charlie's thrusting cock and at last I screamed his name as we shuddered and came together there on the sofa, in front of my gaping husband and Charlie's wife.

There was a long silence. Charlie withdrew slowly, his cock sliding out, still erect and wet with my juices. He pulled me upright and wrapped my dress back round me. I was shivering uncontrollably. Hot, cold, exhilarated, prickling with shame.

The others were silent in the firelight.

I hardly dared, but I had to look at my husband.

'So, guys,' said Charlie, moving away from me towards the stairs. 'Ready to join our club?'

'I want her back now. Once was definitely enough,' Jim slurred, looking punch-drunk. He picked a long blonde hair off his shirt. 'It's my turn. Come on, Natasha. Time for bed.'

I couldn't move. The thought of him touching me, after Charlie –

'I've never seen you fucking anyone like that before, Charlie. You're not supposed to make it special. I can't risk it happening again.' Mandy clicked her glass down on the table, stood up, tugged her sweater down over her jeans. 'Like I said, this weekend never happened.'

'Sorry, Amanda. This was your idea. And you're so wrong, darling.' Charlie came back over to the sofa and pulled me to my feet. 'This weekend has only just begun.'

Unusual start to an affair, but it was never going to be just the once. Because we still do it, every weekend, whether or not anyone's watching.

Primula Bond is the author of the Black Lace novels *Club Crème* and *Country Pleasures*, and of the Nexus novel *Behind the Curtain*. Her short fiction appears in numerous Black Lace collections.

I Spy

Rachel Kramer Bussel

It's a bad habit, a horrible one, worse, in some ways, than smoking or noshing on bacon as a snack or typing in my credit-card number to order that latest must-have gadget when I know good and well I can't really afford it. Some habits are just so bad, they're good. Chief among them is the one that makes me horniest. Or rather, was, until very recently, and it's still what I consider my biggest vice, my most shameful – and therefore sexiest – secret.

Reading my husband's email had become my guilty, horny habit, one I just couldn't give up, and I quit smoking after a ten-year, two-pack-a-day habit. I remember exactly how it started, too. Pierce had forgotten his laptop at home one day and since I'm what's known as a housewife, albeit one with an MBA in business who somehow let that slide once we tied the knot, when he asked if I could drop it downtown at lunch-time, I said I would. After all, that's what I'm here for – to be helpful. But I'm not *that* innocent; I couldn't help sneaking one little peek at its contents, just because it was there right in front of me, as if waiting for me.

That part was easy enough. I opened the computer and his email program popped up, with countless names that were mostly foreign to me. There were a few notes from me, a few co-workers' names I recognised. Then it started downloading his new email, which it must have been preset to do. I watched as if hypnotised, as his inbox unfurled in front of me, full of the day's business news, a note from his mom and assorted penis-enlarging spam ads, plus a few company-wide directives. But then there was one that caught my eye and held it. The 'from' line had a single name, Margot, and the subject line was 'Moan'. Actually it was 'Re: re: re: Moan', meaning that my husband, proper blue-blooded Pierce Scotch, had been the one to start this conversation with Margot. Something told me there was no way this one was about business. What kind of concerned wife would I be if I didn't investigate this?

Now, when you see a word like 'Moan' and a woman with a name like Margot, what else are you supposed to think? I didn't set out to snoop, but once I'd started, I couldn't stop. My suspicions were confirmed when I saw his initial words to her.

I'm hard all over again thinking about you – the way you smell, the way you look, the way you taste. You drive me so crazy that part of me wants to drive over there right now and fuck you silly. Make sure you keep your pussy shaved like it was today. Nice and sleek so I can run my tongue all over it. Or else you're going to get a spanking. But maybe you'll get one anyway. I want to hear you scream for me again, but not so loud that you make security come; if that happens again I'm going to have to gag you. Actually I'd like to see you with a nice red ball between those pretty lips of yours, trying to scream for me. Maybe I'll record you and give myself a little soundtrack during the day. Or not. I'll decide when I see you next, and you'll just have to go along with it, won't you? P

My heart was pounding as I scrolled through the rest of the exchange. It seemed that Margot was all too willing to comply with his request, and had spent the afternoon in a soapy bathtub squeezing her nipples and shaving her sweet, delicious pussy – that is, when she wasn't using her vibrator and dreaming about sucking my husband's cock.

I wanted to slap the bitch across the face, hard enough to see a red handprint form. I wanted to take the kitchen knife in front of me and carve it somewhere on her body. I wanted to slam her face into our dog Jelly's bowl of kibble. I spent several minutes letting my mind wander through a variety of increasingly violent scenarios starring the two of us that would've given any fan of female wrestling a permanent hard-on. But in a deeper part of me, somewhere beneath the growing layers of resentment, I knew that my anger didn't eclipse the arousal that was bubbling up from somewhere deep inside.

Reading his dirty words had made my pussy clench tightly, had made me wet and hot and eager in a way I hadn't been in . . . I couldn't remember how long. Certainly never with Pierce; oh, he fucked me good and hard, but never like that. Never with the kind of raw passion that made you do reckless, wild, outrageous things – like cheat on your wife. Never with the kind of urgency that had him ducking out of work, or hinting at it, during the day, to attack me with his cock. Sure, sometimes he got on top, held my arms down, bit my lower lip. Once he dripped hot wax all over my inner thighs. Once he ordered me not to come for over an hour as he fingered me slowly, mercilessly, the agony of waiting almost worth diso-beying. I'd sensed he had a kinky side, but I was his wife. We didn't talk like that to each other, even if I sometimes longed for it, longed for the kind of submission I'd known with my ex, Roderick.

So, yes, there was anger, but in equal or even greater parts there was interest. Desire. Curiosity. Excitement. I was getting to see a whole other side of the man who I'd thought I'd known everything about, and while some – maybe most – wives would rush to find the most vindictive way they could of leaving him, would forward the messages to themselves or print them out as evidence, I wanted them for another reason – for porn. I had my hand down my skirt and inside my panties before I even thought it through, as I sorted his inbox and found their previous correspondence.

And, to be honest, which I allowed myself to be once the shock wore off, I wanted to watch. I wanted to see her suck his cock, wanted to compare her technique to mine, wanted to see if her pussy was prettier, get her secrets for avoiding razor burn, get her secrets to accessing a part of my husband he'd kept hidden almost as soon as the honeymoon blush had worn off. I wanted to be in on the action, even if only as a fly on the wall. I didn't want a threesome, or a confrontation per se, but if he was gonna have an affair, I was going to at least get to observe it. Maybe I was taking things to a whole new level of wrongness, and, sure, you could say two wrongs don't make a right, but I figured that saying had to go out the window when my pussy was throbbing, demanding attention, my mind racing with naughty images of Pierce and Margot, my new favourite XXX couple. And from that day on, I was hooked.

Thinking back, I remembered that there was a time when he treated me kind of rough. Not as hardcore as he'd been with her, and it was so long ago it had gotten a little fuzzy. But as I sank down on to my kitchen floor and shoved my fingers inside of me, vague memories started to surface. After we'd started seeing each other exclusively, we couldn't keep our hands off one another. We'd grope each other in public, he'd finger me at the movies, we'd be that couple sneaking into bathrooms for quick (though, sometimes, not so quick) blow jobs.

He'd text me naughty one-word messages, things like, Cock or Bad, or commands like Take off your panties and throw them in the nearest garbage can. I'd obey, of course, getting wet instantly not so much from the details but from knowing he was thinking about me that way. It was never too kinky, and when we'd got engaged, I had pictured us taking our twisted fantasies to new heights. I'd wanted to explore that world further, but he'd taken our engagement to mean that we were to scale it back, become more 'respectable', whatever that meant. No, Pierce never said as much, but I could tell. If I dared even hint that I wanted a spanking, positioning myself in such a way that my ass just happened to be within his hand's reach, he'd twist me around or move himself so there was no chance of my bottom becoming sore.

More than the physical part of it, I craved the mental leap from equal to unequal, from loving partner to dirty, filthy whore. In the real world, they may have been worlds apart, but in the bedroom, we could leap that boundary with a single harsh word. All he had to do was say it, but he never did. Pierce pretended like that was just a phase, and now we were all about vanilla sex. Don't get me wrong, I love vanilla – ice cream, and fucking. But I like to mix it up a little, and I had only ever gotten into a truly submissive headspace with Roderick. I'd never wanted to simply bend over and take it from any man wielding a whip, or belt, or hand. Plenty had tried, but I needed to trust someone, to give them my heart before I gave them everything else.

I'd tacitly accepted what Pierce wanted, because, after all, he still had a big cock, still made sure that we did it almost every morning. He never refused my advances, and he still managed to surprise me, with romantic little trips, couples' massages, dinners and unusual dates. He was committed to me, that much I knew, and if he wanted to keep things simple, well, he was worth it. What can I say – I was in love.

And I still loved him, I realised, even though he was cheating on me. That fact mitigated any guilt I might have felt about spying, because suddenly he had given me the key to getting the kink back in our relationship. I came fiercely against my fingers as I pictured this stranger trussed up just like he'd said, then me in her position, then both of us side by side, twin visions of bratty bottoms waiting to get what was coming to us. The idea of being muzzled, of panting and moaning and crying out, only to have the sound trapped behind a gag, made me whimper. I hadn't come like that since our early days; I'd been missing a lot.

I stood up, only to find that the action onscreen had continued without me, unfolding just as their affair had, except this time, I was in on the action. As I looked back up at the screen, in came another reply in the series they were volleying back and forth, making me realise that though I was in Pierce's inbox, so was he – at the office. For about a minute, Margot's missive was in bold, a glossy black veneer tempting me to click on it. Then, accessing his account from the relatively luxury of his desk, Pierce must have read it. It went from bold to regular type, meaning it had been read. Read, as in ready – ready for me. I clicked on it. Today at 2? The usual room? he's asked her. Be there waiting for me on your knees, naked.

Again, I pictured her – in my vision, she had morphed into a sun-kissed, freckled, natural redhead, the opposite of my black Irish colouring – kneeling, waiting to suck my husband's dick with a porn-star-like prowess. Now that I knew they were going to actually get together that day, it was no longer a fantasy. It was real, and that only made me more curious. A part of me was angry, but more of me was fascinated by how it all worked: what they did together, what he'd tell me, how him fucking her affected him fucking me.

I retired to our marital bed and, with the aid of a battery-operated special friend, got myself off again. I pictured them together, staving off the occasional attack of jealousy by tapping into my own voyeuristic fantasies. I've always loved to watch, to ogle, to observe. It's what made me an ace reporter back when

I was covering local culture; I could scope out the hottest graffiti artist, knew all the underground comedy clubs, could spot a future chart-topping busker from clear across a subway station. I was a professional watcher, but I also watched in a more intimate way, storing it all away, hoarding the images like free mental porn. I'd feast my eyes on hot guys at the gym when I swam, their muscles bulging, glistening, hard cocks sometimes visible as they caught sight of a particularly busty or hot woman parading around in a bikini. I'd always wanted to sneak into their locker room and just stand in the doorway, ogling all that beautiful male flesh. I'd look at women, too, gorgeous women I knew were way out of my league, but I didn't care.

The excitement I got from watching strangers was nothing compared with the idea of watching my own husband fuck his mistress. If I couldn't have that, I could at least check out the naughty photos she sent him upon request. One featured her pinching a nipple between perfectly manicured red fingernails. Another was of her ass in a pair of lacy black and white panties, then another where just a hint of her pussy was showing. I wondered if she had someone taking the shots, or if she was doing it herself with a tripod. Didn't matter; I was officially hooked.

So that's how I started snooping on his email. I got his password from that borrowed laptop with the help of my friend Emma, who works in IT and pretty much knows everything about computers, so when he took it back, I was able to keep reading from the comfort and privacy of my own computer. It became my ritual, a better pick-me-up than the cup of hot coffee I indulge in at nine each morning. He seemed to start in on the dirty talk as soon as he got to work, keeping up a steady stream of it while he was supposed to be brokering multimillion-dollar deals. I guess the world of finance only holds so much fascination.

I was riveted to the way they emailed, all breathless, so frantic they had little need for proper grammar. These were not long, fawning love letters like the kind James Joyce wrote to his wife Nora in 1909, the ones I'd stumbled across while researching him for a college English paper and almost had to get myself off right there in the library. They weren't eloquent or even worth saving. But they did let me know that while their affair was strictly sexual, it was not a one-time thing. It was a two-timing thing, an ongoing connection they shared that, had Pierce not happened to forget his laptop that day, I'd be none the wiser about.

I spent two weeks hoarding my little secret, until I finally had to confess to my best friend, Cheryl. The burden of keeping my naughty news to myself was too much, plus I wanted to see what she'd say. Was I crossing a line in spending so much time snooping? Did the end justify the means? And really, when you cut right to the chase, the question for me was whether I was a sick pervert for getting off on Pierce and Margot's affair, tuning in to their Internet musings like this was an X-rated soap opera, rather than my very real life.

I'd even bought a BlackBerry so my spying could happen on the go. There I'd be pushing a grocery cart around the store, trying to find the freshest cut for our dinner, while surreptitiously trying to see what assignations Margot and Pierce had planned, whether they'd stick to their same hotel room or try something new, whether they'd flaunt themselves in an elevator or flirt in public. Whether he'd tie her up, tease her, fuck her in the ass, order her not to come. I had managed to keep it to myself, not letting on when Pierce came home, pretending when I pounced on him that I was just plain old horny, rather than horny from my daily detective work. Who was the real cheater, and what was the real crime here?

I'd somehow lost track, the deeper I got sucked in, only knowing that I needed the spying to fuel my increasingly active fantasy life. Even while Pierce was on top of me (usually with the lights out, a far cry from our early experimentation and, according to his emails, the way he liked to watch every move Margot made), I'd shut my eyes and picture them, picture her petite mouth wrapping itself around his thick hardness. I had to bite my lip so as not to call out her name and give everything away.

When I told Cheryl, she demanded to see a sample of their messages. I showed her the screen:

You are such a fucking little whore. I bet you could take two cocks at once, one in your mouth and one in your pussy. What if I bring a friend with me next time? He has an even bigger dick than I do, one that could really make you gag, though I do my best. Be prepared, my pet, because I'd like to see you try to take on both of us at once. He could probably turn your ass pretty red, too.

Cheryl blushed, then looked over at me with a shocked expression, even though she should know by now that I'm pretty hard to ruffle. 'Well? Are you keeping these for evidence?'

'Evidence?' I laughed, the noise floating over the elegant silver forks lifting delicately over other ladies who lunch. 'Cheryl, I'm not planning to divorce him. Not with masturbation fodder like this. I mean, this is hotter than anything we've done since we got married.'

'You mean you get off on reading this stuff?' she asked, with a look that clearly said, 'That's sick.' At first, she looked horrified, but I could tell she was also intrigued. 'Doesn't it bother you? Another woman messing around with your man? What if she's really hot? What if she wants to steal him away?'

I'd thought of all those things, of course. I bristled, because they were the aspects of this that I didn't let myself think about. 'Well, there's not much I can do about that, is there?'

'You can fight back. You can get all sexed up for him. You can show him why it's wrong.'

But there's where Cheryl was wrong. It was an age-old tale, of women trying to haggle for attention, settling for being told they were second-rate, turning on other women in a frenzied competition for cock. I didn't want any part of that. No, I'd go one better than catching him in the act; I'd turn all my mixed feelings to the one part of my body that could properly process them: my pussy. Which is exactly what I told my friend. Was I jealous? Sure. Was I angry? A little. But any negative emotions were overshadowed by the way I'd become captivated by them, by the mystery of Pierce and Margot, this secret, shadowy couple who existed in a vacuum.

When you get married, everyone knows who you are, the new you: you are one half of a couple. So even when you go out, there's a part of whoever you run into who's filling the other person in, a silent partner. You reap the safety of such a relationship, and when you go out together, even if it's just to the corner store, you get to bask in the glow of knowing that you are this man's Wife. Yes, I still think of it as a capital-letter kind of job, one I'm grateful to have. I couldn't leave him over this; what would be the point? To teach him a lesson? To do the 'right' thing? Well, if anyone was wrong here, I was too. I'd brought any misfortune upon myself.

But more importantly, after that initial flare of white-hot hate, I'd cooled down. I'd turned lemons into sweet, sexy lemonade, and I'd be damned if I wasn't going to drink my fill!

She didn't quite agree, but there was a sparkle in her eye that told me that just maybe she got what I was talking about, got why it was hot to be privy to my husband's innermost dirty thoughts. It was almost like seeing what porn he watched or how he masturbated: here he was, free of any social niceties. On a purely pragmatic level, I understood what he was doing (even though I'd never have chosen it). Should he share those truly dirty, pervy, sadistic thoughts with me, and I rejected them, and therefore him, he'd never be able to save face. You can't bring up your innermost fantasies and then put them back in the box, make them disappear, laugh it off as a joke. If this were something that truly touched him to his core, as, I was realising, it did me, he would want to protect it, keep it sacred, special. Maybe he'd thought he couldn't share this with me. Maybe he'd met Margot and she'd seemed too good to be true. But where he'd underestimated me was in thinking I'd never find out. Thinking I'd be the dumb innocent little wife, the one he could pull something over on. He thought he was so smart, with his cake and his ice cream and eating all of it like he was at some fixed-price buffet.

He thought he was some smooth operator, but I knew better, and what's more, I'd turned the tables on him. Because part of the thrill of having an affair – at least, what I imagined to be the thrill – was doing so in secret, knowing that at any moment you could get caught. That had to be what those who engaged in public sex experienced, too. Even though he didn't know it yet, I was taking the wind out of his illicit sails. I was taking some of the magic away from him and bringing it to me. Sure, I could've had an affair of my own, but I didn't want to, and, frankly, didn't need to, because in a very real sense I already was. I was having an affair with their affair. That was my dirty little secret, my taboo treasure, one I had to hide from my husband just as much as he had to hide his mistress from me.

And then I upped the ante. I decided that instead of being a passive player and just watching from afar, reacting to their trysts and texts, hoping for certain outcomes, I'd go one step further. I'd become an active player in their little game, and serve my own purposes in the process. Because the more intimately involved I became in their lives, soaking up each racy message, savouring each arousing anecdote, the more I wanted out of it. There were some things I wanted to picture, wanted to see, as if they were actors in my own private porno film. I couldn't outright send Margot emails from Pierce's account, because he'd surely know that he wasn't the one who'd sent them, and even if I deleted them from the sent file, if she called him on them, I'd be screwed, and not in a good way.

But I could plant seeds in his mind. I could suggest outings, toys, positions for them to try and me to live through vicariously. Sure, Pierce still fucked me regularly, but that wasn't enough – not for him and not for me. I wanted her there with us, wanted her writhing, begging, aching. Not literally, of course; a threesome was never on the cards, especially not with someone my husband was clearly so besotted by. Some sweet young thing we picked up at a club? That I could entertain, but not the mythical Margot. I didn't want to see her in the flesh; I only wanted to know that she was doing my bidding. So I started closest to home.

'I got pulled over for a ticket today,' I said, noting that Pierce was only half listening, one eye on his cell phone, probably waiting for a text from Margot. 'When he got out of the car, the cop had a pair of handcuffs attached to his jeans. That got me thinking – why don't you try tying me up sometime?' I asked him, posing seductively with my wrists together in front of me.

'Bondage? Honey, our kind doesn't do that sort of thing,' he said with a sniff. I didn't stoop to remind him that I'd only been included in 'our kind' since I married him, nor to impart the knowledge that 'our kind' was probably the kinkiest around.

'But no one would ever have to know,' I whined.

'That's not the point,' he said, and just like that, our conversation was over. I could tell there was no arguing with him once he'd gotten that look on his face, and besides, I didn't want to have to beg to be bound – at least, not like that. The only begging I wanted to do was the erotic kind. We each settled into bed with separate books, and might as well have been in separate beds.

But lo and behold, the next day, Pierce was telling Margot he had a surprise for her.

What is it? Can I get a hint?

Here's your hint: I'm going to play cop and you're going to play lawbreaker.

I almost came right there when I read that. I know my husband all too well, apparently.

Oh, do go on, she wrote.

Maybe I should have been more jealous. After all, Margot was the one who was going to get bound by the handcuffs that, as Pierce's wife, were rightfully mine. But nothing, especially sex, is ever fun when you have to con someone into doing it, and I'd much rather experience his dom side vicariously than have him do it under duress. But words can only go so far when your dirty mind's in overdrive; I wanted pictures. How to get Pierce to think about photographing her all on his own, though? That was an even bigger step than the bondage, because once he documented the affair, it was far easier for news to travel. He could deny anything else, even the emails, saying they were roleplaying, or a friend was using his computer, but pictures don't lie.

I knew they had started to play with the idea of handcuffs. She was dropping hints about her sore wrists, and for just a moment I pictured myself taking part, holding her arms down while he fucked her, playing the role of the mean mistress as he drilled inside her. She was such a submissive slut, it seemed, that she'd surely love it. But never mind me; I had to get Pierce interested in the idea first.

The next night, while he slept, I surreptitiously snuck out of bed and did a little creative web surfing on his computer. Bondage porn site after bondage porn site appeared on the screen, enough so that if he went to check his email or visit espn.com or Amazon, some version of bound, gagged, naked women would pop up. I figured he'd either dismiss it as spam or get a membership, but either way the idea would be planted in his head. I felt like a perverted Samantha on *Bewitched*, playing the witchy wife, but instead of a twitch of my nose, it was a few strokes of my fingers.

Sure enough, the next day Pierce was telling Margot that he was going to blindfold her, stuff her panties in her mouth, tie her arms to the bedpost of their hotel *du jour* and take photos of her.

'You can't do that!' I could practically hear her gasp, then giggle, even though the words were written. Much as people say email lacks character, when you know what you're looking for, you can find it in the written word.

Don't worry, I won't blackmail you with them . . . if you're a good girl, he wrote. I wondered if that meant Margot was married too; if so, we were all tempting fate, all taking chances with our futures in the name of lust. I kind of liked that idea, but then it made me think of Margot's poor husband, who probably wasn't enjoying their tryst quite as much as I was. Then I focused back on the problem, or rather the solution, at hand. My husband's increasingly mischievous side impressed me; if only he knew how good a team we could make. By then, though, I was no longer pining for the man I half-had; instead,

I fully appreciated the good fortune he had shone upon me. I could've gotten stuck with a man who didn't fuck me – or anyone else. Instead, I had an extra-virile man who could conduct an affair, fuck me, and find ways to innovate and improve on his erotic repertoire.

That afternoon, I went to get a massage, at a spa where I knew they gave very happy endings. As the man with the magic hands brought them to bear on my buttocks, then lower, his thumbs caressing my labia, I silently urged him onward. Part of me wanted him to take the part of Pierce and stuff my sticky panties between my lips, add an eye mask to remove my sight, and hold my wrists together while his face plunged into my most private parts. Instead, I shut my own eyes, brought my wrists together over my head, and held as still as possible as he teased my pussy, his thumbs moving closer and closer to my wetness. I finally let go of the image of Pierce and Margot, replacing it with my own private stud. He was a tease, though, giving me only an almost happy ending, his feather-light touch more arousing in its frustration than a full-on finger-fuck would've been. I could've asked, but like I said, if I have to beg, if a man's not raring to go, ready to show me just how much he wants me, I'd rather not. I had a vibrator that's always ready for some action waiting for me.

When I got home, I was climbing the walls. I longed to let Pierce know that I knew, but I couldn't; that would ruin the fun. He wasn't home yet, so I went to the local electronics store and said I needed a nanny cam (I couldn't very well say I needed a perv cam, since the perv, in this case, was me). I installed the shockingly easy to use camera, then subtly suggested to Pierce that we watch some amateur porn that had somehow appeared in our mailbox. 'Imagine if that was us on screen, honey, fucking right here in our bed, captured for all eternity.' I can lay it on thick when I want to.

'Oh yeah,' he said, rather unconvincingly, but as we started watching, I could practically feel the wheels in his brain spinning, churning, itching to get his hands on his hottie so they could star in a little video of their own. He was so aroused that even though I could tell it confused him to be horny for her, then naked with me, he made love to me while I fantasised, this time, about capturing us on film. Maybe someday . . .

For now, I was ready to put my new and improved plan into action, one that might get me everything I wanted, including my husband back. Yes, the two of them, in my head, were hot as hell, but I was starting to feel like my interest in them was unhealthy, veering too close to obsession for my comfort. It was OK as a brief little blip on my masturbation radar, but I was so preoccupied with following their affair, I'd lost all perspective.

The next day, I told Pierce I'd be out of town the following weekend; my sister had invited me to her home in San Francisco, and I couldn't pass up the chance to visit her and my nieces. I'd checked with her and made sure it was OK; I wanted to give Pierce and Margot as much time as possible to soil our marital bed sheets. Yes, it was time for one last hurrah, one that would mark a major turning point, for them, and for me. Bringing your mistress home is never a smart idea . . . and I had finally figured out that it's always the least smart ideas that are the most arousing. The mere thought had me gushing, my vibrator working overtime when I read Pierce's message to Margot excitedly relating this chance to be truly naughty.

I made sure to set the camera with an extended videotape to fully capture every moment they shared in our bed. My escape to San Francisco was short-lived; I was so preoccupied with wondering about my X-rated directorial debut, I barely heard a word my sister said. I hinted to her that something very special was happening with Pierce and me, but didn't want to disrupt her romantic notions by sharing the real truth of our sordid affairs.

When I got home, Pierce was reclining on the patio with a cigar. He looked as handsome as ever, and I felt the stirrings of real lust for him, not just him-and-Margot. I'd been so focused on screwing him by proxy, I'd forgotten about the live cock that lived in his pants. Right there in our backyard, I lifted my dress over my head, pulling myself, and my husband, into the here and now, the glorious, sexed-up present. 'Have a good weekend?' I asked as I tossed the garment dangerously close to the pool. Before he had time to protest, I settled myself over him, grinding against his crotch. The cigar was soon put out as I leaned down and met his lips with mine. My breasts made their way out of my bra and into his mouth, his lips sucking at my nipples.

He stood, balancing my weight around his waist, carried me into the bedroom and threw me on to the bed. I landed hard, the soft thud placating me for a moment. I looked up into the red eye of the camera, still whirring, and winked. Pierce had his clothes off in moments. Maybe taking Margot in our bedroom had reminded him of the passion we used to share. I almost confessed to Pierce about what I'd been up to, but then his fingers were probing my pussy as if he'd never touched me there before. 'You're so wet,' he said, his voice awed. And I was. The next thing I knew, his hands were pressing my wrists down, while I writhed against him in mock struggle.

'Yes,' I whispered as our eyes locked, the power shifting as he took control the way I'd long wanted him to. I let him fuck me with my head hanging over the side of the bed, his strong hands pulling me toward him, my hair flowing down, my screams filling the air and adding a soundtrack to the sex tape I never wound up watching. The next day, he told Margot that he wouldn't be seeing her any more, that his marriage was too important to threaten its existence. It was an abrupt end to things, but I was ready. All that extra passion I'd put into spying became passion I vowed to put into spicing up our love life, whether that meant toys or notes or, most of all, sharing my fantasies and desires. Telling him those dirty dreams I jerked off to, rather than living through them vicariously.

I never asked what changed his mind, and while I sometimes miss his affair, we've started a little email affair of our own, cutting out the middleman, and it's even filthier than their correspondence ever was. I saved the tape, though, locking it in my secret safe. If I'm ever hard up for masturbation fodder, I know just where to look.

Rachel Kramer Bussel is a world-renowned editor and author of erotica. Her short fiction is also featured in the Black Lace collection *Sexy Little Numbers*.

The High Ground

Janine Ashbless

'Hey, Jill.'

I did a double-take seeing Miles dressed like that when he walked into the wine bar. I couldn't remember the last time I'd seen him in a suit, although he does work for a legal firm and of course that was what he'd wear to work. Silly of me, really, but I'd forgotten because Dan and I saw him only at weekends, at the orienteering club or in the pub or over dinner.

'Hi, Miles,' I said, flustered. He looked really good in a suit, I couldn't help thinking. With his tall lean build, high cheek-bones, red-gold hair and the tight musculature of a long-distance runner, he looked positively elegant in formal wear. But the thought was the last one I needed in my head in these circum-stances.

'You're looking nice,' he said with one of his hard little smiles, his gaze flitting over me with a hint of surprised pleasure. I changed my mind: *that* was the last thing I needed to be thinking about. Of course he wasn't used to seeing me in a skirt and heels either. Usually it was tracksuit and sweatshirt. 'So what's up?' he asked and deliberately glanced around the bar full of lunchtime drinkers so as to convey the question *Why are we here?*

'Um.' I wrung my hands. 'I need to talk to you.'

'OK. Have you eaten yet?'

'Not here,' I said, pushing away my empty glass with my fingertips. 'Somewhere more private.'

'Sounds serious.' His pale-blue eyes were steady, his coppery eyebrows drawn together in the faintest of frowns. 'We could walk by the river, if you like. It's a nice day.'

So we walked down to the park together and I let him buy me a burrito wrap from a stall even though I wasn't hungry. I just felt too guilty to refuse, because I knew how much I was about to hurt him. We sat on a bench overlooking the riverbank and the geese grazing the short grass. There was a precise, polite body-width of space between us. Miles checked his watch.

'Are you in a hurry?' I asked anxiously.

'Not too bad. I've got an hour before a meeting with the senior partners.'

'Right.' Had I been looking for an excuse to avoid telling him?

'So what's on your mind, Jill?'

'Ah.' I looked at the rowing teams sculling up the river, the man on the far bank fishing under the shadow of the railway bridge. 'I'm sorry . . . this is so difficult. I think Dan's having an affair.'

'Dan?' His voice was low. 'No. You're joking.'

'He goes out every Tuesday night. He's supposed to be doing a volunteer shift for the Samaritans. That's what he says he's doing. He takes the bus and comes back on the last one after midnight, and he can't talk about anything that's happened, of course.' My voice sounded weak, I thought, as if the words were ashamed of emerging. 'Only, a fortnight ago his mum rang to say his dad had been taken into hospital with a bad chest – it was nothing in the end, he was let out after a couple of days,' I added stumblingly, like Miles cared anything about my in-laws. 'So I thought I should tell him straightaway. I rang his mobile but the phone was off. So I decided I'd ring the Samaritans' number. They'd have been able to put me through to him. I mean, it might've been really serious, mightn't it?'

'Go on.'

'The Samaritans said he wasn't there. That he hadn't done any voluntary work for them since February.'

'Ah. So you think he's doing something else.'

'I know he's doing something else.'

'Jill, I can't believe Dan would be cheating. He adores you. Has he been . . . different since February? Have you two been arguing?'

The revelation, the great big horrible cruel revelation, stuck at the back of my throat, too jagged to force out. I procrastinated by answering his question. 'Not arguing. He has been different, though, now that I think about it.'

'Ignoring you?'

'Just the opposite,' I admitted. 'He's bought me lingerie – he hasn't done that in years. He's been wanting to . . . try things. Stuff.' I went pink, which was stupid in the circumstances, but that didn't stop me blushing. 'A bit kinky. I just thought he'd been seeing things on the Internet.'

That wasn't the entire story, but I wasn't confessing all. Since March our love life had been transformed. After years of us gradually slipping into a dull, comfortable routine, Dan was suddenly once more attentive and very very horny. It was like he'd come more alive. He'd started working out again, bulking up his shoulders and arms. We'd been out for romantic drives in the country that had turned into flushed and frantic sessions in the car or behind a tree. We'd fucked on the kitchen bench, on the dining table, in the shower. He'd bought a vibrating cock-ring for himself and the sexiest green silk basque for me, and spanked my bottom appreciatively when I modelled the matching thong. Men didn't usually behave like that if they were having an affair, according to the women's magazines, but it was all just symptomatic of his guilt, I supposed.

'You weren't worried?'

'No. I didn't think it meant there was anything wrong. I was pretty happy, to be honest.'

Miles bit his lip and nodded.

I looked at my cold burrito wrap without a single bite taken from it. 'I'm so stupid. It didn't occur to me it meant he was playing around.'

'Well, you don't know he is, to be frank. Have you talked to him?'

I shook my head, my eyes blurring. 'I followed him.'

'You what?'

'When he took the bus last week I got in the car and followed it to see where he got out.'

Miles rubbed the back of his neck. I could smell his cologne – something he didn't wear at weekends. At weekends it was all mud and crushed grass and fresh sweat. 'And?'

'He got off the bus at the end of your street.' My voice was hoarse all of a sudden. 'I parked up and watched where he walked to. He went into your house.' I forced myself to look Miles in the face properly for the first time since we'd sat down. 'I'm sorry, Miles. I know you work late evenings. I think Dan's seeing Fiona.'

Miles didn't answer. His expression stayed absolutely under control, almost masklike. Only his eyes betrayed his dismay. He stared at me for a long silent moment, then looked away over the river. He didn't change colour and he didn't lose his demeanour of cold control, but I saw his throat work as he swallowed.

I felt an insane desire to apologise again, but I slapped it down. I had never seen Miles lose his temper and I had no desire to – but I was desperate for some reaction. Something that would make me feel less alone in my turmoil. 'What are we going to do?' I asked.

Miles blinked, his red-gold lashes catching the sun. 'What do you want to do?' he asked. 'Confront him? Kill him? Forgive him? Pretend nothing ever happened?'

'I . . . don't know.'

'Are you asking me to decide?'

I felt a rush of something very close to panic. 'No! I just had to let you know. I don't know what to do.' I licked my dry lips. 'I want to know the truth.' As I said it the conviction solidified within me. 'I need to know for sure what's going on.'

'And you are one hundred per cent certain it was our house?'

I nodded.

'Then on Tuesday tell Dan you won't be home before he goes out to the Samaritans. I'll pick you up from work and we'll watch to see if he really does go and see Fiona. Then we'll both confront them, together.'

I let out a long breath. 'All right.'

'And Jill . . .'

'Yes?'

'You need to think about what you want the outcome to be here. About how much your life with Dan means to you.' Miles stood. 'I'll see you outside your office on Tuesday.'

He walked off.

I sat, stunned. I hadn't expected to see Miles of all men break down in tears or stride up and down raging, but his cool abrupt departure had taken me by surprise. I think I'd expected – I'd wanted – a sense that we were both in this mess together, that he felt the same helplessness and terror I did. There was nothing like that.

Gasping to hold back the tears of frustration, I looked down at my linked hands and saw that I'd squashed my burrito to pulp.

He picked me up as planned on Tuesday, and because we were far too early to lie in wait for Dan he took me to a little Thai restaurant where the waiters knew his name and there we ate delicately spiced prawns and tiny crab-cakes with sweet sauce. He ordered me a jasmine tea in which a large dried flower unfurled in the hot water to release a string of fragrant white and orange pom-poms. We talked about orienteering events we'd been on and those to come and didn't mention either of our spouses.

It felt a bit unnerving, to be planning to catch two adulterers whilst behaving as if we were the ones having a liaison.

'You're so calm,' said I.

Miles lined up his chopsticks diagonally across the square plate, with precise symmetry. 'No one ever won a court case by losing their temper.'

Afterwards we drove back to his house. He and Fiona lived on the edge of town in a leafy suburb. They'd both done well for themselves, he as a lawyer and she as a local government officer in charge of arts projects, and their large Victorian town house was one well beyond the aspirations of Dan and me. We'd been over for dinner many times though, and admired the perfect modernist interior with its leather furniture and colour-co-ordinated ornaments. We were all good friends, even though Fiona didn't run. Tall and curvy with warm dark eyes, she was more the domestic goddess type than the outdoorsy competitor. And she complemented Miles' nature: she gave him humanity.

This time we parked around the corner from his street, down the overgrown lay-by beside the electricity substation where leafy branches obscured the car from the road but gave us a reasonable view of the bus stop. Dan, if he caught his usual bus, would be here within ten minutes.

'How are you feeling?' Miles asked, unbuckling his seat belt.

I pondered a moment. 'Scared,' I admitted. 'Confused.'

'Not angry?'

I shook my head. I'd had moments of anger but each had fizzled out in seconds like a match finding no kindling. How could I explain it to him? Last night I'd come home and found Dan waiting for me with a duvet spread before the lit fireplace, the room illuminated by candles. I'd told myself to go along with it, to give him no reason for thinking that there was anything wrong between us. He'd undressed me and poured me a drink and smoothed baby-oil over my skin and massaged away the tension in my muscles for nearly an hour, until I was a warm and purring rag-doll. Then he'd cuddled up behind me, spooning, and slid his slick fingers up and down between my bum-cheeks and worked them deep into places that did not normally yield to anyone, and when he'd spread and dilated me and reduced me to quivering in every inch of my flesh, he'd slipped his cock smoothly and gently into my rear passage and made love to the deepest darkest parts of me. How could I explain that to Miles, or tell him what it meant? I hadn't tried anal since college, and then it had been interesting but hardly a success. This time I had come over and over and burst into incoherent tears, melting on his cock and his fingers.

In the last few months I'd regained the marriage I'd always craved: intimate, unpredictable, and passionate. But I'd paid a price for it too.

'Not yet,' I murmured.

Miles nodded. 'You love him.'

'Yes.'

'And I love Fiona.'

I didn't doubt that; though as different as chalk and cheese, the two of them were devoted. I stirred, distressed. Fiona had always been warmly, gently flirtatious with just about everyone, male or female. She was one of those people who made you feel better about yourself just because she liked you, but she had never struck me as the kind who would take it too far. And not with my husband. 'How could they – ?'

Miles brushed his lips with the back of his finger, smiling but wry. 'It's funny, isn't it?'

'Funny?'

'I'd always thought that if anyone was going to have a fling, it would be us two.'

My heart seemed to skip a beat and my skin suffused with heat. But it was true. There'd been a spark between Miles and me since first we'd met. I'd thought him attractive from the outset, if a little intimidating. He had those eyes that turn down at the outside corners and I've always found that irresistible. There had been times when those eyes had been very knowing, as if they read the heat concealed in mine. There had been *moments*. Like the Christmas he and I had been bringing logs in from their woodshed, while Fiona cooked the Christmas dinner and Dan on hands and knees coaxed the fire in the dining room to life. Miles had caught me in the back porch under the bunch of mistletoe and suggested a kiss. I'd complied, both of us clumsy and self-conscious and a bit giggly – until Miles had put his arm about my waist and kissed me properly, easing my lips apart, pulling me into his embrace. It was like something hot and soft had exploded in my sex; by the time I pulled away I was sopping wet and blushing furiously and wobbly in the legs. The imprint of his mouth had seemed to burn on mine for hours that day.

'Remember the run across Bishopsfell?' he asked fondly.

I turned my face away, staring out at the foliage that cradled our car. It wasn't possible for me to forget Bishopsfell. It was a green TD5 route, and we'd been competing individually as usual. I'd been running down the hillside toward the tree-line and no one else had been in sight, so when I'd decided I really needed a pee I'd plunged down into the waist-high bracken below the path, pulled down my leggings and dropped to a squat, determined to empty my bladder as quickly as possible. But by the time I'd finished and stood up again, Miles had caught up with me. He'd been standing near the path with an I-know-what-you've-been-doing grin. I'd jogged back up to him, saying, 'You had better not have been watching, Miles!' and swatting backhanded at his ribs with my map in playful reprimand. He'd caught my wrist, and for a moment we'd just stood there, staring at each other, breathing hard, half-smiling, very close but not touching. Then I'd looked down between us. There's not much you can do to hide an erection in black Lycra orienteering trousers, and Miles had been more than half-hard. Blame my endorphin high: I'd not said anything. I'd just put my other hand down and stroked him through the tight material, felt him fill and swell and rise under my hand, seen the hunger in his eyes as he rose to full straining hard-on – and then I'd snatched myself away and run off, laughing, leaving him stranded in the bracken just as the next runner came over the hill.

'You messed up my times that day,' Miles said softly.

'I'm sorry,' I mumbled. I could feel the ghost of his eager cock in my empty palm.

'You never . . . ?' His question hung on the air.

'I love Dan,' I said. 'He's my husband. I want to keep it that way.'

'And he loves you. I promise you that. I know him, Jill.'

'Then how could he do this?' I demanded, the confusion bubbling up in my breast. 'How is it that I'm not enough – that everything we have isn't good enough for him?'

Miles shifted in his seat to face me. 'Well,' he said, so softly that if you didn't know him you might even mistake it for gentleness, 'I can understand, I guess.'

'That's horrible!'

'I mean, I love Fiona, but that doesn't mean that when I'm with you, Jill, I don't feel the need – the very strong need – to wrap you around my cock.'

A jolt went through me, like electricity. 'This is so not a good time,' I whispered.

'No?' He lifted his fingers to my face, stroking my temple and the line of my cheek, brushing my lips softly with a touch like the feather of a fallen angel. I trembled under his caress as his fingertips dipped to my throat. Oh, I could so easily see him as an angel of sin: he was all cold fire and magnetic superiority. But I could see something else too, overlaying the first vision: the skinny ginger kid he must have been once, alone in the playground, far too clever for his own good. His voice was low and hypnotic. 'Then when would be a good time for me to do this?' he asked, leaning from his seat to kiss me.

Our lips were warm together. It was the Christmas kiss all over again, though inside me now as then the effect was rather more like Bonfire Night. For a moment it was almost chaste – then his tongue was on mine and everything was all heat and melting and yielding; my mouth opening to his, my breast quivering under the sweep of his fingers as he sought beneath the claret-coloured fabric of my blouse for my heartbeat. A little whimper escaped my lips as he released me to draw breath. It was a helpless animal noise, the sort that cannot help but provoke the predator. He smiled.

'I love Dan,' I breathed. It was my mantra.

'I know.' His fingers deftly slipped the top button of my fitted grey waistcoat, the main barrier between him and my nipple;

I wasn't wearing a bra beneath that red blouse. 'You love him, and you want to fuck me.'

'Oh God, Miles –'

'It's all right, Jill. I understand. I know.' He kissed me again as he captured the plump berry of my flesh through the silky fabric. I groaned as pleasure danced across my skin, shooting like fireworks through my pulse and my sex.

'We can't.' My voice sounded faint.

'Nevertheless,' said he, licking my throat, biting my earlobe, 'we're going to.' His hand fell from my breast to my inner knee. It was summer and I had no tights on, just smooth skin under his strong grasp. 'Open your legs.'

'Not here.' I was grasping at excuses: the fact that we were out in public, in his car and only a few hundred yards from his house, was a hook to hang my terror on.

'Yes. Here. Open your legs for me, Jill.'

I parted my thighs and he ran his hand up beneath my best work skirt, over my skin, to the tight silky fabric stretched over the hot mound of my pussy. I writhed in my seat, burning with arousal and shame. I put one hand on his arm as if I was going to fend him off, and felt the hard muscle work under my palm. In the secret place beneath my skirt he found lace; an edge; hair; folds.

Wet.

I saw his pupils dilate, his pale eyes darkening. I was slippery with juice already, wet from his kisses, his touch, his voice. Whatever I said, however I tried to prevaricate, my sex was in thrall to him. My body had already surrendered.

His fingers felt cool in my hot liquid slash. Delicately he took the wet to my clit and circled the sensitive nub. I spasmed, arching, biting back a cry as my arousal hit flashpoint, and that wave of heat and need was liberating. It was an immense relief not to have to think any more; I had been doing far too much thinking for the past fortnight. I let the tsunami wash over my guilt and my terror and my loss, and drown them. I sank one hand in Miles' hair and pulled his face to mine, biting his lips. Suddenly we were kissing again but fiercely this time, scrabbling at each other's clothes, stealing the breath from each other as we gasped for air. He wrestled off my panties and threw them aside, and then he hauled me over into his lap.

It wasn't exactly graceful. I had one leg either side of the gear-stick and it wasn't really clear whether I was supposed to be sitting with my back to him or side-on, and we were cramped behind the steering wheel and the windows were steaming up. But he managed to lift me clear enough of his crotch to yank my skirt up to my hips and release his cock from the confines of his trousers before it burst his fly. I didn't even get to *see* his cock – but I felt it go in. Fuck, did I ever feel it. Three strong thrusts sank him to the root in my wet pussy. My eyes watered. His arms encircled me. One hand burrowed inside my disordered blouse to knead my left breast and pinch my nipple. The other sought my sex, at the place we were joined. With it he could feel his shaft filling and stretching my hole. He rolled my clit between his fingertips.

'You want me to fuck you, Jill?' he whispered fiercely in my ear, thighs and pelvis heaving me up and down on his lap and his impaling length.

I grabbed his thigh and sank my nails into it through his expensive suit.

'You want me to come inside you – deep, deep inside?' His voice was hoarse and uneven. He had to take long pauses between phrases; spaces filled with the sound of my gasping and the creak of the car springs. 'Want me to stick my big cock in your mouth and fuck your throat until you choke down my spunk?'

I started to groan breathily.

'Want me to tie you down and spray my cream on your pretty little tits?' He tugged cruelly on one of those pretty little tits and I squealed, lifting myself up and writhing down on his cock. 'Want me to spank your bottom until it's bright red and then ride your dirty ass and come inside it?'

I think I tried to say yes but it just came out as an incoherent wail as I slammed through the barrier into orgasm. Miles, lifting me bodily and pumping me down on his cock, followed suit seconds later. He made no sound at all, but his grip was like iron and his whole frame shook.

I collapsed back against his chest, staring at the fogged windscreen. Outside it was growing dark. My heart was pounding harder than it ever did when I was running cross-country.

'That was . . . That was very good.' Miles nuzzled at my neck, his tongue testing my pulse. He didn't seem particularly inclined to let go of me. But the confusion I thought I'd drowned was waiting for me as my pleasure ebbed, stronger than ever. When my pulse had stopped rocketing I slipped from him and back into the passenger seat, tugging awkwardly at my clothes, fumbling at buttons. I couldn't find my knickers in the footwell; I wondered if they had gone under a seat. My face was flushed and I tried not to look at the man I'd just had sex with. That wasn't really possible though.

'So, are you wildly in love with me then?' he asked, with the special flippant smirk he reserves for really caustic jokes.

'No!'

'The Defence rests, m'lud.' He tucked himself neatly away and straightened his clothes, then added, almost to himself, 'Back to the Prosecution, then.'

'I want to go home, Miles,' I told him. 'Please, take me home.'

'Is that *Take you home so you can have a good cry by yourself,* or is it *Take you home so that I can fuck you properly, at leisure?*'

I met his eyes then, troubled. It would be fair, in a way, wouldn't it – the second option? It would be karma. I could picture Dan and me carrying on mirror affairs, him with Fiona, me with Miles. My husband would have his dirty secret and I would have mine, and at least the world would be in balance. I wet my lips, but I couldn't answer.

'Tempting,' Miles acknowledged. 'Very tempting. But no. We're here now. The bus pulled up while we were busy. Let's go.'

I hadn't even heard the bus. 'No,' I said. 'We can't, not now.'

'I don't see that. This is our chance.'

'I don't want to!' I snapped.

'Well, if you don't,' said he, opening his door and climbing out, 'I will.'

'Miles!' All my worst fears rushed to the fore. 'You're not going to hurt anyone!'

He stooped to look back in at me. 'Some people ask to be hurt, don't you think?' Then he turned away and the driver-side door snapped shut.

Giving up on my lost knickers I scrambled out, nearly falling out of my shoes. 'Miles! Stop!' He was walking away, not listening to a word. I trotted desperately after him and he paused, turning – but only to point the car's remote key. 'Coming?' he asked, looking down into my face with that glacial angelic smile.

'Miles, please –'

'You wanted to know the truth.'

'Don't do anything stupid!'

'You come keep an eye on me, then.'

So we crossed the road and walked down his street together, under the lime trees, just like we were returning to his house after a day at the office. His stride was relaxed and easy. I was too conscious of my missing panties and I kept wanting to check my buttons to make sure they were done up again decently. I was smoothing back my hair as we stepped through into his front garden, playing with the gold necklace about my damp throat as he slipped the key into the lock and eased open the front door.

There was music playing inside the house. Something Middle Eastern, just a flute and a drum. Miles looked up to the first landing of the stairs then motioned me into the hall with a flick of his eyes. 'Upstairs,' he mouthed, closing the door behind us with the quietest of snicks. 'Be my guest.'

Their hall was perfectly tidy as usual, no discarded shoes or heaps of junk mail like in mine. Their stairs, the Victorian pine the yellow of butter, smelled of beeswax polish. I led the way one riser at a time, up into the gloomy twist of the stairwell. I stopped when I saw the first hint of electric light spilling from an open door. There was something odd about the music, I thought; a beat that was somewhat off. I had a terrible sense of intruding, a premonition like Bluebeard's wife that I was about to find something that I had no desire to know.

'You go first,' I whispered, trying to turn back, but Miles blocked my way. A jerk of his chin was enough to order me back to my station. Swallowing, I offered up a silent prayer that Dan not be there. Reluctantly I took another three steps, the faint creaks of my footfalls masked by the music, reached a landing and turned a corner. Now, standing in the dark stairwell, I could see through the open door straight into the lit bedroom on the floor above.

Dan was sitting on the edge of the bed. He was naked, or at least probably so, because his groin was obscured by Fiona who lay face down across his lap, her voluptuous bottom draped over his thighs. She was wearing only a suspender belt and black stockings, with no panties. Dan had one hand buried between her thighs, his fingers working inside her. His other came over periodically to slap the wobbling orbs of her bum-cheeks, and it was clear that this was the source of the irregular beat I had heard over the CD music. Every time his hand descended she made a mewling noise and gasped, 'Yes!'

My heart seemed to grind to a halt. I felt Miles slip up right behind me and his lips brush my ear. 'I do work late most evenings,' he murmured. 'But not Tuesdays. Tuesdays I make a special effort to be home early.'

At last I understood: I'd been played. I could feel the blood draining out of my face. I turned my back on the tableau above and tried to side-step around Miles, but his arm blocked my passage. He was standing a stair below me so we were much more closely matched in height than normal. 'Think about what's sliding down between your legs, Jill,' he said in a low conversational voice, 'and then consider whether your footing on the moral high ground is as stable as you think it is.'

'You set me up.' My voice was quiet because there seemed to be no air in my lungs. 'You bastard.'

His eyes gleamed in the gloom. 'It was Fiona.'

'Fiona?' Behind me the sensual squeals were growing fiercer.

'Fiona wanted to experience the pleasure of being spit-roast. Two men taking her at once: one banging away in her pussy while the other pumped his prick down her throat. That was what she said she wanted. So I set out to find the right man, and I knew it had to be someone who I was sure would be discreet and treat her well and at the same time not fall for her. I didn't want to lose my wife. It had to be someone I could trust.'

'You picked a *married* man,' I hissed, my mouth twisting.

'Actually, both of us would have been more than happy to

include you as a fourth. It was Dan who said you wouldn't be interested.' He waited a beat for me to absorb that, then shook his head. 'To be honest, I had my doubts. I think he just wasn't prepared to deal with watching me fuck you, Jill.'

The noises upstairs rose to a crescendo. Fiona was coming, squealing, 'Oh, harder! Harder!' as she did, and the fusillade of slaps sounded like applause. My heart was beating time along with them. As her wails broke up into giggling gasps I swung on my heel and marched up the last flight of stairs, not bothering to be quiet, straight into the room.

For a moment I was able to see them not as Dan and Fiona, my husband and my friend, but with the eyes of a stranger. A tall curvaceous woman with the most beautiful creamy bottom turned strawberry-pink where she had taken the repeated impact of his hand, her wrists linked by suede cuffs and a short chain, her back emblazoned with the words WARM HER UP written in felt-tip pen. A solid, muscular man balancing her over his lap: hairy-chested, dark curls shiny with sweat from exertion or excitement, his left hand painted in her pussy-juices. They looked utterly rapt in their game, incredibly intimate, fervid with sexual potency.

They stared up at me.

Then I saw them once again as the people I knew, and I also saw something unmistakable in their faces: that Fiona had been expecting my entrance and that Dan had not. The colour was draining from his slackening face.

'Jill?'

'Have you come to play with us?' Fiona asked with a voice like butter and honey, wriggling on to her elbows. Her long hair was sticking to the moist skin of her cheeks and throat.

The blood that had left my head was back with a vengeance now; I could hear its tide drumming in my ears, feel the pulse in my belly and between my legs. I reached to the small of my back and unzipped my skirt, letting it fall to the boards. Under the claret hem of my blouse my thighs gleamed, sticky with Miles' semen, not yet dry. My pussy lips were pink and swollen and my pubic hair was twisted into fragrant wet rosettes.

Dan lifted Fiona from his lap, setting her aside on the bed, his eyes fixed on the juncture of my thighs. If I had faced what I dreaded most by coming into this house, he was facing it now. 'Jill . . .' The single syllable was strained and hoarse.

His cock stuck up from between his thighs, still half-erect, slow to realise that circumstances had changed. I pictured that cock powering into Fiona's tight-stretched hole while Miles fucked her mouth, Dan's face alight with rapture as he stared down at her big ass and slapped those splayed cheeks good and hard. Or had it been the other way round, that first time? Had Miles humped her from behind while she gobbled greedily at Dan's cock? Had he come in her mouth? Had she swallowed his spunk as enthusiastically as she ate everything else? Or had he pulled out and shot his load over her face and throat and beautiful voluptuous breasts, just for the pleasure of seeing her marked with his seed?

I realised I wanted to see that. She'd look good wearing jiz. Dan's semen was thick and elastic, so different from the stuff oozing out between my thighs right at this moment.

'Clean me up,' I told him, hardly recognising my own voice. 'Get down and clean up every last drop with your tongue, and if you make me come I will forgive you for lying to me.' Then I held my breath.

Without a word Dan dropped to his knees and crawled forward, his cock heavy but contrite, and reached out, appalled, to touch my despoiled pussy. I slapped his fingertips away, ordering, 'Mouth only. I want you to kiss me.'

For a moment I thought he was going to rebel. His dark eyes met mine, tormented. But he obeyed – fearfully at first, crouching to lap at my thighs with the very tip of his tongue. I laid my hand on his head, on the familiar contours of his skull, and felt him quiver. Then he pressed his face to my sex and kissed me, insinuating his tongue into my folds to taste me and to taste my lover. I gave a little sigh, something unknotting deep within.

Fiona knelt up on the bed, that catlike smile playing on her lips. Even as my eyes glazed over I managed to rasp, 'You just wait, Fiona. I'm going to give you a spanking you won't forget.'

Then I lost focus on anything further than my pussy, because Dan was spreading my labia with his fingers and licking deep into its inverted cup. I nearly lost balance; I would have staggered except that Miles came up behind me and made a wall for me to lean back against. He slipped his hands under my arms and began to undo my buttons. The dove-grey waistcoat, then the port-coloured blouse. He bared my breasts and cupped them both, testing the firmness of my nipples and how they contrasted with their soft mounds. Fiona licked her lips, her eyes filled with greed. I looked at her lush curves and wondered how anyone with so much to offer could be interested in my more meagre body, but she was crawling right to the edge of the bed now, fixated on my wriggling form held captive in her husband's grasp.

'The high ground losing its appeal?' Miles whispered, doing unspeakable things with his tongue in the whorls of my ear.

I groaned, lost somewhere between Dan's tongue swirling over my clit and the teasing pull on my breasts. I'm a cross-country runner; I know the view from the high ground is unbeatable, but if you want to go anywhere you have to turn downhill at some point.

And you have to be willing to get dirty.

'You bad girl,' Miles chided.

I had my eyes shut when Fiona finally reached me, placing her manacled hands on my waist and stooping to nudge Miles aside and suck at my tits. I moaned at the first touch of her teeth and lips tugging on me, arched my shoulders into Miles' chest and then hooked a leg over Dan's back, giving him deeper access. He pushed up against my open pussy, his mouth making wet noises as he guzzled. God, it felt good: to have him eating me, to have wet on my nipples, to feel her breath gusting hot and cold as she lapped at the engorged points of my tits. I saw Miles' hands reach to her hair, guiding her head from one of my breasts to the other and back again, enjoying his benevolent despotism as he controlled my pleasure.

'Here,' he murmured. 'Now this one.'

My poor nipples were tugged and stretched as she switched from one to the other. Fiona's own big bare tits were dangling free, unattended. *You like a bit of punishment do you?* thought I, and slapped them; not hard, just enough to feel them bounce. Fiona managed a muffled squeal but it didn't sound exactly like protest. I'd never groped a woman's breasts before, but now my nails bit into her satiny skin as I hefted their warm weight. In turn she nipped at my nipples, sending sparks through my whole body, just enough pain salting the pleasure to make it taste even better. As we worked out an equilibrium Miles left my breasts in his wife's care in order to unbuckle his belt and fly, pressing against my writhing bum a cock that was once more stiffly erect. He didn't try to do anything with it though, not just then. He simply enjoyed the friction. And he slid a hand down between my bum-cheeks, stroking me all the way to the sticky terrain of my pussy, all the way to Dan's chin that was jerking rhythmically while his mouth worked at my clit, and into the welcoming hole of my sex. He got his fingers inside me and the sensation of his invasion, of being stretched again, brought me up to a whole new plateau of arousal. I could hear myself starting to make undignified noises. I was getting really close now to forgiving Dan. I couldn't help myself, his mouth was so eloquently pleading his cause, and his supporting witnesses were more than persuasive.

It wasn't enough for Miles. He withdrew his hand, slippery with Dan's saliva, with his own semen, with my sex juices. He pulled back far enough to find the pursed mouth of my anus, and pressed one slick fingertip to its tight aperture. I was on the edge already, every fibre in my body preparing to yield, and he knew it.

'Oh fuck,' I yelped. Explosions of sensation were billowing up my spine and across my skin from my asshole.

'Too right.' It didn't take more than a twist and a push to pop his finger through the ring of muscle, and once inside my guard he could slide all the way into my hot clinging depths. That was the moment I gave up any notion of calling the shots. With three of them pleasuring one of me the contest was unequal, the outcome inevitable. As Miles' finger flexed deliciously inside my butthole I came, thrashing and quivering up and down on my husband's slippery face and rubbing my breasts in his wife's, my cries damn near loud enough to wake the whole neighbourhood.

Three people, I found, is enough to hold you as you let loose with everything you've got. As my limbs went to rubber they took my weight. Miles brushed his lips to my ear again.

'"And Jill came tumbling after,"' he said with a low chuckle. Fiona's lips closed softly over mine and I murmured in pleasure. In the warm waves of my afterglow I wondered what it would be like to taste Dan's come on her tongue.

Oh God, Dan. He was sitting back, flushed and anxious and expectant, his cock fully erect and eager for the next round. I licked my lips as I met his gaze. Part of me was still shocked beyond words at what we'd done, but the stronger part of me was soaring. And, far as I had come today, I had the momentum to keep going a long way yet.

Janine Ashbless is the author of the Black Lace novels *Divine Torment*, *Burning Bright* and *Wildwood*. She has two single-author collections of erotica, *Cruel Enchantment* and *Dark Enchantment*, also published by Black Lace. Her paranormal erotic novellas are included in the Black Lace collections *Magic and Desire* and *Enchanted*. Her short fiction appears in numerous Black Lace collections.

Be Careful What You Ask For

Gwen Masters

Carrie was ovulating.

She could feel it happening. There were small twinges in her belly. Her breasts were tender and her temperature was up. It was the fourth month since their all-out determined assault on infertility began. Nothing had happened during those first three months, and she was starting to think it was all Alex's fault. She was doing everything right, but he still insisted on drinking caffeine and on wearing those jockey shorts instead of boxers . . .

The box of ovulation tests stared down at her from the top shelf of the medicine cabinet. It was purple with pink and blue accents. How fitting. She peed on a stick and then stood there tapping her foot, counting off the seconds like she used to when she was a kid and thunder woke her up at night. One-one-thousand, Two-one-thousand, Three-one-thousand . . .

The stick showed a little purple line. Positive. It was only the first day, and that meant she had a four-day window. They could have a lot of sex in four days.

Alex was lying on his back in their bed, snoring. They had been married for seven years and even now she hated his snoring. It was the reason she never slept in his apartment while they were dating. She kept a stock of earplugs in her beside drawer, right next to the condoms that were quickly reaching their expiration dates. They hadn't used protection in four years. Still nothing.

'Alex? Wake up,' she whispered in his ear and gently twisted his lobe between her fingertips. He snorted and moved away from her, but didn't wake up. She looked down at him for a while and then lay back to look at the ceiling.

Why were they even bothering? It wasn't like Alex would have time for a child. He was always working. His hours had started out at about fifty a week and had just been increasing. When she bitched about how late he came home at night, he explained very reasonably that if she wanted a child, they had to be able to afford one. When he did come home, he usually sat down in front of the television and ignored her until he fell asleep on the couch. It was maddening.

Carrie wondered what it would be like to raise a child on her own if things ended with her and Alex. She wasn't looking for that but she wasn't ruling it out either. Some would call her pursuit of pregnancy in a failed marriage an irresponsible act, and she supposed they might be right. But she was thirty and, last time she checked, she wasn't getting any younger.

She nudged Alex with her knee. He wiggled some more. She pressed her cold toes against his calf and he abruptly flipped over and started to snore louder. In the dim glow from the night-light she could see the red creases on his face from the pillowcase. His hair was sticking straight up from his forehead. His mouth was open and contorted a little where he had buried his face half-way into the pillow. Not all that appealing.

The twinge came again, down low. She was definitely ovulating. She didn't even need that little purple stick to confirm it any more. She knew her body better than ever.

She looked at Alex one more time, then got up and padded through the silent house. Her laptop sat there on the kitchen table, forlorn and lonely. She opened it up and blinked as light flooded the chair in which she sat. One click and she was connected to the Internet. Two more clicks and she entered the chat room.

Alex didn't know about this. Carrie never lied to him, had never once uttered an untruth to her husband, and she was proud of that. But she didn't disclose much either, and if he was stupid enough to think all that time she spent on the Internet was completely innocent, well, that was his own fault.

She typed in her password and there was the chat room. She pulled up another screen, typed in a few letters and *whoosh*. There was the email account Alex didn't know she had. Now Carrie was Carrine. And Carrine was usually the belle of the ball.

Fourteen email messages, all with subjects like 'In the Mood' or 'I Loved Last Night!' She scanned them all and responded to a few, with short messages to keep the fire just high enough. Then she moved to the chat room and smiled when three men – at least she assumed they were men, but she could never really be sure – jumped on her presence.

Carrie invited them into her private room. Then she picked one at random and worked her way through a virtual blow job. She knew just how to do it, just what to describe, just how to use the blend of naughty and downright raunchy to get the effect she wanted. She worked him until he typed that he was going to come, then apparently he did, jacking off with one hand while holding down one key with the other:

mmmmmmmmmmmmmm

Carrie smiled.

The next one wanted the same thing. She played him well, and sometimes asked the third person in the private room if he was enjoying himself. She got a virtual wink in response. Then the second guy came, and signed off so fast he made Carrie giggle. Come and run.

The third guy was patient, slow and easy. He mentioned how much he would love to come in her ass, and she switched gears, created a virtual woman who pulled her panties down and her skirt up, who looked back over her shoulder and winked with a come-hither smile. The guy kept typing, and Carrie knew she had found the one for the evening. The one who would be a good substitute for Alex.

The faceless stranger gave as good as he got, and didn't let up until Carrie slipped her hand down into her panties. She played with her clit and was surprised to realise how wet she already was.

Are you enjoying yourself?

Oh yes. I'm dripping wet already.

Good. That will make you wet enough for me to fuck your ass, won't it?

Carrie shuddered with anticipation. Alex would never do that. He thought it was dirty and wrong and maybe it was, which was the whole point of a good anal fuck.

She got herself close to coming but held off. She wanted to wait until she made Alex come inside her. It might slightly increase the odds of getting pregnant.

The guy on the computer screen was close to coming. She barrelled ahead over his typing, and turned it into a game all about him. She wanted him to come. She had what she wanted, she was horny enough to do it with her husband, and she wanted to get it done so she could go to sleep.

The guy came. She was sure he did, because there were no melodramatics, just simplicity.

Wow! Thank you . . . thank you!

You're welcome.

Will I see you again tomorrow? I would like that.

I would like that, too.

And with a virtual smile, Carrie signed off.

Alex was lying on his back. Carrie climbed into bed and crawled between his legs. He didn't move. Carrie gently licked his soft cock. Slowly it began to grow, and when he was semi-hard, Alex woke up. He took one look at Carrie down there between his legs, and she watched with satisfaction as he rose to full attention within seconds.

'What time is it?' he asked, and Carrie felt a flash of annoyance.

'Time to fuck me,' she said with a sultry growl. He didn't move as she straddled him, as she ran her wet pussy over his shaft. When she sank down on him and took his cock to the hilt, he sucked in a breath and thrust his hips up to her.

'Don't move,' she whispered, and leant down so her hard nipples ran over his chest. She whispered into his ear, 'You like that? My tight pussy waking you up? You want me to ride you nice and slow or nice and fast?'

'Fast,' he said immediately, and Carrie began to pump her hips. Alex started to reach for her but she growled a warning, so he held on to the headboard instead. He watched her bounce above him until his eyes grew heavy with pleasure. Carrie studied his long eyelashes and his messed-up hair and his chest, which heaved now with tortured breaths. She angled her body so that her clit ran right over his shaft. He felt the change and groaned in satisfaction.

Then Carrie really went wild on him, slamming down hard enough to hurt, gliding along the length of his shaft. She was right on the verge. 'I want to feel you shoot inside me,' she taunted, her voice soft, then rising with every thrust. 'I want you to come, I want you to fill me up, I want you to come so hard you can't come again for days, I want you to give me that hot load, right there in my cunt.'

Alex groaned and then grimaced as if he were hurting. Carrie felt him give her exactly what he wanted. She was suddenly sticky and even wetter. She came too, right after he did, and announced it with a roaring cry that made Alex suddenly grab at her shoulders.

'Are you all right?' he asked breathlessly, even before her orgasm faded. She nodded and fell weakly to her side. Her head spun. She hadn't come that hard in a very long time, and for a short while she forgot all about babies and tests and fertility treatments. Long after Alex had gone back to sleep and his breathing was even, Carrie was thinking about that man in the chat room. She was thinking about how it would feel to have her ass fucked. She had never done it before.

A few hours later, Alex was up bright and early. He was far too chipper for someone who rose before the sun did. Carrie sat at the kitchen table in her bathrobe and watched as he ate dry toast and flipped through the paper. His briefcase sat primly on the floor at his feet, like a faithful dog.

Carrie watched him with an air of detachment while she sipped her coffee. She should probably ask him to have sex again, before he left for work, while she was prime for fertilisation. But something about him turned her off. Maybe it was the way he so deliberately chewed his toast, or the way his hair was too perfect. Something just failed to trip the lust trigger.

'I'm off,' he said to her when he finished his paper. His kiss slid off the side of her mouth, in too much of a hurry. She listened to the door close. The engine of his car idled a moment, then revved up and took him out of the driveway.

'I love you too,' she said out loud to the silent house.

She toyed with the computer, not really searching for anything. She opened the email and read the messages with the same detachment with which she had watched her husband. She should probably get a shower. Get dressed. Do something productive.

Then she saw the email. From someone simply named John

Smith. Perhaps the most nondescript name in the world. She opened it, already knowing who John Smith would be.

I enjoyed our time last night, Carrine. I think we're quite compatible in the cyber world. Will I see you again?

A simple email and a simple name. Carrie thought about the way he made her want things she had given up on with Alex. The way he seemed open to anything sexual. She liked that. It wasn't dangerous, she thought. It was just cyber.

Yes, she responded.

Right after she sent the email, her screen beeped at her. A little box popped up. John Smith wanted to add her as a friend. Carrie smiled her first real smile of the day and clicked to allow permission. Within moments they were talking and, surprisingly, sex wasn't the first thing John brought up. He wanted to know more about her.

More? Carrie frowned and took her time in getting a glass of orange juice. He wanted to know more? She just used the Internet as a way to get off. She made a point of not getting personally involved with anyone, other than a few cyber fuck-buddies whose names she didn't know and never would. They were probably married like she was and looking for a release, that was all, and that was just fine. This guy, though. He wanted to know more?

Carrie wanted to tell him.

By the time noon rolled around, she had said things to that invisible man on the other side of the screen that she never would have said to anyone in real life. She had told him things she would never tell her husband. And why not? John Smith didn't know her real name, he didn't know where she lived (other than the somehow illicit delight to learn they were both in the same state, and there was no harm in that, was there?), he couldn't cause her any problems. Why not tell him everything she felt like telling him?

So she told him about growing up in Denver. She told him about Alex. She told him about her favourite foods and her favourite movie and even the damn dog.

She didn't tell him about the problems she and Alex were having. She didn't tell him anything about wanting to get pregnant until he started talking about his own marriage. Twenty years, and no children.

None? Why? she typed.

She never wanted any. There were excuses. Didn't want to ruin her figure or didn't have time. Or didn't want to contribute to overpopulation. Bullshit reasons.

Carrie looked at that for a long time. She wondered why some people were so adamant about not having children, while some were so desperate for them. She thought maybe John Smith had more in common with her than she first thought he did.

I can't believe I'm telling you this, Carrine. I have been angry with my wife for a long time. So I decided to get back at her the best way I knew how. I started going to the fertility clinic. Specifically, the sperm bank.

Carrie stared at the screen.

She would die if she knew. She didn't want children so I shouldn't want children either, but life doesn't work that way. I know there are two children out there with my genes.

Carrie started to respond, then stopped. What the hell could she say?

I cannot believe I'm telling you this.

'No shit,' Carrie said out loud.

Have you ever felt that? Ever been so angry and wanted to do something that you knew Alex would think was wrong, but that you knew deep down was absolutely right?

Carrie bit her lip. Her hands sneaked to the keyboard. Yes.

I hate to do this but my wife will be home soon. We can talk tonight after she goes to bed if you're free.

I'll be free, she wrote. I'll stay up late.

On her end of the Internet connection, Carrie was smiling. She hoped John Smith was smiling too.

Alex walked in that night just after six. He ate dinner, talked about his job at the bank the whole time and didn't once ask Carrie how she was feeling. She mentioned that she was ovulating. 'Wasn't last night enough?' he asked with an air of dismissal. 'It was really good, wasn't it?'

'Yes, it was,' she admitted, and just looked at him.

Alex cleared his throat. He was uncomfortable under her scrutiny. 'I'm really tired, babe. I think I'm going to turn in early. Want to wake me up like you did last night?' he suddenly asked, as if inspired with a solution that would make both of them happy.

Carrie smiled and gritted her teeth behind her lips. She shrugged. Alex read her smile as acquiescence. He kissed her hard on the mouth, then walked down the hallway, whistling.

'Go to bed,' she whispered to the half-eaten chicken on her plate. 'Just go to sleep.'

Thirty minutes later, he did. Carrie flipped on the computer and looked for John Smith. He wasn't there. She went into the chat room and saw a few men she might like to cyber with, but her heart wasn't in it. She wanted to talk to John and no one else.

She tried to sleep. She crawled into bed and listened to Alex breathe. She fluffed her pillow. She got up to get a drink of water. She finally crawled to the end of the bed and flopped ungraciously to the floor, where she pulled a book on fertility from the bookshelf. She flipped to the part about sperm banks, something she had never even glanced at before.

She tried to imagine John Smith sitting in a little room with dim light, looking at a video or flipping through a magazine, stroking his cock while he did it.

On the bed above her, Alex began to snore.

The light from the computer was bright in the little kitchen. One more time she would try, then she would call it a night. She briefly wondered if everything was all right, then chided herself. 'He's nothing but pixels and perception,' she whispered.

She clicked on to the chat room and he wasn't there. But he did pop up in her private messenger. Carrie smiled.

I wasn't in the mood to go to the chat room, she typed.

His words appeared almost immediately: I didn't want to talk to anyone but you.

In the corner of her mind, Carrie saw a faceless man with an erect cock, stroking himself while he stared at the computer screen. She imagined him coming into a little plastic cup.

My real name is Carrie, she typed.

John Smith didn't hesitate. My name really is John. John Myers.

'This is insane,' Carrie whispered.

This is insane, isn't it? John typed, as if in careless after-thought.

So Carrie began to tell him more. She told him about Alex. She told him about falling in love and then slowly falling out of it. She told him about wanting a child and hoping that would save her marriage, but as time went on she knew it wouldn't and she really didn't care. She told him that she had been thinking of him all day, about how he could want a child so badly that he would give to a sperm bank. She didn't know if that was honourable or sad, and she told him so.

John sat in silence for so long that Carrie thought she had lost the connection. She was reaching for the keyboard when he responded.

We're both in New York.

The words hung there between them. Carrie tried to picture

what he might look like. Before she could get an image in her mind, her computer beeped with another message from John.

I'm sitting here hard as a rock, thinking about what it would be like to actually touch you.

Carrie choked back a half-laugh, half-sob.

Stroke yourself for me, John.

She knew he was. She knew he was just as hard as he said he was, because she was wetter than she had been in recent memory, and her fingers were already slipping under her panties. She knew she wouldn't go to Alex tonight. She knew she would sit right here and she would come for John instead.

Do this with me, he implored.

Oh, God, John . . . I am.

Can you imagine my hands on your thighs? Spreading your legs? Can you imagine this hard cock sliding into your pussy?

Do you want that as badly as I do?

Carrie fought to control her breathing. Alex was snoring in the bedroom, oblivious. John Myers wanted to make her come, and she was going to let him.

I want to come inside you, Carrie. I want to come as deep as I can.

She could picture it. She could almost feel it. She played with her pussy and let him spin a tale of what he would do to her, given the chance. She eagerly followed every word on the screen. Her clit was hard beneath her fingers. She played with it, pinched it, rolled it. When he told her how he should be making love to his wife but he was going to come for her instead, he was going to come right now, Carrie went over the edge. She gripped the kitchen table and arched her back in the chair. The sensation flooded her and the whole world went spinning.

Her whimpers went unnoticed by everyone but the dog, who looked up at her with startled eyes. When Carrie caught her breath, she looked back at the screen. Her eyes widened when the words popped up.

Where are you in New York?

Carrie bit her lip. She typed out the word, then erased it. Then she typed it out again. She could almost hear the silence from the other end. She looked up, startled, sure she had heard Alex. But he wasn't there. He was still snoring. She took a deep breath and pressed enter.

Albany.

More silence, then three little words:

Oh, my God.

Carrie watched Alex get ready for work the next morning. She had hardly slept, but she didn't feel groggy. Instead she felt enthusiastic and exuberant. She was a woman with a secret.

As soon as Alex was out the door, Carrie logged on to the computer. John was there.

Where in Albany?

No 'hello', no 'how is your day?' Just a simple question that went right through to places it shouldn't have touched.

East Side. There was no point in hedging around. She knew what she wanted.

I can meet you there.

When?

Today. I can call in to work.

Carrie thought of all the reasons she should say no. She thought of all the reasons she should be careful. She thought of serial killers and rapists and seeing her name on the evening news as that woman who left one morning and never came home. But that wasn't John Myers. He wasn't like that. She knew it might be a mistake, but she felt safe.

Yes.

Yes?

Tell me where.

Carrie was stunned at his choice of hotel. It was expensive as hell, especially on short notice. He assured her he would pay for everything. Just ask for the room number when you get there and come on up. Please hurry, Carrie.

She leapt into the shower. She fretted for only a moment about shaving her legs, decided that they were fine, then changed her mind. Then changed it again. She pulled on jeans and a soft sweater, then changed her mind about that, too. She caught a glimpse of herself in the mirror. She was flushed with anticipation. The sight stopped her and she became very still while she looked at her reflection. She hadn't been this excited in years.

The car didn't start on the first try and her heart leapt into her throat. But the second time was better. The third was the charm. She pulled out of her driveway and glanced back at the house once. She would be a different person when she came back to it, and Alex would be none the wiser.

It was crazy. It was insane. It felt so right, it was absurd.

The hotel was huge. Carrie had driven by it in the past but she had never been inside. She was greeted with perfumed air, an attentive doorman and a front-desk clerk who didn't bat an eye when she asked for the room number.

'John Myers,' she said, and the man frowned ever so slightly.

'Could it be under another name, ma'am?' he asked in a discreet undertone.

Carrie felt a sudden surge of panic. Then she smiled.

'John Smith,' she said, and was rewarded with a smile, a nod and a key to room 402.

She didn't know what she had expected, but John Myers was it. He was tall, just slightly taller than Alex. His eyes were blue and his hair was almost grey. He was just a little heavyset, but not enough to turn her off. On the contrary. Carrie found she liked the idea of someone who wasn't as slim and athletic as Alex.

He was dressed in a button-down shirt that matched his eyes and black dress slacks. No shoes and no socks. He looked down and blushed endearingly. 'I thought I would make myself at home,' he said, and his voice had a husky quality that made her knees weak.

'I knew you would sound like that,' she said.

He smiled. 'Ditto.'

Five minutes after that they were against the inside of the door, John's substantial body pressing her hard against it, his hands inside her blouse and his tongue in her mouth. He tasted like bourbon. She unbuttoned her jeans and pushed them down. As soon as she did it, his finger slipped into her pussy. Carrie clenched his shoulders and rode his hand until they were both breathless with the need for more.

'Here?' he asked.

'On the bed,' she responded, and he picked her up as though she weighed nothing at all. She bounced a little when she landed on the mattress, and they both giggled. Then his tongue was between her legs, on her clit. She curled her fingers into his hair. He looked up from between her thighs and a slow, teasing grin crossed his lips.

'The next time we cyber and I tell you what I'm doing, you will know exactly what it feels like,' he said softly.

He went at her slowly, teasing her lips and playing with her clit. He slid his tongue all the way down to her ass and then back up. He pushed one finger into her pussy, then another.

Then another. She would have bucked up to him but he held her down. He licked her clit in a long rhythm that didn't let up. She had to push her face into a pillow to keep from screaming with pleasure when she came.

'Have you ever come for anyone other than Alex?' he asked her. It sounded strange to hear her husband's name come out of John's mouth.

'No,' she replied, breathless. 'Not since we married.'

Her knees were shaky when she slipped off the bed. She settled between John's legs. His cock was hard, jutting straight out from his body. She knew what he liked after all those nights in the chat room. Her first long lick made him moan. She was surprised that he was so loud.

She worked him sweetly, playing with him until he was on the verge of coming, then backing off and playing him gently with her tongue. Finally he pulled her head back with a gentle tug on her hair. 'Do you want me to come in your mouth?' he asked. 'Or do you want me to fill up that tasty little pussy?'

Carrie shivered in anticipation. She knew what she wanted, but she doubted he would agree with her. 'I don't have protection,' she said.

'I know that, darling.'

Carrie blinked up at him. His smile was calm and steady. 'If you've been trying to get pregnant, you're certainly not on the pill, are you?'

'You mean –'

'Do you want it, Carrie? Do you want my seed inside you?'

She nodded, her eyes wide. John pulled her on to the bed with him. Suddenly his hands weren't gentle. He pinched her nipples and roughly spread her legs. He bit down on her shoulder and she gasped. 'You want that? You want to fuck a complete stranger and let him make you pregnant? You want me to fill up your belly with my come as many times as I can?'

'Yes,' she whimpered.

John slid into her with one deep thrust. Carrie clawed at his shoulders until he took her arms roughly and pressed them to the sheets. She wrapped her legs around him and buried her head in his shoulder as he fucked her. Fucked was the only word for it. It was hard and deep and just on the edge of vicious. She knew there would be bruises to hide from Alex. She didn't care.

'Come for me,' she demanded. 'Come inside me, damn you, do it!'

John thrust hard one last time and flooded her. Carrie moaned against his shoulder. John groaned loudly, much louder than Alex ever had. She lifted her hips and ground against him, wanting every last drop she could get.

John collapsed over her, and for the first time she minded the weight. She could hardly breathe. She pushed him off with a sigh and a satisfied giggle. John's eyes opened just slightly.

'Wow,' he said.

'Yeah, wow.'

'Want to do that again?'

Carrie slithered down the bed and closed her mouth around his cock. Within a few minutes he was once again rising to the occasion. She sat up and stroked him lazily as he got harder. They watched each other as she did it. John occasionally reached up to trace one pert little nipple.

'Know what I've been dreaming about?' she murmured sleepily.

'Tell me.'

She closed her eyes and watched the images in her head. She smiled. 'I've been dreaming about feeling a cock in my ass.

And then I dream about you coming in my pussy. I don't know which one I want more.'

John chuckled. 'Have you ever done anal?'

Carrie shook her head and bit her lip, suddenly embarrassed. 'Nobody would do it with me.'

John slipped a hand down her belly. He slipped a finger inside her and pulled it out, wet and slick with both their juices. He pressed it into Carrie's mouth, and she suckled it as a baby might.

'I've never done it either,' he confessed.

'Really?'

'Unfortunately.'

'Your wife wouldn't let you have her ass?'

'Your husband wouldn't take yours?' John shot back with a grin.

Carrie found a bottle of lotion in the bathroom. It wasn't the best thing they could find to use, but it would have to do. She lay down on her belly and tried to relax while John worked the lotion all over her hips and buttocks. Then he worked it down between her cheeks, and at every brush of his hand she arched a little higher into his touch. By the time he slipped a finger inside, she was squirming all over the bed.

'I want it,' she moaned.

'Not quite yet,' he whispered. 'I don't want to hurt you.'

She clenched the pillows. Then the headboard. She spread her legs and begged. John just chuckled and held back until she could easily take two fingers. They slipped in and out without any resistance whatsoever. Her whole body felt lithe and supple. John's weight was above her and he was bearing down on her, pushing gently. Carrie felt a slow burn and she fought the urge to resist him. Instead she pushed into the sensation, welcomed it, and John's cock eased into her ass with very little pain.

'Oh,' she whispered, and smiled into the pillow. 'That's what I want.'

John pushed deeper. His arms trembled on either side of her head. She leant over and licked one, tasted the skin of his elbow. He moaned lightly and pushed harder. When she felt his pubic hair tickle her cheeks, she ground back against him.

'Now fuck me,' she whispered. She looked over her shoulder and gave him a wink. John laughed out loud.

His strokes were long and gentle at first, designed to get her used to the invasion. Then they were shorter and not so gentle, as the tightness started to take a toll on his control. Then they were much shorter, and deeper, and harder, and Carrie held on to the headboard. She buried her face in the pillow and cried out his name when the thrusts got a little too hard, but she didn't ask him to stop. She did not want him to stop.

Near the end John leant over her and put his weight behind his thrusts. Her ass burned. He growled into her ear: 'You came to a stranger's hotel room and made him come in your pussy. Now he's fucking your ass. That makes you a slut, doesn't it, Carrie?'

John kept whispering in her ear, naughty things that made her come. She felt the throbbing with a bit of disbelief. I didn't think women could come from that, she said to herself, then she didn't think at all, she just moaned and cried out John's name over and over.

John's last thrust hurt like hell, but she welcomed it all the same. He put his weight behind it one last time and this one went as deep as he could go. She felt him pulse inside her. Her eyes widened in amazement. So that's how it feels. John kept pumping his hips until there was nothing left inside him. This time he carefully moved to her side, so that he was still buried but not crushing her. They looked at each other and said nothing at all.

By the time the afternoon sun had crawled across the bed, they had fucked three times. John had put another load of semen inside her as he bent her over the back of the plush couch. She begged him to shoot it as deep as he could, and he did. Then he collapsed back against the wall and announced breathlessly, 'That's it, I swear that's it, it has to be, I cannot go any more.'

Carrie giggled and rotated her hips against him. He slapped her rump gently. 'I'm not a youngster any more,' he reminded her.

'You sure feel like one,' she teased.

He kissed her at the door. His tongue slipped into her mouth and she felt a sudden sense of loss. She didn't want to go back to the computer screen. She wanted to feel him, to taste him, not to just imagine it. John kissed her nose and whispered, 'We will do this again. Let's give it a few weeks, just to adjust. Then we'll meet again. And if you don't think it's a good idea, then we'll just make it coffee. OK?'

Carrie threw her arms around him in gratitude.

Alex came home that night and hardly noticed her. He didn't want sex, which was fine with Carrie. By the time he did want it, four days had passed and the soreness had abated a little, but not enough. She revelled in the feeling of his cock for the first time in years, because it brought back the little aches and pains that John had left there.

Every night she talked to John, but their conversations didn't have the same sexual undertone. They didn't cyber. They saved it up for the next time they would be together. They made plans. One more meeting would make it a full-fledged affair, at least in Carrie's mind. She was definitely ready for that.

* * *

That Friday dawned bright and sunny. Carrie woke up that morning and suddenly lunged for the bathroom. Her stomach rolled and she lost everything she had eaten the night before. Alex had already left for work. How had she slept in that late?

Then the reality hit her. Carrie smiled as she sat there against the cool ceramic of the bathtub. With shaky hands, she dug into the drawer and found the box of pregnancy tests. She peed on a stick and watched as the lines turned pink – both of them, a positive result.

She stared at them and began to cry, big racking sobs that ripped from the depths of her.

My God, what have I done?

She logged on to the computer and John wasn't there. She called Alex at the office and left a message with his secretary, who said kindly that he had stepped out for a few moments. After those few moments turned into an hour, she got in the car to go meet him. She had to tell him. She was suddenly filled with a love for her husband that was startling in its force. They could make it work. Now they had something substantial to fight for, and they could make it work.

Carrie breezed into the lobby of the bank with a smile on her face. The tellers greeted her with friendly hellos. She stepped through her husband's open door and froze.

There sat Alex, smiling and playing with a ballpoint pen. The man who sat in front of him was what made Carrie's blood run cold. She blinked and slowly began to back out of the office. Alex stopped her with a booming welcome.

'Honey! Come on in. I'm glad you're here. I want you to meet the new bank president.'

A tall man with greying hair stood to his full height before her. His blue eyes were radiant. His suit was impeccable. He reached out to shake her hand.

'John Myers,' he said to her very calmly, and Carrie fainted.

Gwen Masters is the author of the Black Lace novel *One Breath at a Time*. Her short fiction appears in numerous Black Lace anthologies.

The Judge

Alegra Verde

He was her husband, after all, and she had the right to do whatever she could to save her marriage. 'Lupe, he doesn't see me any more. I mean, he sees, but he doesn't see. Know what I mean?' Georgy would ask and I would nod. 'Lupe,' she would say between sips of *café con leche*, 'sex with him has become so boring.' She would sip some more, and sometimes there would be a wetness in her eyes when she looked back at me. 'He used to be so into me. Now, it's just a series of quick probes and pokes. I'm so frustrated.' I would squeeze her hand. 'Afterwards, I just lie next to him restless, unable to sleep.' I'd nod in sympathy and sip my *café*.

One day, a couple of months ago, she smiled at me across the little bistro table at Border's and said, 'So, I've decided to do something about it, and I need your help.' I slid my cup on to the table and sat up. 'Anything, Georgy.' And I meant it. Georgy was a good friend and had always been free with a loan for books when I was short of money, a spirit-lifting shopping spree to Victoria's Secrets, or an introduction to a likely publisher. We'd met at a writers' retreat and had connected even though she was more than a decade older than I was.

The fiction workshop we attended was run by a chauvinistic Italian who reminded me of my dad, not just the way he looked with the salt-and-pepper hair and stocky build, but in his insistence that his was the right and only way. I'd endured some particularly brutal criticism of my latest short story and had gone back to my room to bemoan my lot in life when Georgy appeared at my door with contraband, a bottle of Merlot and two stemmed glasses. She'd pointed out the merits of my piece, mimicked the paunch and accented English of our torturer, and kept my glass full.

That night we sat up reading each other's stories and ended up naked and pressed together on the twin cot, which was standard issue in the monastic rooms. After the retreat, we continued to meet once or twice a month to have lunch, or read each other's work, and usually to get naked and romp around in a full-size bed.

I'm just a grad student, English major, but Georgy, Georgina Marín, is a writer. She's published two novels in English and a book of poetry in Spanish. The novels have received moderate success, but the book of poetry, *Cosas Hermosas*, is in its third printing. She has a son and a daughter in high school, and is married to the Honourable Osvaldo Marín, the first Latino to serve as a judge in the 36th District Court. He had recently been re-elected and was serving his second term.

'I love my life. I love my husband,' she assured me as we sat in a back booth of the sports bar downtown. 'But I'm afraid that our fire has been banked to the point of suffocation.'

'But, Georgy,' I argued, 'there are other ways to stoke a fire. This all seems a bit extreme.'

'It has to be something extreme to get his attention, Lupe. He's so directed, so consumed by his life, the campaign, the tedium of court, being a father. It's up to me to try to combat the monotony that creeps into a marriage of twenty years.'

'But to ask me to seduce your husband, a man who has never cheated on you, seems excessive. I really don't think sleeping with me is going to shake him up that much.'

'It's not about one night of sex. I want him to engage in *an affair*, one that involves his emotions as well as his libido, one that will rejuvenate his lust, his memory of passion.'

'So, once *the affair* has ended, he'll stumble back to you guilt-ridden but refreshed, and eager to make amends?' I pursed my lips to emphasise my scepticism.

'Exactly,' she said, ignoring my doubt and lifting her glass, 'and to that end I will serve as your drama coach and the director of this little farce.'

I lifted my glass to hers. 'Sounds like fun.'

We shopped carefully for my first meeting with the judge. We'd gone to Somerset, a pricey mall, one that I rarely visited. But this was Georgy's show and, after all, it was the judge's money and I figured he should get what he wanted. Besides, Georgy said he'd want demure the first time. It would be easier to find demure at these prices. She said that he was confronted daily with underdressed women in his courtroom. There were usually breasts and thighs of all sizes spilling out of tight blouses, mini shorts, skinny skirts and tiny dresses. All manner of women displayed what they may or may not have had in an effort to gain a favourable judgment for their own cases or to distract the judge for their man's sake. Of course, there was also the phalanx of female lawyers who dressed in austere suits that downplayed their femininity. But, Georgy promised, we'd explore those fantasies later.

She said that we should play up my youth, get something fresh that hinted at playful but cried clean. Apparently, the Honourable Ozzie was a real prig at heart but could not deny his lusty Latin soul when truly confronted with a temptation born of his subconscious desire, and Georgy professed to know him deeply. They had, after all, been married some twenty years. Georgy had been a girl of eighteen just out of high school and Ozzie had just graduated law school when they married.

However, they had loved each other long before the ceremony that had bound them legally. She and Ozzie had lived on the same block in Levittown, just outside of San Juan. Their mothers had been friends and Ozzie had gone to school with her older brother, Victor.

As our heels clicked along the pink tiles of the mall, Georgy talked about the first time she noticed Ozzie as something other than the annoyance Victor's friends usually provided. She had been about thirteen.

'He must have been twenty.' She looked at me and grinned.

'The lech,' I cried.

'No, no. He didn't do anything too improper. At first, he just sort of stared at me when he thought no one was looking.' She laughed and I could see it was a pleasant memory.

'It was Sunday and I was wearing this little yellow empire dress with a Peter Pan collar. I was beginning to get a figure then and the dress fit well, cupping my breasts and hugging my hips nicely. I felt quite grown up and although I would normally rush home and change into jeans and a T-shirt, Mami had told me to keep on my church clothes because we were having guests for dinner. I was a little disappointed when I found out that it was just Ozzie and his mother.

'He had just come home for the Christmas holiday. Luckily, the food had been prepared, and my mother and her sisters were setting the table, heating and putting out the pasteles and the yucca, and slicing the roasted pig. I was charged with fixing and serving drinks. That's when I noticed how he looked at me with these sullen, puppy eyes.' Georgy laughed and shook her head.

'What did you do?' I asked.

'I thought he was sick, so I took him a glass of cola and asked him what was wrong. He just stammered something about a long plane ride, took his drink and left me standing there as he headed back to my brother's side.'

We were walking through Nordstrom's, down the aisles of perfume and make-up counters. We stopped at one of the glass and chrome counters and a bright-faced middle-aged woman asked if she could help. Georgy asked to try the Oscar and the woman looked through an array of sample testers and handed her one. 'This is an older scent; I used to sneak it from my mother's dresser. Ozzie really liked it when I wore it.' She took my wrist and sprayed a bit there, waited a moment and then lifted it to her nose. 'Yes, it blends well with your scent. See,' she said releasing my wrist. It was a pleasant smell. I nodded and she ordered an ounce from the saleswoman. She paid and we were on our way again.

We lingered in the lingerie section, my favourite. '34C, isn't it?' Georgy asked as she selected a lacy bra in peach and a matching thong from a rack. I nodded and chose a pale-blue from another and looked around for a matching panty. Georgy was at the counter speaking to the salesgirl who pulled a couple of boxes out from behind the counter. The young woman opened a box and held up something lacy and white that resembled a garter belt. She had my attention.

The salesgirl, a young woman about my age, beamed up at me. 'These are very popular with young brides.' She held up the bits of lace and elastic. 'This should fit your sister perfectly and the white will really enhance her olive complexion.'

'I think so too,' Georgy agreed. 'But I'd like for her to try it and these too,' she said as she handed her the bras we'd selected.

'Certainly,' the young woman said and led us to a very spacious fitting room that had a large cushiony ottoman in the corner. She hung the bras on the hook, handed Georgy the box with the garter belt and closed the door as she left the room.

Georgy took a seat on the ottoman and I began to undress. First, I slipped off my shoes. Then I slid off my blouse, a little silk T that stopped just above my navel. I did it slowly, hoping that Georgy was noticing. She was. There was a gleam in her eyes, and she gave me a smile of appreciation.

'How did Ozzie finally let you know he was interested?' I asked, reaching behind to unhook my bra. Then I let it slide forward to reveal my already hardened nipples.

'He kept peeking at me throughout dinner, casting me these wistful glances which I now know were all about desire, but then I wasn't sure. I thought that maybe he was coming down with something. I thought about how cold it gets in the States. People were always coming home with sniffly noses and coughs.' She laughed, thinking of her naïve thirteen-year-old self. I laughed too, causing my breasts to jiggle.

'Come here,' she said. I walked over to stand just in front of her. She stroked the line of skin between my breasts and I ran my fingers through her hair, rubbing the smooth lines of scalp and threading the long strands of dark hair through my fingers.

'After dinner he came to me on the terrace in my mother's garden. "You've really grown into a beauty," he said. "I knew you would." I was surprised at his attention, but also pleased. I think I said something like, "You have always been a beauty, Osvaldo." I remember he laughed and I was embarrassed. He must have seen me blush because he pulled me to him to comfort me.'

Georgy drew me to her, took my left nipple into her mouth and rolled it around on her tongue as if it were a delicacy to be savoured. After tasting it, she sucked it hard, pulling it forward so that the whole breast seemed to climb into her mouth.

'His hands cupped my breast through the thin cloth and he

breathed sweet words into my ear.' Her hands mirrored her words, only there was no cloth, just the warmth of her fingers against the heat of my skin. As she stood, the fabric of her dress slid up my jeans and along the skin of my belly to slide against my straining nipples and press into the fullness of my breasts. 'Then he kissed me,' she said into my mouth. 'First licking, then nibbling my lower lip. When he had it pulsing, he nipped my upper lip. He slid his tongue over my flushed, tingling lips, and then like a stick of peppermint, he pushed it into my mouth. He slid his tongue over my teeth, licking the inside of my mouth, tasting me. I could taste him too, the wine he'd had after dinner, the spice of Mami's yucca, and his heat.' Again, she mirrored her words until I couldn't get enough of her mouth, her tongue, and I was squirming against her. She ran her hands, now cool and soothing, down my back and slid her hand into the low rise of my jeans to cup the lobes of my ass, her cool fingers pressing and kneading.

'I knew I would marry him then,' she said as she gently pulled out of my embrace and returned to her seat. 'Take off the jeans; you'll have to try the garter belt. Ozzie's of an age where he'll appreciate the kitsch of a garter belt, but find it irresistibly sexy.' I unzipped the jeans and slid them over my hips.

'Did he? Right there in your mother's garden?' I said stepping out of the pants.

'No, I was a good girl. But, he touched me. I was shocked. After we'd kissed for a while and he had me squirming, he slipped his hands under my dress and his finger into my panties. I remember being mortified because I was wet there, but he seemed to like it, sliding his finger back and forth and pressing himself against me. I was so disoriented all I could do was cling to him. And when he said, "Promise you'll save it for me," I could barely speak. He slipped his finger in, stroking just a little, and I pressed myself onto that finger, my untutored body trying to claim what it wanted. But he held me back, and when he added the second finger it felt so good I grew dizzy and couldn't stand any more.'

She lifted the garter belt from the box and handed it to me.

'Take the panties off too. It's much sexier,' she ordered.

'He made you come?' I asked as I tried to figure out which end was up on the contraption.

'Yes, my first, but I didn't know it then. He pulled a handkerchief out of his pocket. He still carried handkerchiefs, washed and pressed by his mother. I was glad of it then. He dabbed it across my panties and wiped my thighs, before cleaning his hands, stuffing the soiled cloth back into his pocket, and kissing me. Then he asked again, "Promise you'll save it for me." I nodded because I still couldn't speak.'

I stood before the mirror with the bit of white frothy lace secured across my hip. It felt sexy just there framing the sparse bits of dark curls that shielded my mound. The salesgirl had been right about how the white made my skin even darker, more sultry, and the slight weight and tug of the thing across my belly with its little straps hanging down my thighs made me feel powerful. I wanted to strut and bend and display my sex. I wanted to touch myself or be touched. I turned around to see how the garment cupped and squeezed my cheeks. I bent over to see how the lips pouted just below my buttocks. I spread my legs to get a better look. Then Georgy was there on her knees behind me, her hands gripping my thighs, her mouth on my nether lips. She licked the rapidly swelling lips, nipping them from time to time with her teeth. After the sting and tingle of each little nick, she would lick and then suck the offended labia. I could barely stand. If not for her firm grip on my thighs, I would have fallen. As it was, I inched closer to the wall so that I could press my palms against the cool wood for support, and Georgy followed me nipping and lapping. The muscles of my sex clinched just as Georgy's tongue pushed into my opening.

My thighs were trembling when Georgy's little teeth nipped my ass and she rose to stand behind me. She pulled me toward her, my back pressed against the silky fabric of her dress. Her fingers tugged at my hard, long nipples and then slid down, down, down until a slim hand pressed low on my belly, fingers trailing in the damp curls there. With her other hand she pressed me forward again, until I was bent at the waist and leaning with my palms pressed against the door. She caressed the lobes of my ass, her fingers sliding down the centre to tug and toy with the swollen labia that jutted out beneath it. Then quite suddenly, she slid three fingers into my well-anointed opening and began to thrust them in and out in a relentless rhythm that had me writhing and moaning and, after only a few strokes, coming into her gifted hands.

What wouldn't I do for this woman? She held me then, her arms around my shoulders, her lips pressed against mine, claiming my mouth. Her hand found and stroked my back, her long fingers running the length of my spine. After a moment or two, she led me over to the ottoman, where we sat, her arm around my hip and my head on her shoulder.

'Georgy,' I began.

'Shhh,' she said smoothing my hair. 'Another time.'

She tapped my hip indicating that I should sit up. 'I think we should take all of these.' She gestured to the bras that I had yet to try. 'And this too,' she said as she unhooked the garter belt and placed it back in its box. She reached into her purse for a handkerchief. 'A habit I've acquired from Ozzie.' She wiped her fingers and handed it to me with a smile. I dabbed at my inner thighs and handed it back. Standing, she dropped it into her purse and closed it with a snap. Then she gathered our purchases and headed toward the door.

'Get dressed. I'll meet you at the counter. We still have a dress to buy.'

I stood as the door clicked behind her.

We ended up with a nubby pink number from Saks. It didn't have a Peter Pan collar. In fact, it was collarless, but it was empire with a short skirt, although not too, and short sleeves that screamed innocent schoolgirl. It went well with my boyish straight hair, adding just the right amount of feminine charm. We had lattes and then I was off to class and Georgy went home to her husband.

It was a watering hole, a posh one, but still a bar where folks flocked after work to nibble at Buffalo wings and celery sticks while chugalugging Long Island Ice Teas and Courvoisier. The music was jazz: Sarah Vaughan, Miles and Mingus. It was music that appealed to the more conservative, mostly older crowd of city administrators, lawyers, their clerks and the judges. I'd never been in here, but I'd been in many other bars that hosted happy hour for fatigued workers. The one near school was called Verne's, but there were no hors d'oeuvres or tapas. The music was usually Fall Out Boys, U2, maybe some reggae, and you had to buy your burgers, but pitchers of beer were cheap. This one was called Flood's and nothing here was cheap.

I spotted him seated at the bar next to one of his cronies. He looked better in person. Georgy had shown me a photo, but I'd seen him around town on the billboards and flyers. He was tall, maybe six feet or so, and broad-chested, but not too. His black hair was only lightly touched by grey and it was combed straight back by a comb with a vengeance, but a few strands had escaped and fallen to dangle just above his left eye. He was laughing and his hazel eyes crinkled at the ends like Santa in the storybook and I couldn't help but smile. He saw me, and his eyes lingered for a moment, but he looked away, took a sip of his drink and said something to an even taller black man who stood near him. The black man looked at me and smiled, but I looked away. He was good-looking too and wore a well-tailored suit that hugged his lean body, but I wasn't there for him.

I took a seat at the bar directly across from the judge and ordered a vodka and cranberry juice. I didn't want to smell like liquor. The tall glass was chilled; I was a little nervous, and the tasty drink was gone before I knew it. Just as I finished it, the bartender was sliding another one in front of me. I looked up at him questioningly and he tilted his head in the direction of the judge and his friend. The friend raised his glass and smiled at me; the judge smiled too but it seemed a sad smile. I smiled back at them both, took the drink and slid off the stool, deciding to stroll around the room before the judge's friend could try to stake a claim. There wasn't much room for dancing, but a couple had found a square of space and were slow dancing. The place was getting more and more crowded and pretty soon there were no seats. The judge's friend had found prey that was more receptive at a table, and Ozzie sat alone, listening to the music and sipping his drink.

I made my way through the crowd and to the bar to stand at Ozzie's side. I swayed a bit, bumping his side, just a touch. He didn't move, but he watched me. The bartender was very busy and I made weak attempts to get his attention.

'Oh, I'm sorry,' I said. 'I don't drink much and my stomach –' I pressed my hand over my stomach. 'Do you think they have something for stomachs back there?' I admit I was scandalous letting a little Puerto Rico into my speech just like Georgy had told me, and never getting too close to him, being respectful. I could feel his eyes assessing me, questioning, but he eventually gave in.

'Seltzer. They may have some seltzer water. But I don't know if that will help. Do you need to sit down?' He slid off the stool. Such a gentleman.

I tried to get up on to the stool with limited success. He eventually had to take my elbow to help me up, and he stayed close to make sure I wouldn't fall.

'Thank you,' I said, putting my hand on my forehead.

'Have you eaten?' he asked, the concerned father.

I smiled inwardly. 'I can't eat that stuff.' I gestured at the picked over trays. 'I'm meeting a girlfriend. She and I are going for dinner.'

'When is she meeting you?'

'At six,' I told him.

'It's nearly seven now. You should probably go on home, especially since you're not feeling well.'

'I took the bus here. She's the one with the car. I'm sure she'll be here soon.' I made another weak attempt to attract the bartender's attention.

'Smitty,' he called in a voice just above the normal tone, 'gimme a glass of seltzer water.'

'Thanks,' I said, giving him a waning smile, 'and it was really nice of you to give me your seat. It's really hot in here,' I said, fanning myself.

'A little,' he said, looking worried.

A glass of seltzer water and ice appeared before me. I sipped.

'¿De donde eres?'

'Bayamón.'

'Ah, I probably know some of your people. I grew up not far from there.'

'Maybe,' I said and smiled. 'My father is Quadalupe Castillo and I am Lupita.'

'*Mucho gusto*, Lupita,' he said, holding out his hand to me.

'*Encantada*,' I said, shaking his hand.

'Come, Lupita. Let me take you home. I don't feel comfortable leaving you here alone. Your father would thank me.'

'I don't know if my father would be happy with me leaving a bar with a strange man even if he did grow up near Bayamón.'

Laughing now, his eyes crinkled like Santa again, 'You're right. I am Osvaldo Marín, an honourable man. I assure you.'

I pretended to squint my eyes at him as though I doubted his word.

'I have children nearly your age and a wife who I adore. You will be safe with me.'

'I really don't feel well.'

'*Venga.*' He gestured toward the door.

I nodded and slid off the bench, his hand still on my elbow. Such a gentleman: he put his body in front of mine as he made a path for us through the milling crowd. All the while, his hand gently cupped my elbow. At one point, his friend, the one who'd bought me the drink, caught his eye, and smiling, shook his head. Ozzie laughed and said, 'It ain't like that, my friend. You mistake me for you.'

The air outside was nice and crisp, autumn. He must have seen me take a breath because he asked if I felt better. I nodded and said, 'Much,' adding that the fresh air felt good. The valet pulled his car up to the kerb, a black Lincoln Towncar that put me in mind of one of those cars that ride behind a hearse, but it was luxurious inside with roomy leather seats that swivelled and reclined and a state-of-the-art sound system. After he'd put me in the passenger seat and made sure that we'd both buckled our seat belts, he asked me where I lived. I told him and we pulled out into traffic. Then he put the music on, and the congas, the pulse of the *merengue*, filled the space and I knew that Georgy was right. This man who drove a hearse, wore crisp, white shirts and grey suits, whose only vice was a few drinks after work, had passion in his soul. His fires were merely banked and it was up to me to stoke them.

'Do you mind if I pick up something at a fast-food place? I've got nothing at home and I'm really hungry.' I knew from Georgy that she and the kids were in New York spending the weekend with an aunt, so Ozzie would have to eat alone if he went home.

'That stuff's not good for you. You need real food.' Without so much as a by-your-leave, he made a U-turn and headed south. 'We'll go to Doña Lola's, it's not Puerto Rican food, but it's close. She makes great seafood empanadas and her *bacalao* is seasoned *como mi madre.*'

I just sat back. I'd eaten at Doña Lola's and knew that she didn't have a liquor licence, but people usually brought their own beer or wine to drink with their meals. So I wasn't surprised when he stopped at a liquor store and picked up a bottle of Zinfandel, a rosé and a small bottle of seltzer water.

'I wasn't sure how you were feeling or what you liked,' he said handing me the bag.

I unfolded the brown paper and peeked in. 'I'm feeling much better. The air helped.'

'Food is what you need. You'll feel much better after you've eaten.'

We were greeted warmly at Doña Lola's. He introduced me as a friend from back home and Doña Lola herself, speaking to him in a lilting Ecuadorian Spanish, smiled back at him over her shoulder as she ushered us to a booth in the back. She'd insisted on preparing her Red Snapper for him with a rice dish from her hometown. While we waited, she sent out a succulent soup with chunks of vegetables and bits of beef. We ate and drank, praised the food and tried to guess the origin of the various Spanish accents that wafted around us. All the while, Latin jazz, the Brazilian bossa nova all mixed up with Chano Pozo's 'Afro-Cuban Drums Suite', washed over us.

As we left the restaurant, his hand was no longer at my elbow but resting on the small of my back. Once we were seated and buckled in, he slid Eddie Santiago into the CD player and 'Lluvia' began to play as we pulled out into the traffic.

'*Me gusta salsa romántica*,' I said easing back into the seat.

'*Mi tambien*.' He smiled over at me. He was no longer sitting stiffly and driving with his hands in the prescribed positions. He had relaxed into his seat and drove with one hand.

At dinner, he'd found out that I was a student, that I didn't have a *novio* and that I lived in a small apartment on campus, alone. He had also confided that I reminded him of his wife. It was the eyes, he thought. No, it was the laugh. Maybe, he finally concluded, it was the lips. He'd refilled my glass after that and let his thigh brush against mine. I had leant in and fed him the rest of my fish. Georgy had made me promise to let him come to me. It was up to him now, and I could hear the gears in his brain churning, weighing the obstacles, the possible penalties, the rewards. I sat back and hummed along with Eddie.

He slid the Towncar into a spot not far from my door and turned it off. I sat up and waited for him to come around to open my door, but instead, he leant in and kissed me. I jerked back, genuinely surprised. He followed, leaning in further, sliding a hand around my thigh and his tongue across my startled lips.

'Just for tonight,' he said as he sat up, turned away, and looked out his window. 'You said you have no one, and I have no one to go home to tonight. I would like to stay with you.'

I waited, let him stew for a minute and then touched his hand. 'Just tonight.'

After helping me out of the car, he followed me like a boy being forced into a confessional, head bowed and silent.

'It's not much,' I said, turning the key in the deadbolt and clicking on the light. 'Living room, kitchen, bedroom. To get to the bathroom, you have to go through the bedroom.' I headed into the kitchen. 'I need water. Would you like some?'

'Yeah,' he said shedding his shoes at the door, as I had done. He dropped his suit coat and tie on the sofa before following me into the kitchen. I filled two glasses with water from the refrigerator; he pulled out one of the vinyl dinette chairs and sat. I put the glass on the table in front of him, but he took mine from me, sipped it appreciatively, then placed it next to his and pulled me between his thighs.

'This dress is very becoming,' he said as he slid his hand underneath it to stroke bare skin, thighs and the cheeks that peeked out on either side of my thong. He cupped, stroked and squeezed before reaching up to pull the thong down, over hips, down legs, and finally lifting it from around my feet and dropping it on the table. 'I've been thinking about fucking you all night,' he said, stroking beneath my skirt again, pulling the cheeks apart and sliding his fingers back and forth in the moisture between my legs. 'But the first time, I want you to keep the dress on. It's a sweet dress,' he said as he bit my breasts through the fabric. Nice round, gnawing bites that added pressure but no pain.

'You want more water?' he asked.

I nodded and he handed the glass to me. I drank and he kept stroking. I handed the glass back. He took a sip before placing it back on the table. Then he stood, took my hand and led me back through the living room and into the bedroom. The light from the living room bathed the bedroom in a thin spray of light and shadow. He led me to the bed and gently pushed my shoulders back on the bed so that my legs dangled off the edge. The hem of my skirt rode high on my thighs. Then he stood back, unbuckled his belt and unzipped his pants. He looked down at me as he stroked himself, his hand running the long, hard length. He stroked and I squirmed, opening my legs wider in invitation. I could feel the dampness between my legs growing. I closed my eyes and, when I opened them, he was kneeling before me, his teeth nipping at the tender inside of my thighs, his nose nudging the trembling mouth of my sex.

'Open for me, Lupita,' he whispered between my legs as he pushed the dress up further, just above my hips.

'So sweet,' he said as he nibbled and licked, his tongue toying with the taut bud that jutted out strong and hard against the hood of my mound. He sucked it and I writhed, capturing his head between my thighs.

'Ozzie.' I was pulling his hair now and he was pushing my legs further apart. I could hear the buckle of his pants jangling as he slid them further down his hips.

'Lupita, I need to feel you. I want to put it in, now. You're very wet and it shouldn't hurt,' he said as he rose up over me.

I nodded and reached up, pulling him down to me.

I could feel him pressing into me. He was using his hand to position himself. He pushed, slow at first, easing in, but there was resistance. I hadn't had many men, and he was bigger and wider than any I'd ever been with. His cock, like his body, was big and long. I could tell he wanted to push through, but he was trying to give me time to adjust. He braced himself above me, leaning heavily on his elbows, and pushed, burrowing further into my wetness.

'Am I hurting you?' he asked, pressing forward, seeking more of the damp heat.

I shook my head and he leant down to kiss my nose.

'You're so fucking tight, and hot. I don't want to hurt you, but it's so fucking good I want to be all the way inside of you.'

He pushed further, sliding forward, pulling back and then sliding further in. And then he kissed me, slipping his tongue into my mouth while his cock burrowed further in, finally ramming its head against my womb.

'Fuck.' He was sweating now. 'You are so fucking wet, *mami*. I just want to rub against this sweet pussy all night.' He gripped my ass, pulled almost out and then slid in slow. Then he flexed inside me like he wanted to make sure he was touching every part of me. After making sure he had touched and stroked and teased every corner, he pulled back out slow and pushed in again, setting up a throbbing rhythm. He was hot and unbelievably hard and each stroke seemed to find and set off a different nerve deep within my sex. I wanted to hold him just there – no, there – to make each sensation last longer. I tried clutching him with my inner muscles, clamping down and squeezing. But that just made him move faster and go deeper. I even tried grabbing his ass to hold him, draw him near, to keep him from pulling out, but my hands got lost in the feel of his skin, the way the muscles in his cheeks worked, how they contracted with each thrust. Knowing that I wanted to keep him there, he taunted me, moving faster, stopping just long enough, causing my muscles to suck at him, to milk his big hard cock. I couldn't think, only feel the fullness of him, and how I wanted to keep him inside me, stroking me like that.

I kissed his head, his hair, his lips, and then he was pounding into me, saying, 'I need to fuck you hard, *mami*. I need to fuck you hard 'cause it's so sweet and hot and I want to come inside you. Can I come inside you? Hold on to me, *mami*, 'cause I'm going to fuck you so hard and fill you so full.' I was so full of him and there were lights bouncing around every time he slammed into me. He seemed to grow and tighten inside me; he got even harder. Then his back arched and he reared up like a big black-maned lion. 'Oh, fuck me, *mami*,' he groaned. I felt a liquid heat filling me, washing over my walls and nerves, causing my pussy to tremble and beat a staccato rhythm against his cock. Shivers racked my body. I closed my eyes and let the lights wash over me.

I don't know how long we stayed like that, but when I opened my eyes, it was getting light outside. Ozzie was snoring lightly, his head rested on my shoulder, and his half-erect penis was still half in. I shook his shoulders and he looked up at me, a sleepy grin on his face. 'A shower,' he said. 'We need a shower and a nap.' He rose and I followed him into the bathroom.

We didn't do anything in the shower. He washed me with his hands and teased me with his fingers, but we were both tired. So we rinsed, dried each other and tumbled into bed. I fell asleep in his arms.

While I was sleeping, he'd gone out for staples and was scrambling eggs with cheese and making toast and coffee with the sleeves of his rather wrinkled shirt rolled up to his elbows. When I stumbled into the kitchen wearing my standard spaghetti-strap slip of silk and a yawn, he steered me to a chair and slid a plate in front of me.

'Hungry?' he asked, sliding a cup of coffee in front of me and a carton of cream.

'I could eat,' I said, reaching for the sugar bowl that I always kept in the centre of the table.

'Good. I thought you were going to be one of those "I don't eat breakfast" girls.' He sat down across from me with his cup and plate.

'I'm not usually, but that's because I'm too lazy to cook and besides there's never anything here to eat.' It was good, the eggs not too well done, the coffee just strong enough. 'But I have no problem when a handsome man wants to use my kitchen to display his culinary skills.'

'I had fun last night, Lupita,' he said, sipping his coffee and watching me. I could imagine him wearing that same look in the courtroom.

'Me too,' I said around a mouthful of egg and toast.

'This is a new experience for me.'

I nodded and took a gulp of well-creamed coffee.

'I've never done this before.'

I couldn't help it. I rolled my eyes.

'No, Lupita.' He got all serious, a pained look on his face. 'I love my wife, and my children.'

I got up and went to him, pressing his head against my breast.

'Don't worry, Ozzie, I'm a big girl. And we agreed it was just for last night.'

He pulled my hips to his, his face still buried. 'But I want more,' he whispered.

I hid my smile in his hair. His words made me happy, not just because Georgy's plan was working, but because I wanted more too. More of this big, passionate, kind man's loving.

He slipped my straps down and lifted me on to the table, my bare bottom pressed into the cool Formica, as he pulled and tugged at my nipples. His tongue slid into my mouth and the knob of his erection prodded my already slick opening. I opened for him, sliding my legs around his hips as he pulled me closer, pressing inward, searing the walls of my already scorching passage. He lifted me from the table, his fingers cupping my bottom as he began to thrust and all I could do was hold on.

* * *

It was Sunday morning and the sun poured through the thin curtains at my bedroom window. Reluctant to greet the glare of the morning sun, I lay there with my eyes closed.

'Aye, Lupita,' I could hear Ozzie moaning.

I waited, still reluctant to open my eyes to the glare.

'Aye, Lupita, you do that so good.' The bed moved, writhed actually. The sheets tugged away from me and the mattress bounced.

Well, I couldn't ignore that. I rolled on to my back and opened one eye. It took me a minute to focus. What I saw brought me fully awake. I even sat up.

André, my neighbour, had his head buried in the judge's crotch and Ozzie, eyes closed, had his fingers buried in André's blond streaked locks.

André looked over at me, his mouth full of cock, and smiled with his eyes.

I bit my lip and shook my head at him. Then I nudged him in his side with my foot, but he kept sucking.

'No, no,' Ozzie was saying and struggling with the head in his lap. 'Let me put it in. I want to feel you.'

His hands were on André's shoulders, gently lifting him up, but then he must have opened his eyes, awakened fully, because he was shoving André, who was still sucking the head of Ozzie's cock.

'What the fuck?' Ozzie was saying as he tried to stand up, pushing hard at André, who finally let go. 'Who the fuck are you?' he asked André who was staring up at him and licking his lips. Then Ozzie looked at me, his face red with embarrassment and outrage.

'This is my stupid-ass neighbour, André,' I said, kicking him in his side, hard. 'He has a key, in case of emergency. I don't know what the fuck is wrong with him. He usually only helps himself to a glass of orange juice or a roll of toilet paper.'

André stood now, looking sheepish. 'He was there, Lupita. Lying there, the two of you, all smooth and clean and naked. His cock stiff and hard, looking so delicious, I couldn't help it. And he liked it. Look at him.' He pointed at Ozzie, who was covering his still erect penis with his large, but not quite large enough, hand.

Ozzie must still have been a little dazed because he stood there with his mouth open, both hands now covering his genitals. I fully expected him to deck André, let loose a chain of homophobic invective and storm out of my apartment. He was, after all, a heterosexual Latino male. Instead, he reached for his pants and struggled to put them on sans underwear.

I shoved André toward the door and went to Ozzie's side, staying the hand that was frantically pulling on his pants.

'I'm sorry, Ozzie,' I said, pressing my body to his. 'André is impetuous, but he's harmless. It's a compliment really. He was so turned on by your body that he had to taste you.'

André stood by the door nodding his head and stroking himself.

I had Ozzie's pants back down around his ankles and I was sucking his nipples. He looked over at André and started to laugh. Then he grabbed my ass and started to stroke it, pulling the cheeks apart and sliding his fingers down the cleft and into the slickness between my legs.

'You can leave now,' he said to André as he bent me over and pushed me face down on the bed. He tucked one of the pillows under me so that my bottom sat up high and the swollen lips of my vagina were clearly visible. He touched the slippery lips with a finger, running it around the sensitive rim before inserting a long finger. Then he was there, plunging into me, his fingers crushing my cheeks as he filled me.

'May I help?' André's voice was strangled. I had forgotten he was there. 'I could suck your balls,' he said as Ozzie slid in and out of me, my juices flowing, coating him as he increased the pace. 'I'm not very big and I have oil. I would go slow, only as far as you wanted. I would make it good for you. If I could fuck you while you fuck Lupita, you would come like you never did before. I would stroke you so good, *papi*. I could make it so good for you,' André was begging and I knew he was stroking himself and imagining what it would feel like to sink his cock into Ozzie's ass because his words were jerky and husky-sounding, but Ozzie didn't stop. He was ramming into me, the hair at his groin rasping against the swollen tenderness between my legs, causing ripples and tingles. I had handfuls of sheets, nearly ripping them, and Ozzie's fingers were melting into my ass as he banged into me, sending shock waves through my body.

Then André's voice was a high-pitched groan and he must have fallen against the door. Ozzie was still behind me; he pounded harder, his fullness locking into place only to be dragged out with equal force. I pushed back into him, hard. He jerked, trying to hold me, but the stroking, pounding and pushing had become frenzied. I couldn't wait for him and my body trembled, clutching him as wave after wave consumed me and my wetness flowed. I could feel Ozzie's thighs between mine, his thrusts slowing, surging forward like slow motion. He was so hard and so full, and then there was a rush of hot liquid filling me and he was falling forward like a tree, crushing me.

After a few minutes, he got up and said, 'I have to go.' *It was too much*, I thought. *Or maybe it was enough. Was he angry?* By the time Ozzie had showered, André had left and I'd pulled on a pair of jeans and a T.

I was sitting on the sofa with a cup of plantation mint tea when he came out of the bedroom, wrinkled but fully clothed.

'Tea,' I offered.

'I can't do this, Lupita,' he said, standing over me.

I sipped my tea.

'I have responsibilities, a reputation.' His hands were bowed as he held them up in something that seemed like a plea.

I sipped my tea.

'I really like you, but I can't . . . We agreed that . . .'

I sipped and worried that I'd failed Georgy. I chided myself that I should never have given André a key. I knew that he had no self-control, but I never really expected him to do something so thoughtless, so selfish. I liked Ozzie. I would miss him. Georgy was lucky.

'It's not you . . .' he began and I couldn't help but laugh.

'It's OK.' I decided to let him off the hook. 'We had fun. Let's leave it at that.'

'Lupita,' he began again, 'I . . .' His hands were pleading again.

I got up to get more tea. 'You sure you don't want any?' I held up my cup.

'No,' he said, shaking his head, 'I'll get something when I get home. Lupita.' He was starting to look pitiful, starting to make a mess of everything.

'Look,' I said, my cup dangling from my hand, 'it was good. Go home, Ozzie.' I went to him and kissed him on the cheek. I would have kissed his forehead *como* his *abuelita*, but he was too tall. Then I moved him toward the door. He turned and kissed me on my forehead before leaving.

A couple of weeks later I got a call from Georgy. She was ecstatic. 'What did you *really* do to him, Lupe?' she asked. 'He's like when we first married, so eager to please, and such energy.'

'I just followed your directions, like I told you,' I said with a laugh. 'I thought you would be dissatisfied because he never came back. It turned out to be a quick bout of sex, no emotion.'

'Well, I was wrong. Whatever you did, it worked. I owe you.'

'No, it was fun. Ozzie's a nice guy, such a gentleman.'

'I'll buy you something nice. We'll go shopping.'

'No, really, Georgy. Like I told you before, he spent a night with me and André ran him off. It's probably the guilt. You know how guilt motivates a man.'

'Maybe it was having André watch. You know, some gay male fantasy. Ozzie has always been so straight. Maybe it tweaked the freak in him.' She giggled.

'Yeah, maybe so.'

'But I'd like to see you anyway, Lupe. I miss you.'

'Hold on, Georgy. I got another call coming in,' I said as I clicked the key in the receiver that switched lines.

'Lupita?' The voice stopped my heart.

'Yes.'

'I can't stop thinking about you.'

'Me either,' I said, gripping the phone too tight. My hand started to sweat.

'I need to see you.'

'When?'

'As soon as possible.' The words were rushed; I smiled into the phone.

'Hold on. I was on the other line. I have to end the call.'

'I can call you back.'

'No. It's not important. Hold on.' I clicked back to Georgy.

'I have to take this, Georgy.'

'When can we get together?' she asked quickly, responding to the urgency in my voice. 'Lunch tomorrow?'

'I've got a paper to finish. Maybe next week.'

'Maybe I can help with the paper.'

'That's cheating.' I laughed, trying to keep it light. 'I gotta go.'

'Call me as soon as you're free. Lupe, I'd really like to see you.'

'As soon as I'm done,' I said, clicking off.

'Hello?' I said, hoping he'd held on.

'I can be done here by three. I can pick up something for dinner,' Ozzie answered.

'I took my key back from André.'

'I'm glad,' he said, sounding pleased. 'I'll cook you something special.'

'Whatever you want. I'll be here,' I said as I hung up the phone.

Alegra Verde's short fiction appears in the Black Lace collection *Misbehaviour*.

The Interview

Justine Elyot

'If he is late, I won't even consider him. I put up with enough blasted lateness in my working life; I refuse to countenance it in my private life as well.'

My husband's irascible remarks are premature; it is still only five minutes to three. Our candidate might be cutting things a little fine, but there is time enough to park a car and cross the gravel drive to the front door before the deadline.

I take my final chance to cast a critical eye over the photographs that came with the application, though perhaps 'critical' is not the mot juste. The man who has beaten the competition to reach this final stage of the selection process is breathtaking to behold. A shot of his face in half-profile, catching the exact diagonal of his cheekbone, the outline of his rather splendid nose and a flash of devilment in his eyes, reveals nothing to disappoint except lips that might be a little fuller. But then, who wants perfection? My husband, I suppose, but he is a peculiar animal altogether.

The accompanying photographs of his taut upper torso, thumbs hooked into the waistband of his jeans, and the full body shot in black and white please my less exacting eye. Isn't there some theory about the relative proportions of noses and, you know, downstairs equipment? I can hear my husband's voice in my head, chiding me for that turn of phrase. 'Call a spade a spade, Jacqueline. And a cock a cock.'

That is what all this is about. Breaking the inhibition barrier that has proved so troublesome to our bedroom life. Perhaps it's an unconventional approach, but Ralph Watson-James is an unconventional man.

We met at a photo shoot for one of the magazines he owns. I was modelling mini-skirts on a draughty fire-escape behind some disreputable buildings in Soho; I think the story was about a Sixties revival. I thought the triple-ply lashes and beehive hair made me look ridiculous, but Ralph seemed not to agree, standing rigidly beside the photographer and watching me with an avidity that made me feel naked.

I posed for a long and shivery hour, wrapping myself around banisters and sitting on the cold metal steps, fearing that the crew below were peering right up my abbreviated vinyl skirt. When the ordeal was finished, I headed gratefully for my bag, needing a cigarette and then perhaps a chug or two of Diet Coke. And then another cigarette.

I slouched against a wall, sheltering the flame of my lighter with one hand while I sucked up the heady poison, relishing the first sweet seconds of giddiness.

'It's a dreadful shame,' said a cultured voice to my right, 'that a flawless creature like you feels the need to destroy her body with those things.'

I was ready with a sharp retort, but it died in my throat when I saw that the anti-smoking campaigner was none other than Mr Watson-James, in whose hands my future career success might well lie.

'Appetite suppressant, you know,' I explained vaguely. 'Can't afford to put on weight in this game.'

'I understand,' he said, coming to lean beside me. 'Though to my mind it is a pity young women in your profession are forced into such abstemious lifestyles. Food and drink are two of the great pleasures of life. Amphetamines can hardly compare.'

I started guiltily. Did he know I used speed to control my weight? If so, how?

'I guess you're right,' I said, nervous now. 'To be honest, I'd kill for a slice of my mum's chicken and mushroom pie right now.'

'Why don't you let me buy you dinner? On the strict condition that you order whatever you like, regardless of fat content. And I shall insist that you have pudding.'

He smiled at me, and an intimation that he might interest me as more than a rich older man enabling my career slipped into my mind.

We feasted at an intimate little Italian place up some dark and rather dusty stairs in one of the narrow alleys nearby. Foods I had long consigned to the recycling bin of history appeared on the chequered cloth before me, an obscene parade of carbohydrates, rich sauces, butter, cheese, red meat, bread, oil. I was going to need liposuction after this, I protested, but Ralph would not sanction avoidance of a single morsel. He watched me forking the mountain of gloopy pasta into my surprised gullet with a little smile of satisfaction, breaking off from his own green salad and tumbler of water to refill my glass of full-blooded red wine when it ran dry.

'So this is your life, Jacqueline?' he said while I half-heartedly scanned the dessert menu. 'You are professionally thin. Is that what you want for your future?'

I stopped dithering between tiramisu and peach semifreddo and shrugged. 'I don't really know what I want to do. This is good for now, I suppose, but I know it won't last for ever.'

'No, Jacqueline, it won't. Your enchanting face will grow lined – especially if you keep smoking – and the table will be bare of offers. You will have to find more and more desperate markets in which to sell yourself. Perhaps your bones will grow brittle through lack of nourishment and you will become frail and elderly before your time.'

Thanks for the cheerful prognosis, I wanted to say, but instead I stared at him.

'Kate still gets plenty of work. So do all the supers.'

'You aren't a super. You're beautiful – perfect, even – but you aren't one of them. And deep down you know that.'

He was right. Deep down I did. I didn't have the stamina or commitment to make it really big. Modelling for me was a way of treading water until my real self decided to make herself explicit.

'You aren't made for this life, Jacqueline,' he diagnosed. 'You are just a little too fragile, a little too precious, a little too naïve. You need to be tended to, like a hothouse plant, given space and time to flourish.'

His words were hitting their mark. I could not find a response, even though my impulse was to say something coarse that would push him away from me. I felt spooked, repulsed and compelled at the same time. I was afraid.

I ordered the tiramisu. By the time the liqueurs arrived, he had proposed and I had accepted.

Of course, we barely knew each other, but we seemed to get along surprisingly well. On a superficial level, I enjoyed the extravagant lifestyle and the kudos that came with being Mrs Watson-James, and I suppose having a beautiful young model on his arm did not harm his reputation around town.

There was more to it than that, though. He had a lot of involvement in the arts, as a sponsor, and he educated me in theatre, opera, ballet and music. Although our respective life experiences could hardly have been more diverse, we found points of recognition and we shared some basic philosophical and ethical principles. Neither of us set much store by the prevailing social attitudes and we tended to follow our own internal moral codes, which happily coincided. He was kind to me and he never denied me anything, though he did make me give up smoking.

There was one thing that jarred, though.

He was very much more sexually experienced than I was. At first, this was a bonus. Our wedding night – which he held on for, not out of a sense of moral obligation but because he savoured the anticipatory build-up – was a wonderful revelation to me. My sexual encounters after leaving boarding school had been underwhelming, usually initiated by coked-up photographers or leering soccer players in glitzy nightclubs, who were much better at scoring on the pitch than off it. Nobody had ever taken this time with me, been patient enough to ensure that I was ready, been at pains to get to know and understand my body. Ralph was a sensational lover.

I was not.

I was hesitant, tentative, anxious. I wanted terribly to be able to perform for him, to prove myself as the lover he had been seeking for all these years, to push him to those limits of ecstasy I had reached with him. But I did it all wrong. I would accidentally bite his penis mid-fellatio; my grip would be too limp at the base; I would get cramps and have to change position, and all the time I was so, so self-conscious.

He wanted me to watch us in the mirror and I refused. He wanted to film us and I refused. He wanted to try some kinkier things, to develop the trust between us, and I just made a face and called him a pervert. I feel awful about it now.

And the one thing I could never, ever bring myself to do – the one thing he really wanted from me – was to talk about it. To tell him what I wanted, explain my fantasies, use the crude language of sex. It was completely beyond me.

'Why can't you talk to me?' he said, exasperated but trying not to be, one gloomy Sunday morning after I had started to cry mid-coitus.

'I don't want you to think badly of me,' I stumbled to explain. 'I don't want you to think I'm that kind of girl. That says that kind of thing. That ... oh, it's because it's you. I have to live with you. I'm kind of in love with you. It makes it hard ...'

I looked away, tearful once more.

'Jacqueline,' he said, gently bringing my face back round to his. He never called me Jacqui or Jax, like everybody else did – always Jacqueline. 'There is nothing wrong with being "that kind of girl". How many times have I told you that?'

A rictus smile and a shrug. Possibly about forty times? I had lost count.

'Well,' he said sadly, taking my hand and stroking it. 'Mere reiteration of the point does not seem to be doing the trick, does it? How can we unlock you, Jacqueline? How can we find the sexual woman lurking inside the frightened girl? Because I know she's there. I wouldn't have married you otherwise.'

'Maybe ... erm ... some kind of therapy?' I suggested.

He chuckled. 'I don't think so. I'm not one for clinical solutions to personal problems.'

'Oh, but that's a silly, old-fashioned view!' I exclaimed, but he put a finger to my lips.

'I'm a silly, old-fashioned man,' he said. 'I know you can't tell me much, but can you tell me when you have ever had a sexual experience that you found fulfilling?'

'You fulfil me!'

'Well, thank you, but I mean one where you felt less inhibited? One where you felt you were expressing your real sexuality?'

I thought about this. It was true that none of my previous

boyfriends were up to much, but there was one occasion . . . the sex wasn't fantastic, but I had found myself saying something I had not allowed to cross my lips before or since . . . 'Fuck me.'

'There was one time,' I said haltingly. 'But it's . . . oh, it's quite disgusting really. I'm ashamed of myself for doing it.'

'Sounds promising. Go on.'

'At a wrap party after a shoot. There was a very attractive man . . . tall, dark and all that, you know. I'd never fancied anyone so much; it was like a magnetic force. I directed all my dancing to him, really sexy moves, you know – and his eyes didn't leave me for the entire half-hour. I thought he might come and join me, but he didn't. It was very frustrating. I didn't want to go up to him – that just looks desperate – so I left the floor and went to the ladies'. He followed me. I said something silly, like "Are you looking for something?" and he said "Yes – you," and . . . and . . . somehow we ended up in a broom cupboard, making passionate . . . oh, not love, but you know . . .'

'Fucking,' said my husband baldly.

'I guess. And it was a bit mad. I was really . . . not myself. I said all kinds of things.'

'What things?'

'Rude things.' I blushed.

'Rude things. So you can do it. It is inside you somewhere.' He kissed me, a long, tender one, and then said, 'Was it because he was a stranger? He knew nothing about you and could not judge you?'

'Yes. I think that was it,' I said in a tiny voice.

'If you'd made arrangements to meet again and embarked on a relationship, would that have changed the dynamic?'

'I don't know,' I said, pondering. 'Because we'd started out that way . . . perhaps we could have carried it on.'

'I see. So what I should have done, rather than wait for you, was take you on that fire-escape the first day we met?'

I giggled. 'Maybe.'

We tried a few more things. Role-playing. Scene-setting. Pretending we had just met that night. None of it worked.

And now, here we are, at the very edge of social acceptability. Mutually condoned adultery. I had no idea such a thing existed, but when Ralph outlined the plan, two months ago, it sounded sane. Ralph has a way of making the outrageous seem normal; it is a large part of how he has built his empire.

'What if you were to find another stranger, Jacqueline? A similarly magnetic, handsome man who lusted after you enough that he lost his reason and was prepared to have you anywhere, in any circumstances? Would that work for you?'

'That's ... obviously that could only be a fantasy,' I stammered.

'Why? Why could that only be a fantasy?'

'Because we're married.'

'Yes, we're married. We are a partnership. As long as we are in agreement on how to conduct that partnership, what else matters?'

'You mean ... ?'

'Jacqueline, I've tried everything. Apart from your therapy idea. I have an inkling that one bout of wild sex with an unfamiliar young man might be all it takes to set that passionate woman free.'

I blinked. Had he lost his marbles? He was older than me, but too young for dementia.

'You want me to go and ... do it ... with another man?'

'Under strictly controlled conditions, Jacqueline, I think it could be the vital step to a healthy sex life. I don't mean that you should prowl alleyways looking for a casual shag. I don't mean that you should endanger yourself in any way. No, what I have in mind is this . . .'

He had placed an anonymous advertisement in the back of one of his magazines. Whittling down the replies, he had set psychometric tests for the ten he considered most suitable. Then, three weeks ago, he had interviewed a shortlist of five, from behind a two-way mirror to protect his identity, even though his face was nowhere near as famous as his name. The successful candidate had been escorted to a GUM clinic for tests; these being clear, he had signed a contract stipulating lifelong secrecy and promising £20,000 on completion of the job.

His name is Aaron, and I both dread and look forward to our meeting.

The clock has made a clicking sound, prior to striking three.

And there is a jangling at the front door.

I catch my breath, take a final mirror check. I look good. My hair is glossy, make-up just-so and the loose silk wrap dress I am wearing – for ease of removal – hints at the expensive lingerie beneath.

'Ralph, I'm nervous,' I say, hearing Fran the housekeeper open the door and a gruff voice below.

'Don't be nervous. You are quite safe. I will stay for the interview and then leave if you wish to take things further. As you know, we will be recording this session for the purpose of CCTV footage if he does anything you do not want, and I will be listening in as well. I want you to enjoy yourself, Jacqueline.' He smiles wistfully at me. I shake my head wonderingly. What a situation to be in.

There is a knock on the door, and then Fran ushers our guest into the room.

'Aaron Lewis for you, Mr Watson-James,' she says.

He is everything I had hoped for. Standing at around six foot two with that manly, arrogant feet-wide stance, he is made for fantasies of illicit trysting.

Ralph stands and approaches the candidate, holding out a hand to shake.

'Thank you for coming,' he says, and they share the ghost of a smirk. Oh, was that a rude joke? I bite my lip and flush. 'May I introduce my lovely wife, Jacqueline?' I allow Aaron to kiss each of my cheeks, picking up a waft of spicy, masculine scent before I stand back and try to look at him. It is difficult, though, my natural inclination being shyness. This man is here to . . . have me.

A strange current prickles up and down my spine at the thought. Handsome Aaron has travelled all this way, jumped through all these hoops, so he can undress me and have his wicked way with me. My stomach flips several times over.

'What do you think, Jacqueline?' asks Aaron in a low voice. 'Will I do?'

'Very nice,' I say.

'You're beautiful,' he says disarmingly. 'I've brought you a present.' He hands me a velvet box, inside which is a jet-beaded choker, Victorian in style.

'Oh . . . it's lovely!'

'Put it on, Jacqueline,' bids Ralph. 'Let Aaron put it on you.'

I move back towards him and hold my hair up out of the way while he fastens the choker at the nape of my neck. His touch is sure and swift; he does not fumble and the brush of his fingers against my neck makes my shoulders shake.

'Suits her,' says Ralph. 'You have good taste, Aaron.' He goes back to sit in the wicker chair by the picture window. The sun outlines him and he looks a little bit godlike, sitting cross-legged in his pale linen suit. 'We've covered everything you need to know in the preceding interviews, Aaron, as you know.

This meeting is purely to establish whether you think you will be a good fit. Jacqueline, is he attractive to you?'

The way he asks the question throws me off-balance a little, so brisk is its tone. He wants me say yes. He wants this to happen.

'Yes. Very,' I say truthfully.

'Do you think he is the man for the job?'

'Do you want to be?' I ask Aaron coyly.

'It's completely up to you,' he replies, but his lips are quirking a little and his eyes tell me not to even think about turning him down.

'Good, good,' says Ralph, clapping his hands and rising from the wicker chair. 'I'll leave you two to it, then. No need to stand on ceremony. The less polite chit-chat, the better.'

He stops on the way out, takes me into his arms and kisses me, very gently, brushing a lock of hair from my forehead. 'Thank you for this, Jacqueline,' he whispers. Then he leaves the room.

I look after him, almost afraid to turn back to Aaron in case I am turned to stone or struck by the lightning of moral vengeance, or something. Is an act of extra-marital sex infidelity, if no faith is being compromised? There is no breach of trust; neither partner is intending to deceive the other. So why do I feel guilty?

'You're conditioned to feel that way,' says Aaron, his eerie mindreading shaking me out of reverie. I am stunned into looking at him; his arms are folded and he has tilted his head towards me.

'You ... think?'

'You're wondering if you have it in you to commit adultery,' states Aaron. 'Even though you've been planning and thinking about this for a long time, when it comes to the crunch, you're bound to think this way.'

'Do you think I'm a bad person?' I ask him tremulously.

He laughs softly and takes a step towards me. 'God, no,' he says. 'We're not supposed to be thinking about anything like that, anyway, are we? We're strangers, remember. No judgments, no inhibitions. At least, I plan to be uninhibited. I don't know about you.'

He has a half-smirk that makes him look like a sexy cartoon villain; the evil squire about to insist on taking his *droit de seigneur*. Suddenly I think I know how to play this. I smile back at him.

'Well, first things first, I think,' I say, walking over and touching his chest. How flat and hard it is beneath the warm cotton of his shirt. 'I know I've seen your photographs, but I've been a model and I know a bit about airbrushing. I want to make sure that what I've seen is what I'm going to get.'

'Oh, really?' He is grinning widely now, all perfect teeth and cheekbones.

'Yes. I think I should undress you. Is the room warm enough?'

'Don't know about the room, but I certainly am.'

I begin to unbutton his shirt, noting that there is a sprinkling of fine dark hair beneath. I send my fingers roving through it, watching my oval nails glide through the growth. They circle his navel then follow the trail down to his waistband, finally wrenching the garment free. He is tall enough that I can rest my cheek against the muscular expanse, and I do so, enjoying the tickle and prickle and heat of it. Meanwhile he has lifted his arms up and is fiddling with his cuffs until he can shrug the shirt off, revealing impressive shoulders and arms.

I breathe in his smell, essence of man beneath the expensive aftershave. My head feels lighter, then his arms trap me in position, pressed up to him, and his hands creep around in my hair. The scalp massage loosens me; I flop into him and sigh happily, putting a hand up to pinch his arms and back and ribs to see if I can find an inch of flesh that is not steely.

'Am I passing muster?' he murmurs, and I detect a faint Northern inflection in his voice, which is low, growly, gritty, earthy.

'Mmm, you feel lovely,' I say, my voice muffled by his chest.

'I've still got my shoes and socks on,' he prompts.

I giggle and drop down to kneel at his feet. 'I feel like a handmaiden,' I tell him, pulling his laces undone.

'I've always wanted one of those.' I pull each shiny brown shoe off each size-twelve foot, then roll the socks down and off.

'You even have nice feet,' I say in surprise, though I don't go so far as kissing them.

'Thanks. Know what else I've got?'

He leans and pulls me upright by an elbow, placing my hands squarely on the belt of his trousers. I look up at him uncertainly, my nerves making an unscheduled reappearance.

'Be my guest.' He nods.

I take a deep breath and flick the end of the leather free of restraint, then unbuckle it. With a flourish, feeling oddly like a rodeo cowboy, I whip it out of its loops, loving the sound it makes, an evocative whoosh, jingle, crack. It feels heavy in my hands, for the leather is of good quality, a little worn but not too stiff. I place it down and attend to the buttons. Oh, yes. There is a bulge.

Contained by soft white cotton, it is nonetheless unignorable. I ease the trousers down over his hips and let them drop to the floor, risking a look upwards. He looks a little distant, lost in a private place. Is this a fantasy of his? A gigolo fantasy?

I know I am not supposed to be curious about him as a person, but I cannot help myself.

'Why are you doing this?' I find myself saying.

'Don't make me break the rules, sweetheart,' he reproves, cupping my chin for a minute and frowning. 'I'm not to talk about myself, and you're not to ask. Same goes the other way round.'

I lift my chin out of his grasp and look him up and down.

'What, erm, what do you want me to do next?'

A cloud passes over the sun and the room darkens suddenly, matching my mood, which is uncertain now that I am close to the feared appendage.

'What do you want to do next?'

'I suppose I should take off your underpants?'

'What do you want to do next?' He sounds so patient, so oddly protective.

'Could we just have ... a little cuddle first? Maybe ... could you kiss me?'

He smiles and draws me in. 'I don't think that's against the rules.'

Unlike the ruthlessly clean-shaven Ralph, Aaron has a trace of stubble and I find I want to rub my face against his sandpapery skin, rub him on to me. His lips are firm, his breath warm, his body warm, his embrace firm, all firm and warm; it is comforting first, then it is arousing. He allows his hands more licence, letting them wander all over me, down to my hips and across my bottom, then his fingers walk slowly up my spine, finally grazing the nape of my neck until I feel ready to kiss harder and longer and fuller.

I try to push him, try to crush him, but it is deliciously difficult to make any impact on that hard flesh; I try to devour his mouth with my tongue but he just captures it and beats me at my own game. I try to merge into him, to force myself through his pores, but the bruising bulge beneath his midriff keeps our centres apart. Sooner or later it is going to demand attention in no uncertain terms, and now is as good a time as any.

'I want to take off your underpants,' I say hoarsely, gasping for air.

'Good.'

I unveil the beast, which is large, maybe larger than Ralph's, though I'm no judge – I rarely look it in the eye. I flinch and look up into Aaron's eyes again.

'Don't you like it?'

'I . . . I'm sure it's . . . very nice.'

'Nice? No, Jacqueline, it's not nice. It's a greedy selfish bastard that will ride roughshod over you to get what it wants. It'll make you feel good, but so does cocaine, and nobody says cocaine is nice.'

'I'm sorry. I've said the wrong thing. I don't know what I should say.'

'You don't have to say anything yet. Touch it. Find your way around.'

The surrealism of the situation is not lost on me. Adonis stands bare-naked in my living room and I'm worrying about the etiquette of handling his . . . um . . . you know.

I put out a hand and tap the side of it. It is hard and stiff and springs back to attention straight away. There is a bead of moisture at its head. I still can't look it in the eye and I blur my vision a little, avoiding its frank stare. My fingers drift downwards, outlining the heavy sacs beneath, then weighing them in my palm.

'Grab it. It won't break,' urges Aaron. I hesitate, so he takes hold of my wrist and moves my hand back to the shaft, prompting me to wrap my fingers around its girth. I find I quite like the feel of it; the skin is velvety and malleable, even as it stands proud, and my hand spans it comfortably. I begin to stroke it, trying not to loosen my grip, moving my other hand down to squeeze the sac.

I look up to see that he has shut his eyes and thrown back his head; an encouraging sign, so I speed up a little. His eyes open and he coughs a little before saying, 'Perhaps you should taste it too.'

'Taste it?'

'Yeah. But you have to ask me. Ask if you can suck it for me.'

'I can't!'

'You can. Just say it! Don't think about it.'

'I . . . can I . . . no, I can't.'

My hand seizes up and I look away, feeling tears well up. Why can't I just say the words?

'OK,' he says, crouching down to my level. 'You aren't ready yet. It's OK. Let's try something else.' He moves back in for another kiss. He knows this works; he knows a good kiss will undo me. He holds on to the back of my head, keeping me in position, then, once my limbs have melted, he sweeps his arm down, hooks it beneath my shoulders and suddenly I am borne aloft, lips still fixed, and carried across to the largest of the sofas.

Once I am deposited on my back, he breaks the kiss and moves down to the middle, tugging at the ties on my wrap dress.

'Hardly seems fair,' he mutters, 'that I'm starkers and you've still got all your clothes on.'

'I suppose not,' I sigh, giggling lightheadedly, as if his kiss has breathed helium into me. What was wrapped is unwrapped, the material falling open easily. I am revealed in my pink and orange scalloped lacy glory. He worships with his eyes for a flattering amount of time, then he places a hand on my stomach. It moves upwards and sideways, and then to the other side, covering every inch of unclothed skin in its explorations. He leans over and his mouth touches my neck, kissing lightly, while his hand crosses the border of my bra and climbs the foothills of my breasts. I shut my eyes and stretch out like a cat in the sunshine, arching my back a little in invitation. I want more of this, as much as he can give.

He understands my unspoken need; his lips begin to pull and nip at my skin while his hands are now on the slopes, above the cups of my bra, moving behind to unhook it. He is no novice, for he has freed my nipples in seconds, consigning the bra and the dress to the floor beside us, and his tongue plunges back into my mouth so I can make no comment on the way his fingers deal with my swollen buds.

He is rougher than Ralph, and his touch lacks my husband's finesse, but the urgency sweeps me along with it and I lock my tongue into his, pulling him in, biting his lower lip so that he makes a muffled exclamation of surprise and extricates himself to smile down at me. 'You're a wild one, under the surface, aren't you?' he says teasingly.

'Oooh,' is all I can say.

'What do you want? What shall I do next?'

I want to tell him that he can put his hand down my knickers and play with my clit if he likes, but the words stay stubbornly on the wrong side of my tongue and I wiggle my hips instead and try to move his hand down.

'Uh uh,' he says sternly, shaking his head. 'You ask nicely, Jacqueline, if you want something.'

'Ohhh,' I protest, but he simply moves his mouth to a nipple and flutters his hands maddeningly around my navel and pelvic area, skimming the elastic of my knickers but never crossing it.

He sucks the nipple until it is slightly sore, sending a buzz of sensation directly down to my groin.

'Please . . .' I moan.

'Hmm?' One finger creeps under the elastic and slides from side to side, waiting for the word.

'Could you . . . ?'

'Could I?' The tip of his tongue flicks my other nipple, preparing to work it into the same over-stimulated state as its pair.

'Touch me!'

'I am touching you, Jacqueline.'

I rear up, trying to force his hand further inside the lace, but he simply slaps my thigh lightly with the other and says, 'Oh, no, you don't. Tell me what you want.'

I compromise. 'Take my knickers down,' I say.

'Good.' He laughs his approval. 'I can do that.' He begins to peel the flimsy things down, breathing heavily on to what is revealed as he makes a slow and majestic progress over my hipbones. The warmth on my mons and my lips is heavenly; I want to push them up to meet his tongue, but I was not brought up that way. Instead I press my thighs together, hoping that he will not see how stickily they cling, while he continues to remove the knickers all the way down to my ankles.

'So then, Jacqueline, now that you are naked . . . gorgeously naked, I should say . . . what next?' He climbs astride me and leans over my face, so close that his white teeth dazzle me. I undulate my pelvis, trying to draw him lower down. His hands rest on my hips, the pads of his fingers pressing into my bottom.

'Trying to tell me something?'

'Oh . . . just . . . do what you want with me!' I exclaim in frustration, knowing that I won't get away with such a vague request, but thinking it worth a try at least.

'Jacqueline, look at me,' he says earnestly. He rests one hand on my mound, so tantalisingly close to the target that I whimper, while his other goes back to play with my swollen nipples. 'What I want is what you want. You can ask me for anything, anything at all. I'm broadminded and pretty kinky when I want to be. I don't think anything you ask will cross my limits. So ask me. I promise I'll say yes.'

'Put your fingers,' I whisper.

'Yes?' They hover lower, ready to dive.

'In my . . .' I push my thighs against his, indicating that I will open them for him.

'In your . . . ?'

'Between my legs . . .'

He reaches behind him and places a hand between my knees. 'Here?'

'No! Don't tease!'

'You're teasing. Say it. Say the words.'

'Oh . . . touch my . . . my clitoris.' I screw my eyes shut, but oh, glory, his fingers home straight in on the hungry bud and he begins to work the whole area with both hands, opening the lips and mapping my folds and crevices surely and thoroughly.

'Like this?'

'Oh, yes . . . like that . . . just like that . . . oh, yes.'

He moves his legs to kneel inside mine, crouching over me with his hands pressing and probing, making the slick sounds of sexual exploration, and I know my juices must be covering his fingertips. He breaks off to tell me, 'You're wet,' and I grunt, unable to acknowledge the words. He ups the ante. 'Why are you so wet?' he demands to know.

'You are making me wet,' I tell him.

'I'm glad to hear it.' Suddenly one of his fingers is pushing into my entrance, demonstrating the oiled ease with which it effects access. 'No resistance at all there. How does that feel?'

'Oh, God, it feels . . . so good . . .'

He pushes another finger in, still working my clit with his other hand, keeping all bases covered and on high alert. Every so often, I begin to pant a little faster and feel a little tremor build, and he slows down, backs off, waits a while before heightening the sensations again. The third time he does this I wail with disappointment and try to force myself on to him, rubbing and rotating against his disappearing hands.

'I can keep this up all day, Jacqueline,' he says, waiting patiently for me to calm down so he can start again. 'I am not going any further until you ask for it.'

'Ask for it?' I groan. 'I am asking for it.'

'I know you are,' he says with a grin. 'No, with your voice, I mean. Say the words. If you want me to make you come with my fingers, say so. Or perhaps you would like to feel my tongue on your clit? Or my cock in your pussy? However you want to come, you can. But you must let me know.'

The way he said the words, casually but in that earthy voice, rings a distant bell, chiming with something in my brain, the part of it that had passionate animal sex with that strange man that one time.

'Oh, I want you to,' I say. 'I want you to ... do me.'

'Do you?'

'Have me.'

'Have you?'

'Take me.'

'Take you where?'

Finally desperate, I spread my thighs as wide as they will go and kick my feet in the air, either side of his ears.

'Put your bloody great cock up here and fuck me!' I shout, beside myself.

He laughs loud and long, swarms up between my legs and places the rounded tip of his stiff length at my well-prepared opening. It is the work of seconds to plunge it all the way up to the end of my channel, holding the backs of my thighs against his palms so that I am at his mercy.

'Well done, Jacqueline,' he growls. 'Now it's my turn to do the talking. I am going to fuck you, and if I don't do it the way you want, you are to tell me immediately, do you understand?'

I nod, transfixed on the end of his hook, ready for the ploughing of my life.

'If you want it harder, say so. If you want it slower, say so. If you want me to flip you on to your hands and knees and take you from behind, say so. Yes?'

'Yes,' I promise. 'I will. Now can you please fuck me?'

'With pleasure.'

For the next fifteen minutes, the only sound in the room – apart from the slap of skin on skin, growing wetter and sweatier; apart from the grunting and the groans of the sofa springs – is my voice.

'Oooh, there. Yes. Slow down . . . just a bit . . . don't bite . . . oh, yes . . . faster . . . and maybe you could touch my clit? . . . and faster . . . harder, harder, harder, harder, OOOOOH.'

I come hard, wanting to say his name, but forgetting what it is, forgetting what my own name is, for that matter. He reminds me, roaring, 'JACQUELINE! YES!' at his moment of climax.

He drops down and plants a kiss on my beaded brow. 'Well done. You did brilliantly,' he says. 'I'm proud of you. And so will your husband be.'

He enters the room shortly afterwards, while Aaron is putting his trousers back on, and kneels by the side of the sofa, rapt and glowing.

'I heard it all,' he whispers. 'You were amazing. Do you think it has helped at all?'

I sit up, and look over at Aaron. 'I think so,' I say.

'Now that I've heard you say those things . . .'

'Yes. You've heard it all now.' I smile at him and let him take me into his arms. We kiss for a long time, such a long time that I do not hear the door click behind my interviewee.

Justine Elyot's erotica collection *On Demand* is published by Black Lace. Her short fiction appears in the Black Lace anthologies *Liaisons, Misbehaviour* and *Sexy Little Numbers – Volume 1*.

Playing the Part

Izzy French

'You – beautiful, dark-haired 1940s siren with deep-red lips. Me – ordinary guy with big ambitions. Let's meet where I first caught your eye two weeks ago. Where you smiled at me. Costa Coffee, Waterloo, 8 a.m., Mon. 24th. I'll carry *Time Out*, wear a red rose in my lapel. You'll know me.'

Lily blew on the window, creating a circle of condensation, feeling her warm breath hit the cold glass. She waited a moment before etching her initials into the fog and gazing through to the ever-growing city. Then she wiped the glass with her sleeve, leaving a smudge behind. They'd arrive soon. And then she'd meet him. She was quite certain he'd be there. He'd always looked the trustworthy type.

Sam had been surprised at her proposed early start. She'd set the clock for 5.45 a.m. She needed time to get ready. There were preparations to make. It wouldn't be quick or easy. Not tomorrow.

'The 6.45? Are you mad? This is becoming a bit of a habit on a Monday morning, isn't it? Got a rush job on or something? I thought opening night was weeks away. And that you were on top of things. As per usual. That you could take it easy from now on.'

'There're things I have to do. You know how it is. People to see. I've got an early meeting. But I'll be home early too.'

'Well, we'd better make the most of the evening then, as the morning will be a dead loss.' He'd pulled her on to the bed, pushing her skirt up over her hips. 'I'll drop you at the station tomorrow,' he whispered, nuzzling into her neck. Sam was always loyal, caring. And forceful.

She smiled now at the memory, squeezing her legs together both in remembrance and hopeful anticipation. The man seated opposite was gazing at her in apparent fascination. Appearing to find her far more interesting than his *Times* he smiled, as though trying to catch her eye. She looked away, watching gleaming mirrored offices take the place of grim tower blocks. Lily loved the city, but her heart belonged to the theatre district. She was happiest when mooching round Victorian passageways, imagining society men waiting at stage doors for chorus girls, whose social status was little higher than that of whores. She would have felt at home then, she was sure of that. But she could embrace change and progress too. And variety kept her alive. Sam understood that too. Married for three years, neither of them had allowed their sex life to dwindle to an infrequent missionary position, like that of many of their friends. They weren't heading for a quickie divorce and a life of unsatisfactory one-night stands.

Last night had been a case in point. Aware of her early start, Lily had been reluctant at first when she felt Sam's hands on her thighs, his breath on her neck. They'd spent much of the afternoon in bed together, after all, fucking, pleasuring each other, slowly but surely. But then she felt his fingers hook under her knickers, slide along her slit and plunge into her cunt. He was brooking little argument. He never did. He liked to be in control. And she was happy with that. To a point. In marrying him she knew she had relinquished a certain amount of personal freedom. That was inevitable. She fell forward on to the bed, arse in the air, inviting him to take her from behind. Tearing her knickers from her, pushing a pillow under her belly, allowing his cock to play around her arse, teasing her, he pinned her down. Sam pulled her hand away when she reached for her clit, held her hands beside her head and plunged deep inside her. He was silent. She gasped at the intense pleasure this quick hard fuck was giving her. Her clit rubbing against the pillow ensured her orgasm soon overwhelmed her, her cunt tightened round him and the waves of her desire heightened before ebbing away to a quiet satisfaction. They fell asleep, still entangled, half-dressed and sated.

Giving the man opposite a quick glance from the corner of her eye, Lily wondered if he could have any inkling of what she was reliving as they were drawn closer into London. She suspected he could. And that he was enjoying some fantasies of his own. He coughed, crossed his legs and dropped his paper into his lap. Surreptitiously she moved in tiny circles against the seat, feeling fabric rub against her clit, warm juices beginning to trickle to the tops of her thighs. She'd dressed carefully today, of course. '1940s siren,' he'd said. 1940s siren she could do. Her suit was original. Charcoal wool, beautifully tailored. The skirt skimmed over her hips, the jacket fitted her snugly around the waist and was broad at the shoulders, as the style of the day demanded. She'd teamed it with a white silk blouse and seamed nylons. The snakeskin bag finished the look. She'd tied her hair into a tight chignon and applied her make-up with care. Deep-red lipstick. Powdered face. Black eyeliner. Blowing a kiss at the mirror just before she left, she felt good.

'I'm a lucky man,' Sam said as he passed, jangling the car keys. 'We need to move if you're to make that train. Though if you missed it, it wouldn't be too great a hardship.'

Lily knew he wanted nothing more than to tear her suit from her. Unbutton her blouse, and release her satin bra. Maybe he could. Later. At the other end of the day. For now she had to go. She had an appointment. Of sorts.

The train began to slow as it approached Waterloo. Lily was beginning to feel nervous. Would he be there? She glanced at her watch. 7.45 a.m. She had plenty of time. She would prefer it if he was there first, waiting. She stepped carefully from the carriage, the tightness of her skirt and the height of her heels constraining her movement slightly. She had to step sideways as she dropped to the platform. It would be fitting now, if she was to be engulfed in steam. But that wasn't to be. Comfort felt like such a twenty-first-century notion. She was dressed for elegance and style, not ease of movement. It struck her now, as it so often did, that clothes could work as such a wonderful disguise. Superficially her outfit looked so charming, quaint. Yet to the trained eye it could also suggest naughty intent. She was forced to walk with a swing of the hips, which she allowed herself to exaggerate, and was unsurprised when the man who had been seated opposite her walked past with a low whistle. Clothes could tell so much more about the person than the naked body, Lily thought. It was why she loved working with them. As wardrobe mistress at a London theatre, she could experiment with her look. Be master of so many disguises. Be whoever she wanted to be.

She turned towards the coffee shop. He was there. Long dark hair tucked behind his ears, he was dressed casually. Jeans, jacket, T-shirt. Red rose in his lapel. Corny but sweet. He was quite beautiful, though she doubted he thought so. That he'd ever given it any consideration. Men rarely seemed to. She admired the planes of his face, his slim build, the ease with which he wore his clothes. He took frequent sips from a steaming mug. Nervous, she thought. Uncertain that his request would be answered. The magazine rested on the small circular table. She waited for a few moments, watching him from behind, before approaching him.

'May I?' She gestured towards an adjacent chair. He looked up at her, his eyes widened; then he nodded. What else could he do? She knew he was unlikely to be rude. To tell her he was waiting for someone, a woman who looked just like her, so would it be convenient if she sat elsewhere?

'Can I get you something?'

'Espresso, please.'

He soon returned with a tiny cup full of dark liquid. She was holding his magazine. Flicking through the 'Lonely Hearts'. He blushed as he took his seat.

'You're not her,' he stammered, sounding unsure of himself. She wasn't surprised. How could he possibly have anticipated this happening? He wasn't prepared.

'No,' she replied.

'But you're very like her.'

She nodded her agreement. Then sat back and waited in silence. The station clock told her it was 8.10 a.m. They both knew by now that she wasn't coming. The other woman. He looked at his watch.

'I must go.'

'Come with me,' she said. He hesitated. And gazed at her. At that moment she knew he would.

'I work at a theatre. Wardrobe mistress. There will be no one there now. Not for hours yet. I can show you what I do.' He stood up. Didn't demur, make excuses, leave. She picked up her bag and walked out to the taxi rank. He followed, tucking his magazine under his arm.

'Drury Lane,' she instructed the driver. He pulled the door shut behind them. Their arms touched as they sat together. The taxi driver gave him a smile and a wink in his mirror.

He thinks we're already lovers, Lily thought. The journey was slow, the driver picking his way through the rush hour. People rushed past, rarely bumping into one another, as though in a carefully choreographed dance, one they did every day. Lily was always struck how little human contact she saw in this city; it saddened her.

It began to drizzle. They were safely cocooned in the taxi. Warm and dry. Lily was happy for the journey to be slow. It felt as though they were getting to know one another, somehow. Silently. A couple of times he turned towards her, as if to speak, but changed his mind. She felt his hand brush against hers, and a frisson of excitement ran through her. His touch was warm. She opened her hand in return, allowing his fingers to tangle through hers. Like a couple on a first date, she thought, smiling. He, uncertain of how the evening had gone, of how he would be received, making tentative approaches. She, responding, letting him know that his advances would be welcomed. But this was the morning. The start of the day. And they had never met before. But they had. She had watched him many times. He was a creature of habit. Drank a large latte every Monday morning before making his way to work. He was a photographer. She'd followed him to his studio one day, when she was dressed anonymously. He wouldn't recognise her. Not now. Her appearance had altered, as it so often did. If he could see how she had looked this time last week, he would be astounded. She would like him to photograph her, one day, if he agreed.

It had been complete chance she'd seen him that morning three weeks ago. She'd received a call late one Sunday night. There'd been a disaster. Some costumes had been lost in transit. She would have to make do and mend. The director had faith in her. He knew she could do it. But the pressure was on. She'd needed a large espresso to kick-start her day, ensure her creativity. And that was when she'd seen him. She was never there at 8 a.m. on a Monday, usually. Her day started much later. She needed to be there for the performances, to give the costumes their final tweak, ensure the fit was perfect. But, by lucky chance, that day she had been there when he was watching the other woman, who appeared to Lily to be oblivious to his gaze. She wouldn't give him a second glance. She had a type, and he wasn't it. And Lily suspected he knew that too, in his heart, but he refused to give up hope, and it didn't stop him looking. She envied the confidence of men. His eyes took in every detail of her look, obviously admiring her rather austere beauty. Lily imagined he had a trained eye. She knew immediately that it was him when she saw the note in *Time Out*. She admired his determination. And she didn't want him to be disappointed. He was too beautiful for that. So she had sorted through the costumes at work, careful to find one that matched what the other woman wore.

His hand was on her thigh now. *Progress*, Lily thought. The taxi drew up to the kerb.

'Drury Lane, miss. Mind your step. It's wet out there.'

Lily handed the driver a note, refusing the change. He helped her from the cab and they darted for shelter into a theatre doorway. The rain was heavier now. Everyone walking past kept their eyes trained on the pavement. No one gave them a second glance. Lily shivered. The rain made her feel cold. He put his arm around her, protectively. She rested against him, feeling his warmth. He turned her towards him, and kissed her lightly on her mouth, drawing back, still uncertain, waiting for her assent. She reached up to him, returning his kiss. He tasted of mint and coffee. His lips were soft. They fitted hers perfectly and they kissed for an age, slowly, softly at first, then more urgently. His tongue explored her mouth, her teeth nibbled his lips. He gave a little cry, of pleasure not pain. This would be unexpected for him, Lily knew that. His hands fumbled with the buttons on her jacket.

'This is where I work,' she whispered. 'Come inside where it's warm.' She pulled a set of keys from her bag and led him round the building. A door took them into a dark corridor. Her heels clicked as she made her way to her room. He tugged her arm and pushed her against the wall. *He's becoming brave*, she thought, *bold*.

His kiss was more pressing this time, persuasive and forceful. He pulled her blouse from her skirt and ran his hands underneath, caressing her skin, sending shivers of pleasure through her. Her body was responding to him. She was wet now. Her cunt needed his attention, but she knew it would be best to wait for that. There was no rush. He began to fumble again, this time with the many pearl buttons on her blouse. Modern clothes were too easy to slip out of, she thought. Men were unused, these days, to unbuttoning, unlacing, undoing. Much of the sensual pleasure had been taken away. Everything was rushed.

'Let me,' she whispered, slowly but deftly opening her blouse. He stepped back and watched as she revealed her satin bra and the cleft between her breasts. His eyes roved over her, feasting on her creamy flesh. He reached forward, hooking his fingers under her collar, pulling it away from her skin. His fingers brushed her collarbone, traced a line up her neck, along her jaw and around her ear. His touch was light but insistent. He slipped her blouse from her shoulders, letting it fall to the floor in a shimmer. He held her shoulders for a moment, turned her, face to the wall, and unhooked her bra, releasing her breasts, then turned her back. He looked at her dark, tight nipples encircling them first with his fingers, feeling the weight of her heavy breasts in his hands; then bent his tongue to them. She sighed as his tongue took one, then the other nipple deep into his mouth. She cried out when his teeth closed on her right nipple, a wonderful mix of pleasure and pain. He held her hands above her head and her skin soon became tender as he pushed against her, rubbing against the rough brick wall. The pain had a sweet tinge, though. She could imagine him caressing it later with his fingertips, soothing the soreness. But still, she didn't want the corridor to be their final destination.

'Follow me.' She held his hand and led him towards the room in which she worked. Instinctively she turned the key in the lock. Now wasn't the time to be disturbed by one of her noisy assistants. She intended to have fun. Flicking the light illuminated the riot of colour and texture that filled the room, piled high around them, in sharp contrast to the darkness they had just left behind in the corridor. He paid little attention, though, not even looking around, choosing instead to lift her on to the large pine table that dominated the centre of the room. He returned to playing with her breasts, admiring their weight and fullness, sucking her nipples. Lily could feel desire surge through her. She loved attention being paid to her breasts. The space between her thighs felt moist. But she was patient. She could wait. She had no intention of rushing this today. It had been carefully planned. She unbuttoned his shirt and pulled it off his shoulders and chest. His body was slim but muscular. Perfect. She ran her hands over his chest, feeling his muscles flex as she did so. She imagined he was strong, could trap her if he wished.

'You taste wonderful,' he whispered, running his hands down to her waist, hooking the fingers of one hand into her waistband. The other had moved to her thigh and was carefully pushing her skirt up. He stopped when he reached her stocking-tops and gave her a grin.

'You took the Forties thing to heart, then,' he said, looking delighted. She dropped to the floor.

'Wouldn't it be easier to remove my skirt this way?' She undid the button and zip, and he inched her skirt over her hips and slid it down to the floor. She had another surprise waiting for him. His eyes widened.

'No knickers. How totally modern.' He placed his hands around her waist and lifted her back on to the table, then pushed his hands between her thighs to part them. Lily had prepared for today carefully. Her pubic hair was carefully trimmed, her skin soft with her favourite, sweetly scented body lotion. She could feel the cool draught across her body, cooling her fiery skin. The bulge of his erection was pressing against his jeans. He was watching her. He breathed deeply, apparently inhaling her scent. Taking her all in. Not touching. Not right now. Then he stepped closer towards her, reaching his fingers to that delicate space on her thighs at the top of her stockings. Her skin was pale, like alabaster, against the dark nylon. It was like a shock darting through her when she finally felt his touch again, trailing up her thigh, pulling her stocking away. Her skin was pliant to his touch, responsive. Instinctively she pulled her legs together, not from modesty, but to intensify the sensation that was growing deep inside her. She trapped his hand, held him tight, but he pushed her thighs apart with some force, exposing her cunt to the air, and to his view. He looked at her pussy; she hoped it looked pink and inviting. She reached down and touched herself, feeling her wetness, parting her lips, offering him a better view.

'Do you want this?' she asked, pushing one finger deep into her cunt, then licking her juices, sweet and ready.

'I want you.' He knelt, and began to taste her again, licking her thighs first, pinching, biting. Idly she wondered if she would bruise. Sam would guess it had been him, hopefully.

He'd reached her lips now, was parting them with his tongue, investigating all her folds, drinking her juice as though it was nectar. She leant back, pushing her cunt towards him. She could come right now, with his face buried deep inside her; she would be quite happy. His tongue was inside her now, then out, darting between her clit and her cunt, moving fast. Her hips gave an involuntary thrust. His hands pushed her thighs further apart, and she felt his fingers push into her as his tongue concentrated on her clit. She groaned with pleasure, tightening and releasing around him. He reached down with his other hand, and released his belt and tugged his jeans and boxers over his hips. He pulled away from her and stood up again, caressing his cock. After kicking his shoes off he stepped away from his clothes, which he kicked towards the corner of the room.

'Fuck me,' she whispered, reaching for his cock, moving his hand away and taking over. She held him firmly, caressed his full length, saw tiny droplets of come ooze from the head of his cock; knew she wanted him to fill her. Now. And he was ready too. She leant back on the table again, opening herself to him, caressing her clit, keeping herself close, feeling her juices run down her hand. His cock nudged at her cunt, parting her lips, and pushed into her, slowly, firmly. He brushed her hand away and replaced it with his own dextrous fingers, keeping their rhythms in time.

'Turn over,' he said. 'Now.' And he pulled out of her. But in seconds he'd flipped Lily on to her front, placing her knees on the table, legs spread wide, exposing her arse and cunt to him, and he entered her again, pulling her hips down on to his cock, plunging into her, his thrusting frenzied and hard. His hand reached for her clit again, and his fingers shot over the tiny sensitive nub, transporting her to ecstasy, her orgasm soon overwhelming her, her cunt tightening round his cock, drawing him into her further still. He was urgent now, long past the point where he could pull back or stop himself. She heard him groan as his orgasm exploded into her, and she felt his come fill her cunt, and the final waves of her orgasm tensed and released around him. The feeling was blissful.

As his orgasm subsided she felt him knead her buttocks, part them, one finger slowly circling her arsehole, then pushing its way in. His cock still filled her cunt, his come was oozing from her, and she ground herself against him, feeling the final waves of her orgasm tighten round his cock and finger, unsure she could take much more. Sensing that her immediate pleasure had subsided, he pulled his finger and cock out of her, slapped each buttock hard, and fell back on to a ladder-backed chair. She turned and eased herself off the table, gazing at his cock resting against his thigh, come glistening in the light. She stood in front of him, their intermingled juices flowing down her inner thighs.

'Bad boy,' she muttered, picking his jeans up from the floor and pulling out his belt.

'I try my best.' He shrugged and smiled, slumped back in the chair, idly playing with his cock. She stepped behind him as he rested, looped his belt through the chair slats, pulled his hands away from the game men love playing and slid the belt around his wrists. Then she tightened and fastened it to her satisfaction. Shouldn't cause him any pain, but, hopefully, it would hold him for a while. She secured his ankles with two chiffon scarves. He didn't show any signs of resistance or surprise. He seemed quite compliant, in fact. Sam would have fought her, resisted. He didn't enjoy restraint, despite his efforts to control her. He expected her to bend to his will. It was an unspoken rule. One accepted by her on the day of their marriage. He would never have understood if she attempted to reverse their roles. She had to step outside her marriage to feel true freedom. And the constraints imposed at home made her relish these moments even more. Her marriage was happy, within its limits, but to appreciate the happiness fully, she needed mornings, days, weekends like this every now and then.

A knock on the door shook her from her reverie. She raised her finger to her lips, asking for his silence. He gave a tiny nod of agreement.

'Hey, Lily, you in there?' The door rattled. It was the director.

'I'll be up with you in a moment, Mark.' She dragged a kimono from a hanger, tied it tightly around herself and slipped her feet into some spike-heeled pumps. She had a reputation for eccentricity. They all knew she liked dressing up. Mark wouldn't begin to guess what she was up to. She unlocked the door.

'Hey, where you off to?'

His voice sounded surprised rather than alarmed. No doubt he thought he could wriggle away from his restraints with little trouble.

'I'll be two minutes.' She gave him a wink, slipped out of the room and locked the door behind her. She wondered what he would think of that. Mark had a couple of questions about the costume changes they were planning. Simple for her to answer. She was a woman on top of her job. She paid careful attention to detail, and was highly organised. She wondered how he was feeling. Alone in her room. Unsure of exactly when she would come back. Or if anyone else would come in and find him there. The meeting with Mark had been planned, of course. She knew he'd interrupt them, but wasn't sure exactly when. She'd taken a risk there. What if he'd summoned her mid-fuck? Would she have gone? What would he have thought? She was testing him. She knew that. For what, she wasn't exactly sure. Loyalty? That was absurd. They'd only met formally a few hours ago. Strength of character? Would he still want her when she returned? Or would he be disgusted that she could desert him there like that, demand release and leave. Would he show his fear and panic? Or would he demonstrate that he was worthy of the risks she was taking just being with him? She hoped he would. She'd chosen him carefully. And she trusted her own judgement. Her marriage was good, too. She wasn't going to risk it for a man who wouldn't take a chance on her.

She wondered how he'd feel about being chosen, rather than doing the choosing. Admit his error with the other woman. Have the humility to accept her. Whether it would be a blow to his manhood. It would be to Sam. And, though Lily loved him, she saw this as a flaw. An insecurity. She wanted a man who could change his mind. Be flexible, and open-minded. Especially open-minded. She wanted Sam too, of course. Nothing wrong with security and a good hard fuck with your husband. Sex on tap. There was a lot to be said for it. But she'd have to toss to decide whether it was better than today's little experience.

Once she'd finished with Mark she went back down to her room and waited outside for a few moments. She was sure she could hear the sound of his breathing. Deep and regular. Was he sleeping?

'You're back.' No surprise this time. Was he a fool to trust a stranger?

'Of course. I said I would be.' She stood in front of him. His cock still rested on his thigh. She untied his ankles. They weren't alone now in the theatre. But that didn't matter. The possibility of discovery added a frisson of excitement to their illicit activities.

'Wrists?'

'Not yet.'

She undid the kimono, allowing it to fall apart. It skimmed over her breasts. Her nipples were erect. His cock flexed slightly. She ran her hands over the gentle curve of her stomach, twisting her fingers through her pubes, delving between her lips. She parted her legs, taking two tiny steps sideways. She found her clit and began rubbing, gently, with the fingers of her right hand. She held her left nipple between her left forefinger and thumb, tweaking and turning it. The sensation was sweet, but not as sweet as when he had done it. His cock was growing, rising from his thigh, thick now, inviting. His face was impassive. He was watching her. Her cunt was beginning to ache for more of him. She sat on the floor and the kimono fell away from her shoulders. She shook herself free from it, and lay back, raising her knees and parting her thighs further. Now she pushed her fingers deep into her cunt, feeling it pulse and tense, announcing her arousal. In one deft movement she turned over on to all fours, her ass facing him, her fingers still exploring her pussy, juices running over her hands. He could see where his fingers had been, where he'd opened her up, where his cock had pumped into her. She felt as though she was on fire. She increased her rhythm, willing herself to come, being turned on by what he could see.

'That's not fair. You're provoking me.' She smiled. She'd wondered when he'd speak. Glancing over her shoulder she could see him struggling against his restraint. He wouldn't escape. She was good at knots. For a girl. This one was deceptively simple, and strong. His cock bobbed as he moved; his erection was hard. He looked ready to fuck again. If only he could move.

'Am I the siren you wanted?'

'You're beautiful.' His voice was hoarse.

'Lips red enough?'

She parted her legs further, giving him full view of her cunt, and her fingers pushing into it, slowly now. He nodded, apparently unable to speak. She turned again, pushing herself to her feet, and stepped towards him, still wearing the spike heels. She fell to her knees, and pushed his legs apart. She stroked his cock, with one finger at first, then her whole hand. Her stroke was deft and firm. The tip was becoming moist. He threw his head back. He was close to coming, she was sure. She took her hand away, reaching for her chignon, allowing her hair to caress his thighs and cock, teasing him. He groaned with desire, pushing his hips forwards, as she'd done before. She knelt, picking up one of the chiffon scarves that had recently bound his ankles, and stood again. She allowed it to fall across his cock, then she tugged on it, quite sure the fabric would create the most wonderful sensation on the sensitive tip of his cock. She knew all about fabric and the sensations it could produce. She was an expert. Taking both ends of the scarf she looped it over his erection, sliding it back and forth, watching him throb with need, his movements involuntary, well beyond his control. Finally she tied the scarf in a knot around his cock, and held it in her right hand, pumping him, knowing the friction would be like nothing he had ever experienced before.

'I can't bear it,' he groaned, signalling the closeness of his orgasm. She pulled the scarf away, letting it fall over her pussy, resting on her pubes. She reached back and pulled the scarf between her legs, sliding it over her clit, feeling the nub tingle with anticipation. She knew how it felt. She'd been here before. Albeit alone. After a few moments she let the scarf fall to the floor and knelt in front of him again, taking him in her mouth, licking, sucking, nibbling; drawing his shaft deep into her throat. She thought he would explode into her mouth, but he held himself, with apparent difficulty. His body was writhing with pleasure and the pain of wanting release. Tasting the salty sweetness that heralded his orgasm, she pulled her head away from him, sucking him between her cheeks and lips as she did. Then she stood and straddled him, offering her breasts to his mouth, which he took with relish, sucking one, then the other, biting her swollen nipples with fervour, making her gasp. Crouching slightly she felt his cock against her pussy lips. She was sure he was desperate to impale her, thrust into her, finish them both off. But she had chosen him. This would be at her pace. Slowly she slid down on to him, his cock parting her lips, finding its way into her cunt again, millimetre by millimetre. She was going to retain control.

'Let me go.' She knew he was asking her to release his hands, so he could touch her, pull her down on to him, maybe. But she wouldn't allow that. She would be merciless. The feeling of his cock filling her was exquisite. She reached for her clit, flicking it with her fingers, stroking, knowing it wouldn't take much to trigger her orgasm. Her whole body pulsed with desire. Once she'd lowered herself on to him she began to twist and turn, allowing him to thrust into her, which he did with urgency. There was no pretence. Their aim was to fuck and come. Their movements were furious now, frenzied. Her cunt was devouring his cock, her fingers flew over her clit, and the first waves of release flooded through her, as his cock rammed into her, and they both shuddered, breathless as their orgasms pulsated through them. Once her ardour had subsided, she rested against his chest, feeling his come running out of her on to his thighs. They stayed like that for a while, comfortable with one another, kissing and caressing softly.

They dressed in silence. She locked the room behind her and led him along the corridor to the street, where she hailed a cab.

'Waterloo station, please.' He spoke this time. They sat in the back of the cab, hands entwined, like shy young lovers, each gazing out of their own window. The streets were quieter. Most office workers were at their desk in a post-lunch slump. The rain had eased. They reached the station and he paid the cab driver. He accompanied her to her platform.

'I'm glad we bumped into one another,' he said. *He still thinks it was chance*, Lily thought. *A happy accident.*

'Can we meet again? I have a studio. We could go there if you like?' His voice sounded tentative. Unsure.

'But I don't even know your name,' she replied, stepping on to the train and taking her seat. He looked surprised, as though astonished that they had shared such intimate moments today but remained strangers in so many ways.

'It's Jake,' he called as an annoyed-looking commuter pushed past him.

'I'll wait for your note,' she shouted. 'In *Time Out*.'

She smiled as the train pulled away from the station and picked up speed. Other men at other times had been disappointing. Not all of them, but some. He had been the best. The most compliant. This time she had chosen well. She thought they would meet again. She would go if he called her. There was, of course, always the chance that she might miss his note. But that was unlikely. Or that he would fail to place it. Which was unlikely too. She had faith in him.

She breathed on the window. The middle-aged, overweight businessman opposite tutted. She ignored him, tracing a shape into the frostiness on the glass. She wondered if the businessman could make it out. She didn't rub it away with her sleeve, but allowed it to fade. When she arrived at the station she could still see the outline of the shape she had drawn, etched on to the glass until the next time it was cleaned.

Tonight Sam would benefit from her daytime adventures. She knew she was deceiving him, but, like the actors she dressed every day, she could act out, pretend. She might even tell him about a fantasy she had. She would speak of a man she met via a lonely hearts column, smiling at the ridiculousness of the whole situation. Tell him of how they went to the theatre and fucked. Sam was loyal and trusting. She knew he wouldn't see it as the truth it was. And would be again.

'Playing the Part' is Izzy French's first appearance in a Black Lace collection.

Vetting the Affair

K D Grace

Kate felt Alan's gaze as she eased the stocking up her thigh and attached it to the suspenders. Sheer stockings and suspenders; that was all she wore. He moved to kneel on the floor in front of her, and ran a large hand up over the swell of her calf easing her legs apart to reveal the sensitive path along the inside of her thigh, a path he began to follow with warm kisses and little nips of his front teeth.

She pushed him away. 'I told you, you have to wait.' Their bedroom was just cool enough to make her nipples stand at attention as she settled herself on the stool in front of the dressing table to put on her make-up.

From where he now sat on the bed, he had a perfect view of her full, bare breasts, bouncing gently as she applied eyeshadow and mascara, as she released the grip and shook her red hair out around her shoulders. She could see the reflection of his cock tenting the front of his chinos. Good. Let him want her. Let him want her until it hurt. Before this evening was over, she planned to make sure it hurt a whole lot worse. She offered him a cool smile in the mirror.

He took the smile for encouragement and came to stand behind her, resting his hands on her shoulders, kneading them with big circular movements until his fingers slipped down over the front of her chest to cradle her breasts. She heard a grunt low in his belly. 'Please don't make me wait.'

He shifted until she felt his penis pressing against her back.

She cupped his hands as they caressed her, relishing the way her nipples pressed into them, feeling the twitchiness growing in her cunt. But as much as she would love to force him to his knees, to command him to lick her pussy, to make him beg before she allowed him to stick his cock where he wanted it, good things came to those who waited. She could wait just a little longer.

She sighed softly and pushed his hands away. 'You're so impatient, Alan. I promise I'll give you what you want and more.' Ignoring his groan of frustration, she moved to the bed, where she had laid out her clothes, and slipped into a lacy bra that held her breasts high and mounded, not unlike the cup of his hands.

'Kate,' he moaned. 'I don't think I can wait.'

She turned to face him, still settling her fullness into diaphanous cups. 'All right, then. Shall I watch while you have a wank?'

He growled under his breath and sank down on the bed, sulking, watching as she slipped into the black dress that fitted like a second skin. She smiled to herself. His hungry stare told her he had just been reminded how good she looked. That might remind him how good she was. She examined herself in the mirror, lingering for the view of her rounded bottom and turning to caress her breasts before running her hands down over her hips.

Then she bent, offering him the full benefit of a view down her deep neckline while she slipped into fuck-me shoes. The way he looked at her made her stomach leap. It was the way he used to look at her, back when he still realised how lucky he was to have her, back when one glance at her from another man could send him spiralling into jealousy and uncertainty.

Back when he found her completely enthralling, both in bed and out. His hunger would make her plans for this evening even more interesting.

He reached out and ran a finger along the edge of her hair where it fell over her cheek. 'You're not going to tell me what's going on, are you?'

She shrugged off his touch and stood. 'I told you, it's a surprise.'

'I don't like surprises.' He pulled her to him, attempting to slide a hand beneath the hem of her dress, up one thigh. But the doorbell rang. 'Shit,' he cursed, as she pushed him away.

She nodded at the bulge in his trousers. 'See if you can calm Simba for a little longer. I'll take care of whoever's at the door.'

At the bottom of the stairs, she took one more look at herself in the hall mirror. She was ready. One way or another, this would be a night to remember.

She took a deep breath and opened the door. Even knowing who she was expecting, her heart still skipped a beat. The dark-haired beauty standing outside was dressed to the teeth. A look of surprise registered in the woman's large brown eyes. 'Mrs Cannon? I'm sorry, I thought . . . I mean I was told –'

'Oh, please, call me Kate.' She forced her voice to remain calm. After all, this was exactly how she had planned it. 'As much as Alan talks about you, I feel like I've known you for ever, Caroline. It's all right if I call you Caroline, isn't it?'

Before she could protest, Kate grabbed her and tugged her into the house, slamming the door behind them, cutting off all escape routes.

'I'm sorry, Alan's secretary said we were seeing clients in the city for dinner, and I was to meet him here.' The woman wasn't a very good liar.

'Oh, I know all about your plans with Alan.'

'You do? I mean, of course you do.' The tinge of guilt around the full red lips and the dark eyes surprised Kate. It made her suspect this woman had never fucked someone else's husband before, and it didn't sit easily with her conscience.

But Kate knew all about their plans for the evening; after all, she had made them. She smiled sweetly. 'Join me in the kitchen. Alan will be down shortly.' She slipped her arm around the other woman's slender waist. Caroline was wearing a clingy red dress, certainly not the kind of outfit one put on to meet clients. She couldn't help noticing the lovely lilting movement of Caroline's small braless breasts swaying beneath the strappy top. One could easily sneak a peek or a grope with those perky tits so enticingly displayed. She suspected Alan did just that whenever he got a chance. She certainly would have. 'Wine, G and T, beer? Name your poison.'

'No, really, I couldn't. I need to keep my wits about me.' The woman's eyes dipped almost imperceptibly to take in Kate's breasts when she thought her hostess didn't notice. Making comparisons, no doubt.

'I'm betting you're a red wine person, aren't you?' said Kate.

'Yes, but –'

'I won't take no for an answer. One drink isn't going to hurt. I've been dying to meet you. I know how important you are to Alan.' She paused just long enough to watch the deep blush climb over the swell of Caroline's breasts, up her slender neck and high on to her cheeks. 'He's lucky to have such a competent colleague. With business being the way it is these days, I'm sure the two of you always have your hands full.'

Caroline seemed suddenly unable to meet her gaze, but Kate continued as though she hadn't noticed.

'That dress is lovely. I've always envied women who could go braless.' She cupped her own breasts and gave the erect nipples a discreet little stroke. 'Me, I'm far too busty. Luckily Alan likes big tits, but if I were a man, I'd be partial to a discreet handful.' She eyed Caroline's breasts and smiled. 'What about you?'

Clearly the woman's budding nipples were enjoying the conversation. Caroline folded her arms over her chest self-consciously. 'I've never really thought about it.'

'Sure you have. The only people who think more about tits than men are women. Don't tell me you're not always making comparisons.' Kate cupped herself again, this time more solici-tously. 'I certainly am.' She laughed. 'In fact, I'm often pointing out tits I admire to Alan, asking him what he thinks. But I'm embarrassing you. Forgive me. I've always been pretty outspoken where sex is concerned. Do you have a partner, Caroline?'

The woman's blush deepened and she shook her head. Kate couldn't help noticing the harder she blushed, the harder her nipples pressed through the thin fabric of the dress. 'Boyfriend? Girlfriend?'

'There's no one. With work, I don't really have time for a relationship.' There was a breathlessness to her voice that took Kate by surprise. It was the kind of breathlessness one has when one speaks a truth she would rather not speak. Could it be that Caroline didn't see Alan as a conquest, ready to divorce his wife and marry her, father her children and give her the fairy-tale life?

But then Caroline was a senior accountant. She didn't need Prince Charming with a big income to set her up for life. Kate knew that thanks, in no small part, to Caroline and Alan, the accounting firm they worked for had managed to stay solvent and even prosper through the credit crunch and the hard times that followed.

'Alan tells me you're an astronomer,' Caroline said. 'He says you showed him the moons of Jupiter through your new telescope, and after that he was completely besotted.'

What was no doubt an attempt at friendly conversation felt more like a slap. Kate had no intention of discussing the intimate moments of her marriage with Alan's lover. As she offered Caroline a glass of wine, she turned her ankle in one stiletto and tripped, sending a spray of Merlot across the woman's neck and the slopes of her breasts.

Caroline gasped and jumped back, practically falling on to the stool at the bar.

'Oh, God, I'm sorry.' Kate forced an embarrassed laugh. 'I'm good with planets, but not so good with heels and wine glasses. Here, let me help.' She grabbed a damp cloth and wiped at the woman's undulating geography.

Caroline froze and her back stiffened. Kate hadn't planned to fondle, but it was hard to do otherwise as the woman's breathing accelerated until the roundness of her tits rose and fell against Kate's hand, and her nipples pressed through the dress like large pearls. She made no attempt to push Kate's hand away. There was a subtle but definite shifting of her hips on the stool. Kate could fully understand why Alan wanted to fuck her. Right now, she wanted to fuck her too.

'Katie, honey, I know you want us to wait, but I'm horny now and . . .' Alan froze in his tracks at the kitchen door.

Caroline let out a little yelp and tried to push Kate away, but Kate had her trapped between the counter and her body. She continued to wipe at her breasts, pushing one of the straps off her shoulder. 'Hello, Alan. This is your surprise.' Her thumb strayed across Caroline's nipple and the woman whimpered. 'I thought it was about time the wife met the lover, don't you agree?'

For a moment the room was so silent, so unmoving that Kate could have sworn she heard Caroline's heart pounding, though it was probably her own. Then Alan spoke in a rush of words. 'Kate, honey, I can explain. We didn't plan for this to happen. It just –'

As he came to her side, she slapped him across the cheek with a resounding thwack. Both he and Caroline gasped, and silence fell again, but only for a moment. 'You made me a promise a long time ago, or have you forgotten?'

'Forgotten what?' He rubbed his cheek, and Caroline worried her bottom lip with her straight white teeth, looking as if she was about to cry.

Kate pulled herself up to her full height and glared at him. 'We said we understood that someday we might want to fuck someone else, to experiment. We agreed we were fine with that so long as we promised to bring our lovers home for approval. We promised to share. Remember?' She swallowed the lump in her throat, now dangerously close to betraying emotions that hadn't been there when she had rehearsed the plan in her head.

'For fuck sake, Katie, we were completely pissed at the time. You can't expect me to think that you'd –'

'That I'd what? That I'd rather know what the hell you're up to, that I'd rather know who you're fucking? I don't like surprises either, Alan.'

'Mrs Cannon, Kate, you have to believe. We never intended –'

Without warning, Kate turned and slapped Caroline. 'You shut up. You have no right to speak to me. Neither of you do. I'm the one in charge tonight, and if either of you walk out of this house before I'm finished, there'll be no making it right. Do you understand?'

They both nodded dumbly.

'Good.' She picked up her wine glass and gulped a good half for courage, then set it down quickly so they wouldn't notice how she was trembling. She had them where she wanted them now. She only hoped she had the nerve to see her plan through.

Anger forced its way through the thin veneer of calm she struggled to re-establish, and she grabbed Alan by the hair, making him cringe, forcing him to look into her eyes. 'How long?'

'Not long,' Caroline answered. 'Believe me, we never –'

'I'm not talking to you, Caroline.'

The other woman bit her lip.

'It started when you were at the observatory in Chile,' Alan replied, holding her gaze with difficulty. 'Things were bad at the office. I was missing you. It just happened.'

'Oh, please! Don't lay this on me.' She choked back tears. This wasn't the time to show weakness. She released her grip on him and gave him a shove. 'You knew the rules. Why didn't you bring her home to me?'

He heaved a sigh. 'We never intended to let it happen again.'

'But it did.'

'Katie, please believe me. I love you. I never wanted to hurt you.'

She turned her attention to Caroline. 'Now that I've met her, I could almost believe you picked her out especially for me, Alan.' She forced an unconvincing laugh. 'She's smart, she's beautiful, she's not needy. You never liked needy women.' She slid the other strap down over Caroline's shoulder and cupped her breasts through the fabric. Caroline didn't move. 'Her tits are exactly the kind you know I like. Do you think about that when you're sucking them and fondling them, when you're fucking her, watching the way they bounce and sway?' She gave Caroline's breasts a brisk slap and, in spite of herself, a sigh escaped the woman's lips.

Kate chuckled softly. 'You like that, don't you, Caroline? Did my considerate husband pick a lover who has secret longings to be with another woman? Do you fantasise about big tits?' There was a collective gasp in the room as she unzipped her dress, stepped out of it and guided Caroline's hand to her breasts. 'It's all right. You can touch them. We're all friends here, aren't we?' She felt Caroline's small soft hand contract against her left tit. 'That's a girl. You see how nice that is, how much you've been missing out on?'

Alan moved to her side. 'Kate, stop this. It's wrong.'

'Is it?' She grabbed his hand and placed it on her other breast. 'Is it any more wrong than fucking someone behind my back? Besides, just ten minutes ago you couldn't keep your hands off my tits. Now I'm letting you have them, but you have to share.'

'Kate –'

'Undo my bra,' she commanded.

He did as she asked, and she was once again in nothing but suspenders, stockings and fuck-me shoes. A quick stroke told her the chinos were straining hard to hold Alan's package. The hands on her breasts were kneading and caressing, and she struggled not to lose herself too quickly in the pleasure of their touch. She wasn't finished yet. She eased Caroline's dress down over her tits and returned the favour, hearing the woman gasp as she lowered her mouth to suckle each large dark nipple in turn.

'This is insane,' Alan rasped just before he dropped his mouth to Kate's heavy breast.

'But you don't want me to stop, do you?'

His hand worked up the inside of Kate's thigh, but she slapped him away. 'You can have my cunt when I say. Not before.' She slid the hem of Caroline's dress up and the woman lifted her arse off the stool to make it easier, without stopping her fascinated caressing of Kate's tit.

'I want to see where he fucks you, Caroline. Does he eat you out before he sticks it in you? He's good at eating pussy. Did he tell you what he did to my cunt while we were watching the moons of Jupiter? I'd keep him around just for that, but no doubt you know he has other talents.'

Caroline gasped as Kate slipped a hand down the front of her thong and with little tickling strokes fondled her well-shaved mound, before wriggling her fingers between soft heavy lips. 'I like shaved pussies. They show off every swell, every slippery fold.'

Caroline wasn't listening. She was squirming and rocking on the stool as Kate probed deeper into her pout. 'You two are very naughty to keep this from me,' Kate said, rubbing her thumb in tight circles over Caroline's hard clit. 'Undo his trousers,' she commanded.

'Excuse me,' Caroline grunted, trying not to buck off the chair.

'You heard me. Undo Alan's trousers. I'm sure you've had plenty of practice. Come on, free his cock and let's see what happens. You –' she grabbed Alan by the collar and pushed his face back to her cleavage '– I didn't say you could stop sucking my tits, but since you're here –' she guided his hand between her legs '– you can have a little feel, but just a little one.'

With a zip and a swish of fabric, Caroline shoved Alan's trousers and pants down over his arse, letting them fall to his knees, releasing his heavy penis into her hand. Kate slapped her away. 'I want him in your mouth. You like to suck cock, don't you, Caroline?' She hooked a finger in the woman's thong and pulled her up from the stool, making her flinch and whimper as the crotch fabric bit into her slit. 'Come on. Let me see how you do it.'

'Alan, sit here.' She paused to stroke his bobbing erection as she arranged him on the stool. Then she pushed Caroline's face towards his cock, but when the woman started to kneel down, Kate yanked the thong again. Like a bit in a horse's mouth, the pressure against Caroline's pussy gave Kate exquisite control. 'Not on your knees. Bend over. I want to see the cunt he fucks when he's not fucking mine.' She watched with her heart pounding in her chest and thumping in her cunt as he shifted his hips, offering his lover easy access to his needy penis.

Without hesitation, Caroline took the whole length of him into her mouth and began to cup his weighty balls, always so heavy when he needed to come. Both Alan and Caroline lost their look of utter misery, and their accelerated breathing told Kate that their bodies were betraying them – again.

She quickly dispensed with Caroline's thong, admiring the way her lovely bottom was lifted at just the right level for Kate to view her cunny, bare and pouting, like a peach pulled apart to reveal the juicy, tender flesh. From the counter-top Kate took a wooden spoon with a long handle and brought the bowl of the spoon down with a sharp smack against the hillock of Caroline's pale buttock. The woman whimpered and cringed. Ah, but that begging pussy only seemed all the more swollen and needy for the red mark now marring the smooth skin of her bum.

Kate spread Caroline's cheeks and bent to lick a trail between the swollen lips down to the node of her clitoris, making the woman squirm and groan around Alan's cock. She'd tasted her own pussy on her fingers and on Alan's cock, but this was different, this was a yielding, sopping cunt, another woman's cunt, her husband's lover's cunt. Alan's eyes were the size of saucers as he humped Caroline's mouth and watched his wife licking her pussy, something the two of them had often talked about in their hottest love-making sessions.

Kate pulled away, her face shining with Caroline's juices, and grabbed Alan's face. She kissed him hard, letting him taste the flavour of his lover on her tongue. 'You see how much more fun it is,' she said, nipping his bottom lip hard enough to make him flinch.

'I want to fuck you,' he gasped. 'I want to fuck you, Kate.'

She brought the spoon down hard across his left pec just above his engorged nipple. 'You don't get to choose. You've been naughty.' She bent and bit him until she felt him cringe, then she worried his nipple between her front teeth, feeling his body tense, his chest expand against her.

When she pulled away, she grabbed both of them by the hair, yanking Caroline from Alan's cock and pulling him up off the stool. 'Bend over,' she ordered her husband. In her stilettos she was almost as tall as he was, and she brought him up on his toes before forcing him down so that his face was inches away from her muff, his cock jutting out from his body. But when he reached for her, she tightened her grip. 'This is not for you.' She gave herself a stroke.

Caroline's face was suddenly pale.

'Don't be nervous, Caroline. I know you've never eaten pussy before.' Kate laughed a throaty laugh. 'Ah, but you've wanted to, haven't you? Well, you're about to get your chance. On your knees this time.' She sat down on the stool, which was still warm from Alan's bare arse, and spread her legs, hearing his gasp as she guided his lover's head to her aching cunt. 'That's right, Caroline. You're a woman. You know what we like. Now do it to me.'

At first, Caroline held her breath, her tongue moving tentatively over Kate's clitoris then down between her lips. Kate tightened the grip on her hair and pulled the woman closer, feeling her moan against her pussy, her hips rocking and shifting. 'You need to come too, don't you, Caroline? I made your pussy hot, didn't I? Alan, play with her cunt.'

He started to move behind his lover, but Kate grabbed him.

'Not like that. You're such a bad boy that I want your arse here where I can punish you if you don't do exactly as I say.'

It took him a few seconds to get the position right, but he was much taller than Caroline, so he could easily bend over her arse and lick her cunt. The moans of pleasure from Caroline translated into delicious vibrations against Kate's slit, where Caroline was beginning to get the hang of pleasuring another woman.

How often had Kate fantasised about having her husband's lover lick her pussy? But the fantasies had never included the betrayal. Caroline seemed desperate to make her come. Perhaps it was her penance. But betrayal wasn't so easily absolved.

She reached between Alan's legs to cup his balls, to feel the weight of them, to feel his breath catch at her touch. They'd been married for ten years. She knew exactly how he liked her to play with his balls, how he liked her to reach out a finger to stroke the underside of his distended cock as she did so. She couldn't help wondering what techniques for pleasuring her husband Caroline used in their secret trysts. Did she pleasure him as Kate did, or was there something exotic, something more enthralling about the way she loved him?

In front of Kate, Alan's anus clenched each time she cupped him. She leant down and gave it a tentative lick, feeling it tighten beneath her tongue, and his body convulsed. For a second she thought he had come. He pulled his face away from Caroline's pussy and gasped out loud. 'My God, Kate! That's amazing. Don't stop.'

His demand ended with a sharp intake of breath as she brought the wooden spoon down hard across his arse cheek. 'I told you,' she growled against his still clenching hole, 'you don't get to choose.' Caroline peeked up to see what was going on and added her own little gasp.

Kate gave him another lick. 'You've never licked his arse,

have you, Caroline?' The woman shook her head, eyes large, pupils dilated. 'You can watch, as long as you keep your fingers busy in my cunt.'

Caroline nodded enthusiastically, and Kate went back to work on Alan's puckering arsehole, at first only circling it with her tongue, then pushing the tip into it, feeling it grudgingly yield to her efforts. All the while Caroline's gaze remained locked on what she was doing. Suddenly Kate had an idea. She handed the spoon to Caroline, expecting her to lick the handle, but Caroline had something else in mind.

She pressed the bowl of the spoon against Kate's splayed vulva, with a gentle spanking motion that made Kate whimper and rock back and forth, gushing girly juices against the spoon and the chair. Then Caroline turned it and dipped the handle into Kate's pussy, twirling it about until it rubbed teasingly against her G-spot.

Kate's concentration was deliciously divided between Caroline's ingenuity with the spoon and her own growing fascination with Alan's puckered hole. The sensations were swiftly approaching overload, but she struggled to hold back her orgasm. She wasn't yet ready to give either of them the satisfaction of pleasuring her to release.

'Give me the spoon,' she commanded.

Caroline obeyed and watched wide-eyed as Kate spat on the tight grip of Alan's anus.

'Help me.' She placed Caroline's hand on Alan's arse cheek and nodded. The woman gently separated his buttocks and Kate pushed the handle of the spoon into Alan's grudging hole.

He bucked and pulled away from Caroline's pussy. 'Oh, God! What the hell –'

Kate smacked his bum hard with the flat of her hand and kneaded his arse cheek as she swirled the handle of the spoon deeper into his anus. 'Shut up and take what I give you, you cheating bastard!' The venom in her voice surprised her, surprised all of them; she could tell by the way the two lovers froze, struggling to calm their breathing lest even that make Kate angry. The lump in her throat and the sudden mist over her eyes made her even more furious. Damn it! She would not lose control, not in front of these two. In her anger, she smacked him again, harder. She heard his intake of breath, somewhere between pleasure and pain, but he said nothing.

She pulled the spoon out and hurled it across the room with such force that they all jumped as it thwacked hard against the wall. She nodded to Caroline. 'Get his clothes off of him, all of them.'

The woman did as she was told. He yielded meekly to her efforts until at last he stood before them naked, eyes downcast, hands hanging loosely at his side, erection dark and bulging.

'On your hands and knees,' Kate commanded. Alan obeyed immediately, wincing at the cool tiles against his knees. She stood in front of him, opening her legs so he had a good view of her cunt, as she slid her fingers, then her hand, over the whole of her vulva, pressing her palm between her spread lips and grinding against it. When her hand was slick with her juices, she brought it to his lips, as though she were offering a titbit to her favourite dog. He suckled and moaned, nuzzling her cunt-scented palm while involuntarily thrusting his hips. Caroline watched in fascination.

When she was sure she had their full attention, Kate came around to his side and sat on his back as though he were a sofa, opening her legs wide, making sure he felt her swollen wetness sliding against his spine where it could do his rigid cock no good whatsoever; where he could smell her, feel her, but get no satisfaction. She motioned Caroline down on her knees in front of her, admiring their reflection in the chrome of the refrigerator as she did so. 'Alan, you get to watch while your lover makes me come. That's all you get to do. Caroline, you get to lick my pussy until I come, that's all you get to do. And I get to do whatever I want to the two of you until I'm satisfied, until you've made up for all the times you didn't include me.'

Caroline was sobbing as she buried her face in Kate's cunt, and Kate might have felt sorry for her if she had been able to think, but Caroline was penitent in the most delicious ways. She raked the fingers of both hands down over Kate's tightly trimmed muff, causing a tremor to run up her spine. Then with thumbs alternately swirling around Kate's protruding clit, she suckled and slurped each lip of Kate's labia, tongue dipping in and out of her slippery opening until Kate lifted her legs, placing her heels on Alan's back so she could bear down better, so she could get more of her cunt into Caroline's face.

She was so caught up in the delicious feel of her rival's tongue that it took her a while to realise Alan was speaking to Caroline, instructing her.

'Use your middle finger up inside her, up against her G-spot. She loves that. Mmm, listen to her. She purrs like a cat and rocks her arse and her buttocks get so tight.'

Kate felt Caroline nod and mumble against her clit, as she slipped a finger up inside her.

'Good, now another one. She can take three fingers, but then she comes. She can't help herself, not when I'm sucking her clit at the same time. Make her come. Make her come hard, Caroline. You can do it.'

Kate could feel Alan's hips rocking beneath her. She reached one hand down and stroked his penis, felt the groan vibrate up his back. The room suddenly blurred.

'Oh, God! Oh, God!' The words repeated themselves like a mantra. As Caroline inserted a third finger and Kate exploded in orgasm, she realised the words were her own, spoken between sobs, as she fell over backwards. Alan collapsed beneath her, then rolled out from under her and pulled her into a tight embrace.

'Get off me! Get off me, you bastard! You had her. I had no one. I was alone. How do you think that felt?' She pounded his chest. 'I didn't know what the hell was going on. You shut me out, and I wanted you so badly. Then I found out.' She shoved at him and landed a knee in his belly, barely missing his cock.

He gasped and fought for breath, but didn't let her go. He surrounded her with all of his strength and held her until she stopped struggling, until the room was silent except for their harsh breathing and the pounding of her heart.

At last he spoke, his voice rasping and heavy with emotion. 'I'm sorry, Katie, I'm so sorry. I should have remembered. I should have kept my promise. I never wanted to hurt you. I love you. That hasn't changed. It never will. I just didn't know what to do.'

She sniffed hard and wiped her nose on the back of her hand. 'Well, you do now.'

'Yes, I do now,' he whispered, lifting her chin and placing a timid kiss on her lips. He held her gaze. 'Please, Katie. Please let me make you come.'

Carefully, cautiously, he rolled on to his back, his erection standing out from his body, one hand resting at the base of it next to his balls. With the other, he helped her straddle him and, with a familiar caress of her clit and stretching of her labia, shifted his hips as she eased herself on to the length of him.

'Jesus, you feel so good,' he gasped. He reached up and gently cupped her breasts, brushing her nipples with his thumbs the way he knew she liked it.

The intensity of pleasure that had been denied her in recent weeks made her come almost immediately, her release trembling through her vulva, snaking up her spine and over the crown of her head, making her feel as if her whole brain had just opened to an intense, tingling warmth. She closed her eyes and felt the tension of her husband's need carefully held under control. She knew his control. He was exquisite. He could stay on the plateau for ages, keeping her coming until she was exhausted and sated before he would empty himself into her. No doubt he'd done the same for Caroline.

Caroline! Her eyes fluttered open to find her husband's lover, her clothes bundled in her arms, tiptoeing towards the kitchen door. 'You!'

Caroline stopped in her tracks with her back still to them. Kate could tell by the way her shoulders were trembling that she was crying. 'I didn't say you could leave, did I?'

There was no response.

Alan froze in mid-thrust.

'Caroline, did you hear me? Put down your clothes and get over here. I'm not finished with you.'

Kate could see the hasty attempt to wipe her eyes, as the other woman dropped her bundle of clothes, squared her shoulders and turned to face them.

For a long second the two women held each other's gaze. Everyone held their breath. 'You need to come too, don't you?'

Caroline nodded, moving cautiously towards them.

'Then straddle Alan's face. Let him lick your pussy. He likes that, and so do you. Do it facing me, so I can enjoy those lovely tits.'

Caroline knelt and opened her legs, easing herself down until her heavy pout was within easy tongue range of Alan's mouth.

'That's a good girl. Now, make her come, Alan. Make us both come, and I'll make you come.' Kate wasn't entirely sure whether she heard it or imagined it, but there was a collective sigh of relief and a little whimper as Alan's tongue snaked tentatively over Caroline's cunt and his hips once again began to shift sinuously beneath Kate. 'Good,' Kate breathed, reaching out to caress Caroline's breasts, thumbs pressing on her rebounding nipples. She leant forward and took Caroline's mouth. It was soft and warm, with the briny flavour of Kate's cunt. Their tongues danced, each tasting of the pussy of the other, each exploring hard palate and soft cheek, until at last Kate pulled away with a gentle nip of Caroline's upper lip. She could see how close her orgasm was; she could feel the building strain in Alan's body with each thrust, with each grip of her pussy against his cock.

Caroline came first, falling into Kate's arms, causing her to clench down hard on Alan's cock, and the two of them came together, Alan emptying a nearly endless load of warmth into her convulsing cunt.

'You see,' she whispered, when he was done coming. 'Didn't I tell you it would be better this way? Better for all of us.'

Short fiction by K D Grace appears in the Black Lace anthologies *Liaisons* and *Sexy Little Numbers*.

Visit the Black Lace website at
www.blacklace.co.uk

BLACK LACE – THE LEADING IMPRINT OF
WOMEN'S SEXY FICTION

TAKING YOUR EROTIC READING PLEASURE
TO NEW HORIZONS

Black Lace Booklist

Information is correct at time of printing. To avoid disappointment, check availability before ordering. Go to www.blacklace.co.uk.
All books are priced £7.99 unless another price is given.

BLACK LACE BOOKS WITH A CONTEMPORARY SETTING

☐ ALL THE TRIMMINGS Tesni Morgan   ISBN 978 0 352 34532 5
☐ AMANDA'S YOUNG MEN Madeline Moore   ISBN 978 0 352 34191 4
☐ THE ANGELS' SHARE Maya Hess   ISBN 978 0 352 34043 6
☐ THE APPRENTICE Carrie Williams   ISBN 978 0 352 34514 1
☐ ASKING FOR TROUBLE Kristina Lloyd   ISBN 978 0 352 33362 9
☐ BLACK ORCHID Roxanne Carr   ISBN 978 0 352 34188 4
☐ THE BLUE GUIDE Carrie Williams   ISBN 978 0 352 34132 7
☐ THE BOSS Monica Belle   ISBN 978 0 352 34088 7
☐ BOUND IN BLUE Monica Belle   ISBN 978 0 352 34012 2
☐ CAMPAIGN HEAT Gabrielle Marcola   ISBN 978 0 352 33941 6
☐ CAPTIVE FLESH Cleo Cordell   ISBN 978 0 352 34529 5
☐ CASSANDRA'S CONFLICT Fredrica Alleyn   ISBN 978 0 352 34186 0
☐ CASSANDRA'S CHATEAU Fredrica Alleyn   ISBN 978 0 352 34523 3
☐ CAT SCRATCH FEVER Sophie Mouette   ISBN 978 0 352 34021 4
☐ CHILLI HEAT Carrie Williams   ISBN 978 0 352 34178 5
☐ THE CHOICE Monica Belle   ISBN 978 0 352 34512 7
☐ CIRCUS EXCITE Nikki Magennis   ISBN 978 0 352 34033 7
☐ CLUB CRÈME Primula Bond   ISBN 978 0 352 33907 2   £6.99
☐ CONTINUUM Portia Da Costa   ISBN 978 0 352 33120 5
☐ COOKING UP A STORM Emma Holly   ISBN 978 0 352 34114 3
☐ DANGEROUS CONSEQUENCES Pamela Rochford   ISBN 978 0 352 33185 4
☐ DARK DESIGNS Madelynne Ellis   ISBN 978 0 352 34075 7
☐ DARK OBSESSIONS Fredrica Alleyn   ISBN 978 0 352 34524 0
☐ THE DEVIL AND THE DEEP BLUE SEA Cheryl Mildenhall   ISBN 978 0 352 34200 3
☐ DOCTOR'S ORDERS Deanna Ashford   ISBN 978 0 352 34525 7
☐ EDEN'S FLESH Robyn Russell   ISBN 978 0 352 32923 3
☐ EQUAL OPPORTUNITIES Mathilde Madden   ISBN 978 0 352 34070 2
☐ FIONA'S FATE Fredrica Alleyn   ISBN 978 0 352 34531 0
☐ FIRE AND ICE Laura Hamilton   ISBN 978 0 352 34534 9

❏ FORBIDDEN FRUIT Susie Raymond ISBN 978 0 352 34189 1

❏ FULL EXPOSURE Robyn Russell ISBN 978 0 352 34536 3

❏ THE GALLERY Fredrica Alleyn ISBN 978 0 352 34533 2

❏ GEMINI HEAT Portia Da Costa ISBN 978 0 352 34187 7

❏ THE GIFT OF SHAME Sarah Hope-Walker ISBN 978 0 352 34202 7

❏ GOING TOO FAR Laura Hamilton ISBN 978 0 352 34526 4

❏ GONE WILD Maria Eppie ISBN 978 0 352 33670 5

❏ HIGHLAND FLING Jane Justine ISBN 978 0 352 34522 6

❏ HOTBED Portia Da Costa ISBN 978 0 352 33614 9

❏ IN THE FLESH Emma Holly ISBN 978 0 352 34117 4

❏ IN TOO DEEP Portia Da Costa ISBN 978 0 352 34197 6

❏ JULIET RISING Cleo Cordell ISBN 978 0 352 34192 1

❏ KISS IT BETTER Portia Da Costa ISBN 978 0 352 34521 9

❏ LEARNING TO LOVE IT Alison Tyler ISBN 978 0 352 33535 7

❏ LURED BY LUST Tania Picarda ISBN 978 0 352 34176 1

❏ MAD ABOUT THE BOY Mathilde Madden ISBN 978 0 352 34001 6

❏ MAKE YOU A MAN Anna Clare ISBN 978 0 352 34006 1

❏ MAN HUNT Cathleen Ross ISBN 978 0 352 33583 8

❏ THE MASTER OF SHILDEN Lucinda
   Carrington ISBN 978 0 352 33140 3

❏ MIXED DOUBLES Zoe le Verdier ISBN 978 0 352 33312 4 £6.99

❏ MENAGE Emma Holly ISBN 978 0 352 34118 1

❏ MINX Megan Blythe ISBN 978 0 352 33638 2

❏ MS BEHAVIOUR Mini Lee ISBN 978 0 352 33962 1

❏ THE NEW RAKES Nikki Magennis ISBN 978 0 352 34503 5

❏ THE NINETY DAYS OF GENEVIEVE Lucinda
   Carrington ISBN 978 0 352 34201 0

❏ NO RESERVATIONS Megan Hart & Lauren Dane ISBN 978 0 352 34519 6

❏ ODALISQUE Fleur Reynolds ISBN 978 0 352 34193 8

❏ ONE BREATH AT A TIME Gwen Masters ISBN 978 0 352 34163 1

❏ PAGAN HEAT Monica Belle ISBN 978 0 352 33974 4

❏ PEEP SHOW Mathilde Madden ISBN 978 0 352 33924 9

❏ THE PRIVATE UNDOING OF A PUBLIC SERVANT
   Leonie Martel ISBN 978 0 352 34066 5

❏ RUDE AWAKENING Pamela Kyle ISBN 978 0 352 33036 9

☐ SARAH'S EDUCATION Madeline Moore	ISBN 978 0 352 34539 4	
☐ A SECRET PLACE Ella Broussard	ISBN 978 0 352 34531 8	
☐ SAUCE FOR THE GOOSE Mary Rose Maxwell	ISBN 978 0 352 33492 3	
☐ SEVEN YEAR LIST Zoe Le Verdier	ISBN 978 0 352 34527 1	
☐ SHADOWPLAY Portia Da Costa	ISBN 978 0 352 34535 6	
☐ SPLIT Kristina Lloyd	ISBN 978 0 352 34154 9	
☐ THE STALLION Georgina Brown	ISBN 978 0 352 34199 0	
☐ STELLA DOES HOLLYWOOD Stella Black	ISBN 978 0 352 33588 3	
☐ SUITE SEVENTEEN Portia Da Costa	ISBN 978 0 352 34109 9	
☐ TAKING CARE OF BUSINESS Megan Hart and Lauren Dane	ISBN 978 0 352 34502 8	
☐ TAKING LIBERTIES Susie Raymond	ISBN 978 0 352 34530 1	
☐ THE THINGS THAT MAKE ME GIVE IN Charlotte Stein	ISBN 978 0 352 34542 4	
☐ TO SEEK A MASTER Monica Belle	ISBN 978 0 352 34507 3	
☐ THE TOP OF HER GAME Emma Holly	ISBN 978 0 352 34116 7	
☐ UP TO NO GOOD Karen Smith	ISBN 978 0 352 34528 8	
☐ VELVET GLOVE Emma Holly	ISBN 978 0 352 34115 0	
☐ WILD BY NATURE Monica Belle	ISBN 978 0 352 33915 7	£6.99
☐ WILD CARD Madeline Moore	ISBN 978 0 352 34038 2	
☐ WING OF MADNESS Mae Nixon	ISBN 978 0 352 34099 3	

BLACK LACE BOOKS WITH AN HISTORICAL SETTING

☐ A GENTLEMAN'S WAGER Madelynne Ellis	ISBN 978 0 352 34173 0	
☐ THE BARBARIAN GEISHA Charlotte Royal	ISBN 978 0 352 33267 7	
☐ BARBARIAN PRIZE Deanna Ashford	ISBN 978 0 352 34017 7	
☐ THE CAPTIVATION Natasha Rostova	ISBN 978 0 352 33234 9	
☐ DARKER THAN LOVE Kristina Lloyd	ISBN 978 0 352 33279 0	
☐ WILD KINGDOM Deanna Ashford	ISBN 978 0 352 33549 4	
☐ DIVINE TORMENT Janine Ashbless	ISBN 978 0 352 33719 1	
☐ FRENCH MANNERS Olivia Christie	ISBN 978 0 352 33214 1	
☐ NICOLE'S REVENGE Lisette Allen	ISBN 978 0 352 32984 4	
☐ THE SENSES BEJEWELLED Cleo Cordell	ISBN 978 0 352 32904 2	£6.99
☐ THE SOCIETY OF SIN Sian Lacey Taylder	ISBN 978 0 352 34080 1	
☐ TEMPLAR PRIZE Deanna Ashford	ISBN 978 0 352 34137 2	

BLACK LACE BOOKS WITH A PARANORMAL THEME

- [ ] BRIGHT FIRE Maya Hess   ISBN 978 0 352 34104 4
- [ ] BURNING BRIGHT Janine Ashbless   ISBN 978 0 352 34085 6
- [ ] CRUEL ENCHANTMENT Janine Ashbless   ISBN 978 0 352 33483 1
- [ ] DARK ENCHANTMENT Janine Ashbless   ISBN 978 0 352 34513 4
- [ ] ENCHANTED Various   ISBN 978 0 352 34195 2
- [ ] FLOOD Anna Clare   ISBN 978 0 352 34094 8
- [ ] GOTHIC BLUE Portia Da Costa   ISBN 978 0 352 33075 8
- [ ] GOTHIC HEAT   ISBN 978 0 352 34170 9
- [ ] THE PASSION OF ISIS Madelynne Ellis   ISBN 978 0 352 33993 4
- [ ] PHANTASMAGORIA Madelynne Ellis   ISBN 978 0 352 34168 6
- [ ] THE PRIDE Edie Bingham   ISBN 978 0 352 33997 3
- [ ] THE SILVER CAGE Mathilde Madden   ISBN 978 0 352 34164 8
- [ ] THE SILVER COLLAR Mathilde Madden   ISBN 978 0 352 34141 9
- [ ] THE SILVER CROWN Mathilde Madden   ISBN 978 0 352 34157 0
- [ ] SOUTHERN SPIRITS Edie Bingham   ISBN 978 0 352 34180 8
- [ ] THE TEN VISIONS Olivia Knight   ISBN 978 0 352 34119 8
- [ ] WILD KINGDOM Deana Ashford   ISBN 978 0 352 34152 5
- [ ] WILDWOOD Janine Ashbless   ISBN 978 0 352 34194 5

BLACK LACE ANTHOLOGIES

- [ ] BLACK LACE QUICKIES 1 Various   ISBN 978 0 352 34126 6   £2.99
- [ ] BLACK LACE QUICKIES 2 Various   ISBN 978 0 352 34127 3   £2.99
- [ ] BLACK LACE QUICKIES 3 Various   ISBN 978 0 352 34128 0   £2.99
- [ ] BLACK LACE QUICKIES 4 Various   ISBN 978 0 352 34129 7   £2.99
- [ ] BLACK LACE QUICKIES 5 Various   ISBN 978 0 352 34130 3   £2.99
- [ ] BLACK LACE QUICKIES 6 Various   ISBN 978 0 352 34133 4   £2.99
- [ ] BLACK LACE QUICKIES 7 Various   ISBN 978 0 352 34146 4   £2.99
- [ ] BLACK LACE QUICKIES 8 Various   ISBN 978 0 352 34147 1   £2.99
- [ ] BLACK LACE QUICKIES 9 Various   ISBN 978 0 352 34155 6   £2.99
- [ ] BLACK LACE QUICKIES 10 Various   ISBN 978 0 352 34156 3   £2.99
- [ ] SEDUCTION Various   ISBN 978 0 352 34510 3
- [ ] LIAISONS Various   ISBN 978 0 352 34516 5
- [ ] MISBEHAVIOUR Various   ISBN 978 0 352 34518 9
- [ ] SEXY LITTLE NUMBERS VOL 1 Various   ISBN 978 0 352 34538 7
- [ ] MORE WICKED WORDS Various   ISBN 978 0 352 33487 9   £6.99
- [ ] WICKED WORDS 3 Various   ISBN 978 0 352 33522 7   £6.99

- ❑ WICKED WORDS 4 Various — ISBN 978 0 352 33603 3 — £6.99
- ❑ WICKED WORDS 5 Various — ISBN 978 0 352 33642 2 — £6.99
- ❑ WICKED WORDS 6 Various — ISBN 978 0 352 33690 3 — £6.99
- ❑ WICKED WORDS 7 Various — ISBN 978 0 352 33743 6 — £6.99
- ❑ WICKED WORDS 8 Various — ISBN 978 0 352 33787 0 — £6.99
- ❑ WICKED WORDS 9 Various — ISBN 978 0 352 33860 0
- ❑ WICKED WORDS 10 Various — ISBN 978 0 352 33893 8
- ❑ THE BEST OF BLACK LACE 2 Various — ISBN 978 0 352 33718 4
- ❑ WICKED WORDS: SEX IN THE OFFICE Various — ISBN 978 0 352 33944 7
- ❑ WICKED WORDS: SEX AT THE SPORTS CLUB Various — ISBN 978 0 352 33991 1
- ❑ WICKED WORDS: SEX ON HOLIDAY Various — ISBN 978 0 352 33961 4
- ❑ WICKED WORDS: SEX IN UNIFORM Various — ISBN 978 0 352 34002 3
- ❑ WICKED WORDS: SEX IN THE KITCHEN Various — ISBN 978 0 352 34018 4
- ❑ WICKED WORDS: SEX ON THE MOVE Various — ISBN 978 0 352 34034 4
- ❑ WICKED WORDS: SEX AND MUSIC Various — ISBN 978 0 352 34061 0
- ❑ WICKED WORDS: SEX AND SHOPPING Various — ISBN 978 0 352 34076 4
- ❑ SEX IN PUBLIC Various — ISBN 978 0 352 34089 4
- ❑ SEX WITH STRANGERS Various — ISBN 978 0 352 34105 1
- ❑ LOVE ON THE DARK SIDE Various — ISBN 978 0 352 34132 7
- ❑ LUST AT FIRST BITE Various — ISBN 978 0 352 34506 6
- ❑ LUST BITES Various — ISBN 978 0 352 34153 2
- ❑ MAGIC AND DESIRE Various — ISBN 978 0 352 34183 9
- ❑ POSSESSION Various — ISBN 978 0 352 34164 8
- ❑ ENCHANTED Various — ISBN 978 0 352 34195 2

BLACK LACE NON-FICTION

- ❑ THE BLACK LACE BOOK OF WOMEN'S SEXUAL FANTASIES — ISBN 978 0 352 33793 1 — £6.99
  Edited by Kerri Sharp
- ❑ THE NEW BLACK LACE BOOK OF WOMEN'S SEXUAL
  FANTASIES — ISBN 978 0 352 34172 3
  Edited by Mitzi Szereto

To find out the latest information about Black Lace titles, check out the website: www.blacklace.co.uk or send for a booklist with complete synopses by writing to:

Black Lace Booklist, Virgin Books Ltd
Random House
20 Vauxhall Bridge Road
London SW1V 2SA

Please include an SAE of decent size. Please note only British stamps are valid.

Our privacy policy
We will not disclose information you supply us to any other parties. We will not disclose any information which identifies you personally to any person without your express consent.

From time to time we may send out information about Black Lace books and special offers. Please tick here if you do <u>not</u> wish to receive Black Lace information.   ❏

Please send me the books I have ticked above.

Name ....

Address ....

....

....

....

Post Code ....

Send to: Virgin Books Cash Sales, Black Lace,
Random House, 20 Vauxhall Bridge Road, London SW1V 2SA.

US customers: for prices and details of how to order
books for delivery by mail, call 888-330-8477.

Please enclose a cheque or postal order, made payable
to Virgin Books Ltd, to the value of the books you have
ordered plus postage and packing costs as follows:

UK and BFPO – £1.00 for the first book, 50p for each
subsequent book.

Overseas (including Republic of Ireland) – £2.00 for
the first book, £1.00 for each subsequent book.

If you would prefer to pay by VISA, ACCESS/MASTERCARD,
DINERS CLUB, AMEX or MAESTRO, please write your card
number and expiry date here: ....

....

Signature ....

Please allow up to 28 days for delivery.